CORN HOLLOW

To: Torilley,

To a bookeeping magic
woman, a woman of
endurance en my
field. Enjoy the journey
through history with
reading Corn Hollow.
Regards,
4/9/17   Lavenue My head

CORN HOLLOW

A Journey of Sorrow and Triumph

LaVerne Hillis McLeod

Purple Feather Press

Cover painting © 2016 Chelsea Belle Davey
Editing: Memory Perry and Joyce Krieg
Created with Vogel Graphics
(Formatting, E-book and Printing Conversions)

First published in October 2016

Published by Purple Feather Press
Post Office Box 566
Big Sur, California 93920 USA

Library of Congress Cataloging-in-Publication Data

Corn Hollow: A Journey of Sorrow and Triumph
Includes bibliographical references.

ISBN: 978-0-9976531-0-6 (Paperback)
ISBN: 978-0-9976531-1-3 (E-book)

First Edition

Printed by Ingram-Spark USA

DEDICATED TO:

*My deceased parents, Albert and Lula Hillis
*My husband, Kenneth McLeod
*My son, Tobias Hillis McLeod

Mother was wise, thrifty, bold, beautiful, always learning something new, the best homemaker and interior designer in the county, and always loved her children.

Daddy was strong, knew how to make a living for his family, a Mr. Fix-it guy who also loved nature and especially the backwoods. His fearless qualities shall never be forgotten.

My husband, Ken, who stood by me in the midst of all the strife and tension that came about during my writing stages. He deserves a medal for his emotional tolerance of enduring my repeated presentations of *Corn Hollow.* Being born of Scottish and Norwegian descent, *Corn Hollow* brought him closer to understanding the African American perspective in the rural south both pre and post the Civil Rights Movement in America.

My son, Tobias, a constant support for my creative endeavors, a teacher and coach, who understands the effort I had to put forth in order to write this novel. He will lovingly pass along African American tales and heritage to his wife, Maribel, of Latina heritage, and my grandchildren, Toni and Kenneth II (and any others born after the first publication of this book).

CONTENTS

Part I Pre-Civil Rights

Part II The Civil Rights Movement

i. **Acknowledgements**

I wish to personally thank the following people for their contributions in helping me create *Corn Hollow*. Even though I was so inclined to write this book bit by bit, it was with the help of a lot of others that continued to push my writing buttons.

I want to express deep appreciation and recognize Oscar Nolan posthumously. Just about every time that I bumped into him at a local supermarket and even in my last visit with him on his death bed, he encouraged me to continue to write. His constant inquiry was always, "How's your book coming?" I am thankful for his prodding.

Recognition also goes to the support of the first readers, - Helen Rucker, Dr. Nancy Knapp and Jasmine Bangoura who read my manuscript and gave me helpful comments. Several others were sparks that also helped fuel the fire of creation of *Corn Hollow*.

Gratitude goes to Betty Withrow, Ellen Pendleton and Sharon Pieniak, good listeners and reminders of my publishing possibilities. Deep thanks must go to my editors, Memory Perry and Joyce Krieg. I am grateful to Vogel Graphics for the technical knowledge and creative patience in combining all the pieces into a finished product.

The visual perception for the cover of *Corn Hollow* was painted by Chelsea Belle Davey. I am in gratitude to her for her talent and skill.

And lastly, I give credit to the divine spiritual energy that kept me connected to this endeavor.

ii. Testimonials

"1, who rarely read fiction, finished this manuscript in one sitting. From the first few pages, I cared about the narrator, her family, and her central question: 'How come white folks don't come into our house?'

"My caring was rewarded, and renewed, by a wonderfully braided narrative of alternating foreshadowing and flashbacks, rich with opposition survival lore (unspeakable horror/pain met with practical wisdom, personal talent, and community coping.)"

Dr. Nancy Louise Knapp, Ed.D., who holds degrees in history, counseling, and administration, and has experience as a graduate school professor, school superintendent, magazine/book editor, speaker and consultant.

"This novel takes us back in time in the south to emphasize the personal struggles and joys of a black family during the Civil Rights era. The author uses very interesting and creative descriptions in depicting all of the extraordinary events. This is truly a creative as well as a historic novel."

Memory Perry, MA in English from Mills College.

"I like chapter 9, The Bus, and how the situation demonstrates Tamara's naïve nature concerning overt racism in public and in private life. Also I liked the threads in *Corn Hollow* that keep emerging with the black hair straightening issue and beliefs about having a light skin tone."

Jasmine Horan Bangoura is a Southern Oregon University graduate who holds a Bachelor's Degree in English and Education. She has editing experience working as an intern.

iii. Forward

As a child of the South, I can identify with the protagonist in *Corn Hollow.* Although a work of fiction, I could relate with the author, LaVerne McLeod, even more. LaVerne and I met at the Panetta Institute's Monterey County Reads programs, she a volunteer reader in her Big Sur community, and I as a volunteer with other Panetta Institute programs. We instantly knew we had much in common after a long conversation about reading and teaching youngsters to love reading.

I had the opportunity read her book, *Corn Hollow,* and immediately knew much more about LaVerne. Her writing not only gives one a glimpse into what it is like growing up in the rural South of yesteryear, but you get the feeling that you know exactly how her protagonist felt. The conditions she was forced to live with, how the sounds and smells of her childhood condition, and her unique survival techniques, helped keep her sanity intact. Even dealing with her own family members influenced her.

Although my growing up in the South was different in that I did not have the rural background, I can still see how both, LaVerne and I would grow up as adults. We came to California, ended up as confirmed Civil Rights and community activists, and engaged in some of the same types of activities. My early Louisiana experiences with segregation and its overwhelming discrimination also led me to be of service to the people around me.

In *Corn Hollow,* LaVerne has given us not only a historical view of the rural South, but also a personal view. The reader can experience the taste and feel of an era not many people knew about and maybe couldn't even imagine. Her insights bring us into close proximity with experiences we will never have and can only hope to have through LaVerne's words. Surely, any reader will find this book a "powerful read."

Helen Rucker, - Monterey County Civil Rights Activist, Educator and Community Leader. At age 83, Helen is currently very active in her community.

iv. Introduction

Through the voice of protagonist Tamara Banks, the author's intent is to show the reader the undraped, true lifestyle, trauma and triumph of a rural black family living in Corn Hollow, Tennessee. Exploring the years 1954 to the early 1970s, Tamara begins her journey from her child voice.

As an African American female, raised in the rural South, Tamara Banks retains and reflects on her childhood memories as well as her adult experiences. These past glimmers motivated her to speak out in this novel. Tamara and perhaps you, the reader, notice how black women, family, and community dealt with joys and sufferings in a historically oppressed time.

Amidst Tamara's voice, the author reveals the ethnic views and insights of this era along with its rural agrarian events. The reader can take into account, emotionally and historically, how three women in the Banks family overcome their relationships with sexuality, personal prejudice, and personal growth from different experiential aspects.

There are messages in *Corn Hollow* for everyone of every nationality. One might even dive into the contents on the pages and hold its meaning from a guilt-free and emancipating perspective.

Allow your heart to unfold as colloquial and dialectal language flows throughout *Corn Hollow*. This manner of communication is like the dangling silk of an ear of corn inviting you to step into that moment in history.

Part I.

Pre-Civil Rights Movement

Chapter 1

The Banks Ladies

"Hey, Tamara, bet you can't make your momma spring her eyes open so to see the whites all round the black ball."

"Bet you I can, Luella!"

Momma Zettie, who we mostly call Momma, and Cousin Hortense, who is also her best friend, were sittin' in the porch swing talking. Luella is Hortense's youngest and kinda like a sister to me. They live down the road a piece from us.

"Bet you I can!" I repeated as I ran toward the porch. I knew how to win that bet. "Momma," I said when I was standing beside her, "why come white folks don't come inside our house?"

I watched her eyes get bigger and bigger. "Is you gone mad jumpin' round like that and askin' that foolish question? You know why white folks don't come in our house," she said, her voice filled with rage.

I froze. So did Luella, who'd followed me to the porch. Every time I ask Momma about white folks, she gets mad and springs her eyes open. I sure wish I knew why.

"You know better'n to ask 'bout that," she continued. My sister Althea, whom I often called Big Sis or Thea, and had been scissoring blooms beside the porch, now joined us. She looked right at me, then turned to Momma. "Can I press my hair today?"

Momma turned her head, not knowing who to holler at. "Take them flowers in and put them in some water in the Maxwell House coffee can on the back porch. They gotta look good for the Community Circle."

As Luella walked inside, she turned to Cousin Hortense. "Did that girl ask what I thought she done asked 'bout her hair?"

Momma Zettie was so worked up that she started to sweat. She pulled her apron up and wiped her forehead, then stomped toward the house. The screen door slammed and Momma was inside, waving her pointer finger in Althea's face.

"Girl, you crazy? You been listenin' to that radio too much. Brother Block always talkin' 'bout havin' that sleek, bleached look."

I could see Althea through the screen door, slouched in our dead granny's chair and pullin' her fingers like a comb through her nappy hair. "But Momma, you got real light skin and everyone thinks you a pretty woman, saying you yellow, and your hair is all soft curls."

"If I ever catch you talkin' like that again, I whip you so hard you wish you was dead! That radio's poisonin' your thinkin' with all that talk 'bout that Brown family who done put their own kid to hard sufferin' just to go to the white folks' school, sayin' it's too dangerous for her to

16

walk through that railroad yard to the colored school when the white folks school is just a little piece from their house. Tryin' to be white folks, that's what it is. Now you wanna change them naps to start lookin' like 'em. Bet you put your sister up to asking me that question, too."

"I did not put her up to it! And I heard on the news that some states are letting colored kids and white kids go to school together in South Carolina, Virginia, and Delaware."

"You better mind your own business 'bout that there Dellewhere or whatsoever they call it. Them coloreds in them states better mind theirs, too. Take what we can and go 'bout our business. That's what we coloreds knows is best. Turn that radio off and take care a them blooms," she said as she stomped back toward the porch. I had to jump back quick to keep the screen door from hittin' me in the face.

I watched Althea rise from the chair and move toward the radio. "All she thinkin' 'bouts being so beholdin' to them white thieves who cheat us out of our cotton pickin' money," she said. A loud voice rumbled from the radio: "... historic times. Brown versus ..." before it was switched off.

Momma turned back toward the screen door. "Gal, I hear you sayin' somethin' under your breath?"

"Hear me say what, Momma?"

"I wasn't talkin' to you, Tamara. Get outta my sight fast fore I done pulled out a peach tree switch and take it to your butt."

Luella said, "Yes, mam" at the same time I did and we ran down the porch steps and hid beside the porch. Momma Zettie and Cousin Hortense sat back down in the swing.

"That gal don't know when to stop. She searches and is so damn curious and go 'gainst all the elder rules. I fears for her when she grows up and can't do what she wants. Gots to figure out how to keep her tamed down. All them questions. Her sister ain't too far from Tamara, neither, tryin' to copy their ways when she's black as tar."

Luella and I didn't want to get caught listenin' so we snuck off to the fence near the walnut tree. Perched on the fence, we could look down the road that led to the cotton fields, the melon patch, and the corn rows. I kept thinkin' 'bout a piece of that sweet, green-striped "Dixie Queen" watermelon my Daddy Al, also known as Alfonso Banks, called them.

"Now why Momma had to go and be like that, Luella? Me and Thea ask questions a lot, but I don't never see her swell up like that 'bout other questions. You know what she always says when someone else gets all swelled up 'bout a question?"

"No, what, Tam?"

"She say the heat got to 'em. Maybe the heat got to her."

It was a summer day, a Saturday afternoon. Earlier the sky had cried down buckets of rain. The Bermuda grass was sparkly and the sycamore and walnut trees' leaves were bent over waiting for the sun to dry off their backs so they could stand up again in the Tennessee sun.

"Maybe you should ask her that question again on a cold day, Tam."

"I guess she doesn't think I'm old enough for her to tell me real answers about white folks, even though Althea says she tells me things so I can be ahead of my age. Sometimes I know what she's talkin' 'bout and sometimes I don't. Anyhow, let's figure out a way to open up one of them small Dixie Queens next time you come over."

Now and then I'd just stare at Momma 'cause she was so beautiful. She tried hard to keep things secret from me and hoped I'd stop asking about certain things.

A couple times, she told me to just go look in the mirror and stop with such foolishness. Being almost six at the time, I actually went to the chifforobe mirror and peered at a tall, skinny me. I was nearly four feet tall and so wide shouldered that my appearance when standing led folks to believe I was older than I was. My lanky body was held up by two "sticks," as my older brother, James — I call him "June Bug"—called them. He told his friends that my legs were so bony that they seemed like those desert scenes he sometimes watched on the black and white where mirages would appear and disappear. My legs, he claimed, vanished like that when I ran. My skin was a creamy brown and my slightly wide nose bore more closely to my Daddy's than to Momma Zettie. Folks said the twinkle in my eyes came from the fire that sparked my spirit. My adventurous nature made Momma despair and even made Daddy Al raise up his eyebrow a little. Oh yeah, lookin' in the mirror made me feel good. But it didn't answer why white folks never came inside our house.

My sister, Althea, on the other hand, figured she knew the answers to all that interested her. A daydreamer and critic, she idled away almost all of her childhood and adolescence condemning Corn Hollow and almost everyone in it. She was courageous and accepted the consequences of that. There was something real strange about the way Momma acted around Althea. Her hints indicated that it had something to do with Althea not having a medium or light complexion. I honestly thought Momma despised dark skin, especially in her children, since Althea, the darkest, was constantly reminded of this by Momma when she was angry. "Gal, you black as tar." Momma Zettie blamed her skin tone on Daddy Al's father, who was disdained for his ashy, coal-black color.

In spite of this, Althea's spirit seemed to come from her preoccupation with wishing she were somewhere else and doing anything but what people in Corn Hollow did. She thought of life in Corn Hollow as callous and difficult. To be spared the peach tree switch to the back of her calves, Althea usually tried to muzzle her mouth in Momma's presence. She escaped reality by hiding from Momma and secretly reading used novels that came from the school-house. She treasured *Jane Eyre*, whose hard orphanage life and quest to prove herself equal to a society she did not belong to, touched my sister's heart. Althea often told us she'd wait for the man of her dreams, even if he didn't arrive until he was old and blind. The haughty attitudes and tones of her heroines, as well as what they wore, stuck with her. This all sent June Bug into wild laughter.

She wished she had a dictionary so she could look up the hard words she didn't know. The only dictionary in Corn Hollow was bedraggled and had pages missing, but it was kept locked up in the Corn Hollow Elementary School. Since it was field work time, Althea had to wait until crop lay-by when coloreds attended school. I found it quite humorous to see such a skinny, full-breasted girl whose high cheek bones gave away our paternal grand-mother's Cherokee ancestry, try to be someone she wasn't. June Bug could get her to smile about her foolishness, but he couldn't stop her.

Chapter 2

Community Circle

In spite of Althea's lack of concern for the County Fair, she had to be involved for she and I were like servants for the fair committee better known as the Community Circle. That Circle meeting was Momma's pride and joy. She could be in charge of something where everyone looked up to her and she could show off her house and good country manners.

"Now you girls did a fine job on scrubbing this front porch. Just keep your tongue and don't you start ..."

"Hey Momma, them girls being put to some good use?"

"Now mind your business, June Bug. Go help your daddy."

I did a quick eye review of our work. Even the finely graveled tar paper siding that wrapped the front porch part of the house, simulating a fake brick effect, was mop scrubbed. Now you couldn't see where dust had kicked up on it nor on the porch planks. The smell of Purex remained as the sun gave way to moist remnants of drying puddles on the lowest end of the porch.

Momma prepared to take charge of this group and could be heard from the front porch side of the house practicing her opening words.

"We are here for the sole purpose to ensure that Corn Hollow coloreds are properly represented at that fall Grentwood County Fair."

Besides listening to Momma say this, all I clearly remember from the meeting was how the usual parade of eleven Corn Hollow coloreds entered our house.

With Althea and me as front porch greeters, a lot could be said for our front porch for it served so many purposes like a room of its own. On this Monday afternoon, the porch was a stage and even a prelude to display one's true self before composing and entering into my Momma, Zettie Mae Banks' living room.

Mr. Parker walked up three steps and onto the front porch panting like our dog Pluto, while his wife, Miz Cotillion, constantly smacked her lips against the right side of her toothless jaw. Her eyes looked straight ahead as her wrinkled forehead gave way to what seemed to be on her mind at the time. It seemed quite fitting that the Parkers chose the the cushy armchair and the small cushy chair that was pulled next to it, otherwise occasioned by Momma. The Parkers, along with Mr. Jake and Miz Iola Barnes, were the obvious elder figures of Corn Hollow. When the Barnes entered the living room, they happily placed their curved, crooked backs on our sofa as their heads protruded forward to not miss a thing in sight and to hopefully hear everything.

Unlike the frail and sickly Parkers, the stout and robust Barnes elders lived across the field from our sharecropped cotton area. The Barnes had such an odd way of dealing with things, especially their money saved from the sale of Mr. Jake's brother's place when he passed and had no heirs other than Mr. Jake. Noticable was their huge carpet bag that accompanied them wherever they went, even to church. Mr. Jake and Miz Iola were the experts on raising rare chickens as well as having the best "princess feathers" and lilac flowers at the County Fair. Folks usually bet on Miz Iola's fine poultry and dried arrangements as ribbon winners. Momma and Miz Iola had a great friendship. Miz Iola taught Momma everything about raising chickens. However, the only thing that Momma was more interested in was her own vegetables/flower gardens, and all her community work. Momma often said that "chickens are for eating, not petting and showing."

"Hey, Thea, since Momma is real quiet and peaceful, maybe while everybody is arriving, it might be a good time for me to ask Miz Iola or Miz Cotillion what I asked Momma two days ago, don't you think?"

"I wonder too, Tamara."

The parade of Circle folk continued. Mr. Daniel, a tall, handsome, baseball cap-wearing man who always wore his tan khaki shirt and pants, walked on the porch with his semi-plump and stocking-rolled to her stout knees wife, Miz Siddie Goodson, and she always approached with compliments.

"What lovely bouquets. I bet you, Althea, picked these. I know they from them starts I gave Zettie Mae last year."

It was so hard for me to say "Yes Ma'am" because Miz Siddie grumbled it with her teeth closed and I despised her fakery. Then Mr. Daniel, who stood six feet tall, led Miz Siddie to one of the remaining seven sea-grassed, rope-woven chairs. He had a special relationship with the white sharecrop bosses, Mr. Clifford and Clifford's brother, Mr. Jeffers. Mr. Daniel nearly had his left foot cut off by a John Deere plow, and could stand up no more than fifteen minutes before falling down unless he had his leaning cane. He was known to be a flirter and a whiskey drinker. Chiefly, he mastered what I later found out that folks called being a 'Tom' for Mr. Clifford and Jeffers. The favor to Mr. Daniel was never forcing the issue of Miz Siddie working in the fields or cleaning their houses. How I felt about Miz Siddie could be overlooked. It was Mr. Daniel that was outright dirty and lowdown. I saw him staring at my sister Althea's ten-year-old legs and chest, gazing backwards behind Miz Siddie.

After entering the living room, I heard him say something to Momma. "Your girls are growing up, Miz Zettie Mae."

"Yes they are, Mr. Daniel."

"Tom."

"Was that Mr. Jake or Mr. Clarence who whispered that name? Althea, why didn't they call him Mr. Daniel?"

"I'll tell you some other time. Quiet, the preachers are coming in now."

The Community Circle is the only time that our Corn Hollow, soft-spoken African Methodist Episcopalian minister, Reverend Stokes, and the stuttering Reverend Issac Tate, of the General Baptist Church, do not try to outdo or out-pray the other while in the same room.

Miz Quintilla Hickle, full with child, slowly paced and tumbled herself in a hard, straight-backed chair. She always spoke at the Circle for her husband, Mr. Leo Hickle, who flat-out refused to come to a meeting. His high tempered nature had overpowered and destroyed some previous conversations. The Hickles were a big sharecropping family. Mr. Leo talked about owning his place like us Banks so he wouldn't have to do repair jobs at the Clifford and Jeffers estate compound, be a substitute cotton ginner when needed and work with the Angus cattle in crop lay-by seasons.

Walking directly behind Miz Quintilla was Mr. Dave Dove, who held his head more than humbly low. Mr. Dove was quieter than any of the other members. He often helped Mr. Clarence and Miz Cotillion Parker with their chores in exchange for Miz Cotillion's home-cooked meals whenever he wasn't busy with Clifford and Jeffers' Angus cow trough cleaning and fence mending with Mr. Leo Hickle. Miz Quintilla and Mr. Dave Dove represented others that Miz Siddie called 'outcasts' in Corn Hollow that weren't allowed to attend the meeting or wouldn't come even if they had been invited.

At the time I didn't know what an outcast was. It didn't take too many more annual meetings for me to figure out by listening carefully to Miz Siddie Goodson that other folk and chicken talk seemed to upset her.

"Since we are here for the County Fair, we got to do something about that yellow Fairly Farrow around the fairgrounds with her most recent inbred on them hips."

Miz Cotillion Parker's neck hunched out with her head turned sideways.

"Miz Siddie, I ain't concerned about them. What about my chickens?"

Mr. Clarence nudged Miz Cotillion with his elbow.

"Be quiet so I can save us a lot of 'barrassment. My wife here done accused Miz Iola of stealing one of them

Guinea fowls. Cotillion only wanted to raise two chicks and not a whole henhouse of them."

Momma, Mr. Jake, and Miz Iola knew that Miz Cotillion was senile so they only raised their brows a bit. Mr. Jake raised a finger to talk.

"This matter can be cleared out because Zettie Mae, your son, June Bug, and Hortense's boy, Isom, chased off Fairly Farrow's neighbors' possum hound that belong to that Snake Dewitt before the dog nearly ate up the whole thing. They put it in a sack and brought it to me thinking it was one of Iola's chickens. I told them to take that one to Miz Cotillion's as this here is a pullet. Iola only got full grown guinea hens and some pearl guineas but this one did not belong to Iola."

I put an ice cold lemonade in front of Miz Cotillion and tried hard not to listen to the conversation. Instead, I let my mind focus on the beauty of the bouquet blooms. Partially due to Althea's love for flowers, our living room looked so pretty all set up with vases of mop-headed lilac and periwinkle hydrangeas picked on Saturday. Their paper-like petals ignored the summer heat and were still intact, even though it was Monday. What made the bouquets unusually beautiful were the starch-stiff doilies that stood in lacy scallops around the base of a camouflaged bottle and can. I stopped to listen for a second and the chicken upheaval was still on the rise. Maybe there will be the right time coming real soon so I can ask my question.

"Where is that sack, Cotillion, that them boys brought over to us?"

"I put it in the smokehouse. Was that what them boys was telling me when I was in the garden? Huhn. I kinda recollect."

Miz Siddie pulled her shoulder shawl back and crossed

her arms across her chest.

"What in the hell that snake-eater, Snake Dewitt, doing letting his dog loose on them chickens? He done gone wild and so is his dog. And I saw him with the whore Attie's son."

"Watch your mou-mouth, cause preachers and kids not needing to hear them words, Miz Siddie."

"Sorry, Reverend Tate, and sorry if them kids heard it."

Momma's left fist clinched onto her skirt sorta under her leg where her chair seat ended, revealing cotton gabardine fabric protruding through her hunched knuckles.

"Folks gotta stay away from Attie's boy. He bad business."

Momma started clawing her skin through her skirt as her princess slip lace started to show at the skirt hem. Wonder why Momma is doing this?

"He was born dangling them feet first and had to be cut out of Attie. The sign of the devil, don't you agree, Quintilla?"

"I agree, Siddie."

"Ladies, that's only what some say," and then Momma grunted in her throat and looked at Reverend Stokes as both preachers fanned their faces with their hankies. I poured more lemonade into the preachers' glasses as Reverend Stokes was about to speak. Instantly, an idea rushed into my head because Momma said the elders knew everything.

"I think that Mr. Dave can surely speak for them folk. What about it, Dave?"

"No sir. I talk later only because maybe it's all not finished up yet."

Reverend Stokes patted his hankie under his chin and pointed towards Miz Cotillion, who with repetitious monotony sucked air over her toothless gums that made annoying clucking sounds similar to chickens. She wanted to speak but Miz Siddie spoke out first.

"Why come we spend our valuable time talking about scum?"

"And why come white folk don't come inside our house?"

There was a dead silence.

I stared at Miz Cotillion in hopes that this elder would answer me. I saw Miz Siddie put her arm out in front of Momma as Momma, uncontrollable, spilled her drink. Her eyes had swelled open and were coming back to their regular size.

"Don't bring another glass into this living room, gal. Althea, bring me a rag and clean up my spilled lemonade."

I tucked my head and started walking out when I overheard Mr. Daniel mumble to Momma that he needed to talk to her after the meeting. I looked back and saw that everyone was sweating and swiftly fanning or wiping sweat off their faces. They pretended that I had said nothing. Yet I noticed that Mr. Daniel stomped the end of his cane down on the linoleum twice. Mr. Clearance turned.

"What did she say?"

Miz Cotillion just dropped her chin and quickly hunched her shoulders and gave an eye to Mr. Daniel. Miz Quintilla put one hand on her head and the other rubbed her belly. Momma then announced that I was just playing. The Barnes twisted their mouths.

Was this like last Sunday's Sunday school lesson, Moses commanding Aaron and his sons to burn a sacrificial offering that became extremely hot before his people to cleanse his sins? Reverend Stokes loudly whispered to Momma that he will get me to learn some Bible verses just as I was thinking about Sunday school.

"Yah sir, Reverend, I'll have her over to see you tomorrow morning and I'll send her by your way to Reverend Tate with some comfrey poultice for Miz Melviner's sores."

"Mighty kind of you, Miz Zettie Mae."

"Wish I could do more for your wife, Reverend."

"Let's continue." Momma's voice sounded wavy and she pointed to Mr. Daniel.

"Back to them other folks. There is some good thing them folks do. For example, Snake Dewitt hauls everybody's livestock to the County Fair, not to mention them real sweet watermelons he passes to both the A.M.E. (African Methodist Episcopal) and the Baptist churches when we gather in the pasture for fun. And that boy named Till, just does whatever chores his Momma Attie says do."

Peeping around the corner, I saw Momma breathing out hard and then less hard. She seemed more relieved about what Mr. Daniel just said she seemed mad at me. Mr. Daniel sat back and was quiet and seemed to be smiling and entertained at the circle. As Corn Hollow Tom, Althea said that he didn't care what people did. He only reported it to his bosses, Jeffers and Clifford, and his job was done.

Momma excused herself to go get something. Althea whispered to Momma Zettie in the dining room.

"Momma how come we don't see if some of the Fairly boys put some of their elderberry and walnut hull paintings in the County Fair exhibits?"

"Gal, you daydreaming. Get some more lemonade in that pitcher and shut your mouth."

I saw Momma holding onto a quilt square as she had let go of her skirt and started rubbing the wrinkles out with the palm of her hand.

"OK, we done talked about the guineas and about what Mr. Dewitt can do for the County Fair. Let's move onto other items. I vote for the Patch Star quilting pattern this time. Don't you like that one, Quintilla?"

Miz Quintilla straightened her back upright and as she warbled, the woven sea-grass chair bottom made the wood slightly squeak. She propped her arms across what might be the backside of her unborn baby.

"Well is that the one with the star in the middle and some patches on each corner and a big four-way patch inside the star?"

"That's the one, Quintilla. But didn't we use those patches year before last? How about the Flying Geese one?"

"Now, Zettie Mae, we ought to let them geese fly away because them white quilters won with that patch last year and we don't want to seem like we can't do somthin' new."

"You got a point, Iola."

Althea made her move by placing a glass plate of dessert on top of the Four Queen pattern that was in her hand. She scooted the hydrangea vase and the doily to one side of the coffee table. Of course, it would take the nature of my sister's regal thriving to accidentally suggest without words.

"Who done that up, Zettie Mae?"

Before Momma could answer, a rally of supporters could have cared less where the square came from because they chose it.

"That one there. I know that one and hope we use it. I know it will be used well by Clarence and Cotillion and we be proud to let our eldest have it. And did you know that since I started my preaching at Corn Hollow Baptist, my wife Melviner's family used to make all our quilts like that each year in different material scraps. And I always loved to see her unwrap them as her Grandma taught her Momma to make them 1-2-3-4 Queens as she always smiled out of her mouth. Wish she was well enough to do that again."

Everyone in the room lowered their heads. Miz Quintilla giggled.

"Of course it's about Four Queens and my Grannie used to say to me to never forget that women are Queens."

Mr. Daniel cleared his throat.

I pulled back from the doorsill when I saw Thea coming inside the dining room to fill up the glasses some more.

"Thea! Althea! They using your quilt piece." Althea dropped her bottom lip.

"Momma saw me clipping from her old pile of quilt scraps and she said nothing. I even asked her for purple and navy thread and she lent it to me."

"Don't cry loud, Althea, or else Momma will probably try the peach tree switch on both of us. They might be finished. And what's wrong with them, Thea? They all act like they hate me and Momma knows you sewed up that square."

"They act like their heads heard a school bell rang and they better escape what's being said or done or else they'll get a lashing."

Rising to stand up with his walking cane, Mr. Daniel spoke up.

"Let's keep it the way it was last and the year before that one. And Dave, can you tell Snake Dewitt to be ready with his truck by helping them fix that u-joint on it? Ain't nothing like Alfonso Banks taking in the hogs. Quintilla, I know Leo do the cow raising. Mr. Clarence can take on his billy goat and you, Miz Iola, will have some of our

31

prize-winning chickens to ribbon up the showcase, not to mention your princess feathers."

"Thanks, Mr. Daniel. Now on to canned goods. Surely enough, them string beans going to stand up this year in the jars. The peaches, tomatoes, beets, carrots, and other Mason jar fillings been talked about all year. Is there anything else?"

"Yes there is, Zettie Mae, and we keep pushing it under the rug about Fairly Farrow, Shad and Bernicia Hall, and that devil sinning, Attie Cole. Unless they have some good to add to the colored part of the Grentwood County Fair, then we can't include them."

Revered Stokes had to remind Miz Siddie of the passed-down tradition.

"Now Siddie, you know Miss Attie's grandma and yours and our grandma was real close. She passed down them good salve cure recipes and we might need her help with them come some epidemic. Them Farrows too quiet to come out but Miz Farrow can make some more pumpkin sauce and we encourage her to enter it. Shad and Bernicia Hall that cut up amongst themselves can do us all some good. Probably be gone by next June so until then, let's tell them to help Snake Dewitt get them livestock in and out of his truck on County Fair day."

Dave Dove scratched his head. "I'll handle it with all of them."

"Hey good folk, the meeting is almost over and I ain't got to talk about it here, but Hortense got a surprise to end with some kids in that entertainment talent show."

After prayers, the meeting was adjourned. Mr. Daniel and Momma were on the front porch talking even after everyone had left, while Miz Siddie stroked her hand over the yard flowers.

"Guarantees that nothing else will come up from that gal's mouth. I'll keep her in her place. And I do know how them boss sharecropper brothers think about us coloreds. Pig knows which tree to rub against."

"Them old creole saying tell the truth. Good day Miz Zettie Mae."

I had no idea what Momma was talking about. "Althea what did I do? Why is everybody mad at me? I just asked..."

"Don't say it, Baby Sis. Just rest on it"

"I know you want me to be quiet but I know who will answer my question."

Chapter 3

School in My Gut

From where I perched my butt, after being assigned a "watcher," was the edge of our one-room schoolhouse's front porch alcove just above the fifteenth and last porch entrance step. Only a week after the Circle meeting we were back at school. Keeping my head to the left as June Bug and Isom had demanded of me, I was to shout out if I saw any sign of small road dust clouds as I listened for crinkling tires rolling over crimson road rock. This left me removed from any thoughts of quilt patterns, serving elders, or anything else. And with such a great unfolding day, I thought there could not be a better day than this one. Yet on the other hand, all I wanted was recess rather than to look out for Miss Fruke. Suddenly, a slight summer breeze moved through my braids, knocking my plastic and metal hair-tip barrettes against the back of my neck.

Just sitting up so high and looking to my right and seeing the big surrounding hills gave me goosebumps as the shadows were cast from the trees that lifted above the back of the school that sat against the reddish clay hillside exposing some of its forked-veined roots through eroding hillside clay. My mind was in the place of running away with thoughts of being on a castle balcony looking for a royal visitor. This was one of the things Thea said she used to do when she was younger and had to be the watcher.

"She's here, everybody. She's here!"

Miss Fruke, the medium-weight, blonde, ring-curled, school-teacher of the white children, lived up the hill near Clifford and Jeffers in Corn Hollow. She was ever so bold as she would actually step foot in the Corn Hollow Colored Elementary School that housed grades first through eighth. She took the attitude that she repeated to any dissident: "A house of learning is like a House of God to me and I have every right to enter it." Miss Fruke was influential in both the white and black community. She was more than happy to link with my schoolteacher and cousin, Raymond Delmar.

Cousin Delmar traveled at least fifty miles daily for work because he lived in the town where he did some preacher work just for coloreds to "stand up," as Thea once told me. Anyways, all the kids called him "Cousin Delmar," regardless of kinship. In actuality, he was really a distant cousin to us Banks on Momma's side. Cousin Delmar and Miss Fruke were meeting for their bi-annual book negotiations as part of the seven and a half broken-up agricultural school months during this crop growing season.

I always enjoyed Miss Fruke's visits to our school. However, I couldn't help but reminisce how good it felt for me to throw clods of dirt at June Bug after the first half-a-mile enroute to school this morning. My brother kept rattling his mouth.

"Yeah, Isom, she asked that foolish question in front of the Circle."

"You mean she really had the gall to open up her mouth and say that."

June Bug looked sideways at me and continued to speak.

"Shucks, gal, aim straighter and you might get away by brushing me with that dirt. And look at Thea, she gone pouting about something. Something is wrong with them girls."

June Bug and Isom chuckled uncontrollably. All I could see were two shirt bottoms flying off in a mist of dust, avoiding my repeated scoops. I never figured it out before school that day, but June Bug and Isom knew better than to poke fun at Thea in front of her face.

Nonetheless, the driveway gravel crinkled as Miss Fruke was slowing down to enter the school driveway. Her demeanor and her beautiful clothes always distracted me from thought. She wore a blue organza dress with bits of fine lace on the collar edges, along with her sincere and loving smile that glistened to about a half mile radius and shone on all of us. Miss Fruke's voice weakened as Cousin Delmar's voice softened. I noticed the sisters Verdie and Luella meet eyes with the other. They sort of smirked as Cousin Delmar and Miss Fruke mutually lit up at the sight of the other.

Cousin Delmar was obviously a Negro, endowed with

37

green eyes and big strong shoulders and a small nose. His features could make any man jealous if he even said, "Good Morning" to his wife. Cousin Delmar's charm and rhetorical charisma were irresistible.

"Tell me the answer to number four history questions Cousin Delmar."

"Now is it wrong to drop the zeroes when multiplying this pattern?"

"Kids, it's almost dismissal time, so until we have finished with our talk, you kids can have a long recess. I'll tell you when to come back inside. And, oh! Tell June Bug to unload those boxes of books in Miss Fruke's car and bring them inside now!"

Althea ran and whispered something in Cousin Delmar's ears.

"Okay, Althea. Go brush up on that 'mother' assignment I helped you prepare for Miss Fruke."

"Bet I know what she asked you, Raymond. She must be Althea, the one you told me about last time. She's the one that wants to be sophisticated. Well, I've got the perfect novel for that one. It's one I have been reading over and over myself. Tell me if she likes it at all. And I can't wait to hear her paper."

Cousin Delmar and Miss Fruke sat down at the big table that was at the right front side of our one room schoolhouse. In the left front side was where our potbellied coalfed stove was placed.

"What were they doing when you took the books in?" Luella held her hands on her hips as she confronted June Bug.

"They were talking about books, what they always talk about. Don't try making something to what it ain't."

I walked towards the edge of the schoolyard so I could

look into the mud puddle. The sun glittered and shimmered on the mud puddle like amber coins sparkling and waving their shine to invite me to pitch a rock into it to move the sparkles into rippling circles. Apparently, my brother June Bug and Cousin Hortense's son, Isom, had the same idea as they walked to where I was standing. June Bug frowned and cocked his head to his right shoulder and spoke as he stared into the water.

"Wonder what those fellows are doing, Isom? I keep noticing that truck going back and forth and up and down the road. They slow down like they going to stop and then speed off and turn round again."

"Yeah, I see it. The kids are starting to stare and look. Let's make sure that they act like they don't see those guys and don't act scared. Maybe they'll go away. Isn't that the little boy in the truck bed that sweeps up at the General Store?"

"Yep, definitely from the sorghum hills where all the poor whites of Corn Hollow live and where Fairly Farrow's real folks come from."

WHAP!! A baseball barely missed Isom's left ear. Althea came running fast down past us, following the ball as it rolled ever so slightly into the road near the truck.

A voice called out from the truck. "No boy. Don't jump outa tha truck bed to fetch a nigger ball."

It was too late, as a white boy wearing a tattered plaid shirt and no shoes retrieved the ball.

"Here, gal. Whatsen your name?"

"My Momma named me Althea. What's yours?"

"Alvin. Trig Alvin."

"Well thanks, Trig Alvin."

"You can just call me Alvin."

I saw Alvin's eyes follow up Thea's dress as it sorta

pulled up with the wind as she slid down the small embankment to the road. It reminded me of how I saw Mr. Daniel look at her legs just before the Circle meeting.

June Bug hollered, "Thea, keep your butt up here on this schoolyard. Them guys look like trouble."

"That one named Alvin was not trouble. He got my ball for me."

June Bug and Isom started to mumble amongst themselves. Something came over my gut and felt like somebody had poured hot water in my belly and all I could do was breathe real hard until the heat left.

"We gotta seem like they don't scare us a bit. Don't look now, but notice that guy on the passenger side. He keeps holding up a stick and hitting it into his palm and skeeting tobacco in between his teeth."

I saw that myself and that's when my stomach felt bad. I threw another rock and slowly moved towards the center of the schoolyard. After a long recess, Cousin Delmar rang the clamored cow bell. Eveyone of us ran faster than usual into the schoolhouse.

"Sit down everybody and Althea will read something. Thea, you are up."

"Yes sir, Cousin Delmar." Althea began to read. Simultaneously, the truck wheels that carried the white, angry, looking men peeled off with a long, grinding noise as the rubber swiftly sped over the gravel.

"What's that out there?" Cousin Delmar looked directly at June Bug and Isom.

"Just some guys in a truck and they gone now, Cousin Delmar."

"Huhn!"

Miss Fruke had such a twinkle in her eyes watching us eagerly enter the school. She hardly heard the screeching wheels.

"Everybody sit down and be quiet."

I couldn't keep totally still so I sat at a back desk and started to draw.

It's about a character description or writing a story about a person: She was age seventeen and a true attestation of a first-rate beauty queen in the colored community. As a youngster she loved to hand-sew the finest cotton sack dresses and adorn them with pockets of old lace. Her slightly swelled nose accented her long, semi-straight French braided wavy braids that shrouded her shoulders like a corded blanket. Zettie Mae was her name. She walked with a slight twist to one side, which created quite a stir as the young men talked about the rumpling, tiny, red flour sack roses that seemed to glide and sway on her hips.

Any floral patterned sack dress would match Zettie's coal-black eyes that complemented her lightly-tinted yellow skin tone that often appeared in the summer as a crispy, light tan, sun-burn. Her family line mulatto heritage still peered through the third generation of white and colored mixings.

Even her speech, though distinctly Negro, was not the flat-tongued guttural Southern twang that often emitted in colored talk. Zettie Mae could make idioms and isms sound proper. A lot of her mother's Creole linkage combined with her Grand Pappies Estate Master blood line accounted for her unique appearance.

Two years passed by and Zettie had her choice of suitors. She chose the one man who would later make her a widow at an early age due to lack of medicine and surgery for colored ills.

After being nearly raped by a local deacon shortly after her first husband's death, Zettie gave in and needed pro-

41

tection so she married the one kind man, Alfonso Banks, who always helped her at no cost and finished her cotton crop harvesting while she was still moaning and grieving over her beloved.

Zettie Mae, though affable to and by the Corn Hollow community, never let her heart open to Alfonso. She grew resentful of his presence even though they had three wonderful children.

The elder son was James "June Bug," who followed behind the steps of his "Daddy Al." June Bug was not attached to his "Momma Zettie," as everyone in Corn Hollow addressed her, no more than through her fine suppers.

Clap-clap-clap! Through the clapping I could hear June Bug say, "Why she bringing in all that stuff 'bout Momma and saying I don't like her, only her food?"

Isom grinned. "It's only a story fellow and that's Thea, you know."

Thea brushed by June Bug's seat and whispered to him to never make fun at her when she is truly sad. Miss Fruke almost had watery eyes as she kept clapping.

"Come here, Thea." Miss Fruke hugged Althea and then went down the line and hugged all of us.

Cousin Delmar stood up. "Now anybody got a question before Miss Fruke leaves?"

I raised my hand. June Bug was seated directly in front of me and his height guarded me as I was drawing. Before I could raise my picture from my desk, June Bug's hand was on it and mumbling under his breath.

"Don't you dare draw pictures of white folk coming into our house."

"Miss Fruke comes into our schoolhouse and how you know it's our house?"

"Because, silly girl, 'The Banks House' is what you

wrote as your title."

"Oh."

"If I show that to Momma Zettie, she'll whip your butt really good. Tear it up now so you don't keep getting into trouble. You just act like you wanna be whipped and Momma don't seem to be in a good mood lately."

I looked up at Cousin Delmar and his face appeared red, like a dark beet.

"Well children, let's wave bye to Miss Fruke and then look at the surprises she brought us."

The moment I said thanks and good-bye to Miss Fruke and then seeing the round red taillight of her '54 Ford turn the corner to drive further uphill, gave me momentum to rush to the big table to see what she had given us. Everyone had the same thing on their minds as we examined and found the books that we wanted to read or just picture view.

"Come here, Tamara. What was that commotion between you and June Bug?"

June Bug was eavesdropping and rudely intruded.

"I'll tell you, Cousin Delmar. She asking things at home to Momma and the Circle meeting, things that start up trouble. I guess you don't pay any attention to the radio. Althea listens to it mostly and over she comes with words about the colored Rosa Parks' courageousness in Alabama, segregation violation putting the Civil Rights Movement into play."

"Excuse yourself, Thea. I am talking with Cousin Delmar and Tamara."

Althea ignored June Bug's comment and walked away.

"Just look at this picture, Cousin Delmar, and Lord knows what them rascals up to that kept driving in front of this schoolhouse while Miss Fruke was here. Maybe you can talk some sense in Tamara's head so I don't have to tell Momma."

Tears ran down my cheeks.

Cousin Delmar bent his knees while his tall trunk looked me eyeball to eyeball.

"No need to cry." He wiped my eyes with his thumb.

"But what did I do wrong? What's the real answer? Miss Fruke comes inside here, so why can't white folks come inside our house? I just drew a picture of Momma and Daddy in our living room with Miz Clifford and Mr. Clifford talking and drinking Kool-Aid with us."

"In due time, Tamara, you will understand all about these things and answers don't always come out because you want one. Promise your Cousin Delmar that you'll enjoy your life as a child and don't worry about that now. Just get older and I will tell you some answers. Go and pick out a book to take home and read. You can give us a school report when you finish it. That will raise your grade."

"Okay, Cousin, like Althea's paper on Momma?" Cousin Delmar knodded his head up and down.

As everybody was either turning pages or reading a page or so, Althea walked over to Cousin Delmar with a despondent face. At the same time, her eyes lit up as she was personally handed a second novel by Charlotte Bronte, one that she hadn't read: *Shirley*.

June Bug and Isom were even keyed up because Miss Fruke always made sure that she included some books about tractors and machines especially "for those well-mannered boys." Momma would hint to us that if Miss Fruke had been allowed, she would love to have June Bug and Isom as her godsons and drive down the road and deliver them new clothes every month.

44

We were ever so lucky to have a colored schoolhouse perched to one side of the foothills of the Olellean Mountains adjoining Corn Hollow that curved forty miles to the town of Olellean. Just five years prior, it used to be the white school and folks say that Miss Fruke charmed Mr. Jeffers and Clifford to build her a new schoolhouse and asked for the old one to be for the coloreds.

Anyways, it would be several months before seeing Miss Fruke again. Often as I played in the schoolyard I would think about Miss Fruke and the day those men kept driving by the school. I even dreamed about them. I could clearly see the men in the truck. One wore a black and blue plaid shirt and it was his arm that kept moving the stick as if he was beating on a drum. His hair was a white, bleachy-colored blond that looked waxy and stringy as fronds flopped over one eye. The other man in the truck wore a white tee shirt and leaned against the steering wheel as he slowed the truck down and turned his head to reveal a mean, cold stare accompanying his long chin and his tan, full-of-holes straw hat that wobbled on his long head. When the thought of those men would come to my mind, I could hardly breathe. My guts twittered and then I would awaken from my dream. One other time I witnessed this heavy feeling, and I was not the only one who seemed afraid.

Chapter 4

Bad Batch

Feeling better and better from Cousin Delmar's calmness, even though he didn't answer my question, eased me up a bit as I sucked on a stored-away sassafras twig. I hid the twig last fall when June Bug an Isom dug up sassafras root for Momma. She would make handmade lamp stands from it. The twigs from the root were chipped off. If there was anytime to have something for myself, it was now.

Bam!! Bam!! Bam!! "Look, Daddy."

"What in tarnation is that confounded noise? Some big, fancy car got a runaway muffler. Gal, I gotta git back to chopping wood."

"Even now, Daddy, when it's still hot weather?"

"Don't ask me questions, gal. Just pick up them wood chips from the pile I got here." chop, chop, his axe pounded.

It was a big-shot car as the elders would say time and time again. It just had to be white folks coming to our house.

"Daddy, could it be Mr. Clifford?"

"Not him. He would be in his pickup truck."

"Daddy, Al, it's Mr. Chet. He is getting out of his car and his face is real red."

I had never heard my Daddy stutter until that day. Having filled my chore bucket with wood pile chips, I was startled at the roar of the car engine as it noisily charged down our road towards our house. I knew it was Mr. Chet Gunstein, owner of Parson's Liquor Store who had a big nose and a gnarly white face. No one else in Grentwood County had a big-grilled, fin-swaying Cadillac that glazed over the big ruts in our dirt road. Daddy Al called out to June Bug and said something to him about corn tomorrow and gestured to the wagon. Meanwhile, I hid myself just inside the yard as Daddy and Mr. Chet talked outside the fence gate.

"What-wha-wha Mr. Chet what-what Mr. Chet want? It ain-ain-ain't time yet."

Daddy was so nervous that he pulled out his handkerchief from his back pocket and started wiping his forehead.

"Yes sir, Mr. Chet?"

I saw Mr. Chet ball his fist in a knot.

"Hey, Al! Now see what you done made me do?"

My mouth flew open as I followed his arm. He raised his right arm and slammed his fist on his own car hood. I was so afraid he was going to hit Daddy. Mr. Chet's voice tone was full of rage and then he started speaking each word clearly from then on. He just shook his pointing finger at my Daddy. I wasn't sure that Daddy was breathing. Both of them were dripping with sweat. I wondered if Daddy Al felt his gut twitter as I did when I saw those men at school in that truck.

"It's gotta be a better batch. Number five was tasty. That number six was like a cork and burnt corn. No more of that. You hear!?"

"It won't be that way Mr. Chet."

"Good, now let's sit down."

As Daddy and Mr. Chet sat down on stumps, I eased away from behind the tree. I heard Mr. Chet mumbling about Clifford and Jeffers having some men up at his place and needing some of Al's "white lightning" to juice their spirits. Both Mr. Chet and Daddy continued with wiping their foreheads with their kerchiefs as they tipped back their sweat-band-soaked hats.

"There's some lemonade in the icebox. Daddy Al, you and Mr. Chet can come inside and I'll pour up some glasses."

Daddy Al conjured up a fake cough. "She don't know any better, Mr. Chet, just real kind-hearted."

"Then better tell her about them matters, Al-fonso."

I disappeared from the stumps and still felt Daddy's cold, steel eyes telling me without words that I had said something wrong. Daddy and Mr. Chet talked and laughed out loud. They shook hands as if they were both white men. Mr. Chet left without coming inside and with cordial pleasantries.

"Tell your Misses Zettie a good day to her."

"And I stop by with my wrenches before the sun goes down today and have a look at that muffler."

"I knew I could count on you, Al."

It was time to find Luella. "You got to come with me to the corn patch tomorrow."

"Why?"

"Because June Bug told Daddy Al, that's enough wood to load up on the flat wagon for the corn tomorrow."

"Whose big car was that, Tamara?"

"It was …."

Just then Thea came outside and looked at me.

"Why are you crying, Tamara?"

"Thea, it's, cause not Mamma, not Daddy, not June Bug, not you and not Cousin Delmar will answer my question. I invited Mr. Chet and Daddy into the house where it was cooler. It seems like you all hate me for just asking. *bo-whooo, sniff, sniff.*"

"It's okay, just don't ask anymore."

"Why?"

"It makes you cry and I don't want to play with a cry-baby."

"Okay, I'll try not to ask that question."

"You just keep stumbling onto a lot of trouble, Baby Sis. And you think it's about entertaining white folk in our house with lemonade."

"Lemonade is the best drink in the world."

"Not in Daddy Al and Mr. Chet's world. Their drinks are more bitter and cost a lot more. The kind of drink they talk about should not be, because taxes can't be collected on the kind of drinks they talking about."

"What?"

"Nevermind, you have stopped crying."

"So now will you play hopscotch with me Thea? And you too, Luella."

Chapter 5

Moonshine Whiskey

T he next morning Luella and I met at the porch swing very early. We told Momma that we were going to find cantaloupe for her since it was Saturday and all. Plus, the melon area was next to the cornfield.

"I could hardly sleep, Luella. That moon was bright in my eyes. Gotta have fun and stop thinking about asking questions to grownups, so Cousin Delmar says. Let's go."

Upon hearing a distant noise in the back of the cornfield, we followed the sounds. It was unmistakably that of Daddy Al.

"I hear Daddy!"

"Why is he in the backwoods this late on Saturday, Tamara?"

"Let's see!"

"See what?"

"I don't know, but let's go see."

"We'll get our legs stung with the peach switch."

"Besides, at home they just get mad and Momma points her fingers and glare through me and I stop hearing her. I just watch how she stomps and pants. Now Daddy won't see us if we take through the cornfield."

"You know, pushing through these thick stalks of corn is like pushing a piece of paper through a keyhole until you see the light in the other room and you know it went through."

"You are beginning to sound like Althea."

"Since you say that, I better put that in a paper and read it to Miss Fruke. It goes like this: *We saw beautiful colors. There were long, green bamboo-like towers with draping donkey-eared green leaves and cobs covering themselves with yellow nuggets with a red parched-over glow that revealed yellow hairs flinging from the top of what looked like a million ears of corn. I started to get scared and tears were rolling down my cheeks. Wherever we looked: behind us, in front of us, to the left and to the right, there was nothing but corn. Even looking up, there were just tall hanging corn silks that dangled from the stalk, leaving only green sprays of light that seemed to be dwindling away by the seconds through the nearly rising full moon* and I have to end it there."

"And you get an A-plus ... " I paused to chuckle "on and A-plus."

"Let's run to the end of the corn row, scream, get found and take the switch if we have to but first we have to push back our tears and stop trembling. Grab my hand and let's run down this tunnel of corn stalks."

"Ouch!"

"It's just a fall and we are dirty now and just another thing for Momma Zettie to chew us out for."

"Tamara, we gotta pray to the Lord to not let us die in the cornfield. You can't keep your eyes shut and find a way outa here too."

"Oh no, look up, Luella, about one hour or less is the only thing left to see our way and the moon will be headed up then. Daddy told me about the summer sky and where the sun falls as it seeps low through those corn stalks in the west."

"I hear him Tamara. Get down."

"Quit pushing my shoulder down. See, we done fell flat on our face and why you put your hands over my own lips, girl?"

"Sh-eeeee. I see Daddy Al and the other men in the clearing beyond the last row of corn."

"Yeah, I see 'em too. Looks like they setting up stuff… sorta like hog killing except it ain't."

"You mean it isn't. Don't tell me who I sound like now."

"What? Just look. What's all them clinking jars they are putting in the wagon?"

"I've heard that sound somewhere else before, but I can't remember."

"Don't worry about your memory. Let's see what we can see and head on back towards the house before Momma starts hollering for us. I see Mr. Dave stirring something in a big wide pan. Look like a great big bag of Momma Zettie's cornmeal because she marked it with a red tie rag at the top. She and Cousin Hortense grated them corn cobs to death last summer from the fall bunch."

"Wait! Something white being poured in. It's not water,

but I can't tell what it is. Something brown going in now and water is being poured in too."

"Hey, aren't those buckets the ones we use during cotton chopping time?"

"Looks like more buckets are being poured in. They lit a fire under it that's propped on some rocks. Now Mr. Dave stirring it real fast and hard."

"Let's go."

"Not yet."

"It's probably hot by now but I don't see any steam. All of Momma's pot stirrings with water in it on top of the stove always have steam coming up."

"Look now. That barrel has a big shiny worm thing going round and round near that real big shiny jug the color of our special kettle. A long shiny thing that hooks with a barrel and another wooden barrel sits with a top on it. That little old pan is now catching something that's dripping in it. Why are the men so quiet and watching the drip and drop into that catch pan? Their eyes are big and they are saying nothing. They are all taking off those beat-up hats and scratching their heads."

"This batch can't be messed up."

"Now Al, it ain't done yet."

"Tamara, they threw powder in that little barrel and put fire under the wood chips and small wood logs for a burning."

Whoosh!

"The men all jumped back. They poured something in tin cups from that flat pan and turned it up to their mouths."

"Quiet, Luella. They're talking now."

"Say Dave, once Daniel Goodson got drunk and he told me 'bout how Clifford sends Fairly Farrow's children away for nearly two hours with a sack of candy and he and Fairly cut up. And Daniel at the turnoff saying to folk who wanna pass by that turning row, that the barbed wire stretched over the road half this day to let the cows go across to the south pasture to graze."

"Yeah man, Daniel tell it all when we drunk on white lighting. And he only drinks with me on account of he gotta say something to somebody. Daniel Goodson know all about them white folk and can answer 'bout anything of them."

"Yeah, Al we know about that too, but you quiet about holding your mouth 'cept for them old tales. You ain't holding in nothing new, you drinking your moonshine whiskey from that tin can. You knowd when Clifford said that."

"What you talking 'bout?"

"Ain't nobody can wear these boots but me" is what I am talking 'bout. Something been done or going to be. And you know I don't want to be beholding to that 'Tom' since he hides up Clifford's dirt."

The men started laughing and all the talking just continued. We couldn't tell who was saying what.

"It's getting pretty hot back here."

"Why, you think this is hot? It is cool, man. Where I came from, you can't even leave a water dipper in the sun because the heat melts it right down."

Daddy Al proceeded to remark, "I can tell you what I used to hear from my papa. He says that down there in the bottom where his daddy lived, all the fence posts bend over in the middle when the sun comes up, and the logs and stumps in the fields crawl away to find some shade. And he said that it was so hot when they pumped water that nothin' but steam come out. So they caught the steam and put it in the ice house at night and turnsa it back to water."

"Y'all hear something in them stalks?"

"Dave, you either too hot or my 'white lightning' done got to you."

"Let's go, Tamara."

"Yeah, Luella, I never heard Daddy talk so loud in my whole life. Let's tiptoe outta here like we two wild squirrels down the corn patch that way. Go, Luella."

"I see the house in the distance. Now you stumbling over that sassafras root, Tamara."

"I can't see much. Look back and see that big flame. It went out by itself and they hollering and whooping. Let's keep going."

"Tam-a-rah, Lu-ella!!"

"We're coming, Momma."

"Y'all panting like dogs. Where you been?"

"Outside playing."

"You find me a cantaloupe?"

"Not like you want it, Momma."

"You so dirty. Gone and change your clothes and wash them hands in the wash pan fore you come to the table and we'll say grace. Your Daddy and June Bug be late for supper."

"Where are they, Momma Zettie?"

"Thea, they doing late chores with Mr. Dave and some others. Eat up. Save six pieces of fried chicken in case Mr. Dave join them for dinner."

My eyes and Luella's looked like Momma's when she's mad except we are not mad.

"Now why Mr. Dave?"

"Shut up."

"What you kids say?"

"Nothing, Momma. Them collard greens and cornbread

look good. They go right down as they are nice and warm from the cook stove."

Biting into my drumstick, I leaned and whispered to Luella that Momma was not mad at us. "It's spooky."

"Y'all kids clean up this kitchen."

Daddy came into the kitchen and said, "Zettie Mae, it's going to be a long night but a good one. We gots to make a lot more so I'll be in the clear with the bills and you won't be wearing them flour sack dresses to church. The fellers that's help to me then have a good yield of change in they pocket."

"God bless my hubby Al. Since you had a good night, can't you just give me some man time?"

Momma and Daddy exchanged words that I couldn't hear. Althea got closer to the front room wall where the door was nearly propped opened. Momma swelled up and slammed the living room screen door, plopped in the porch swing with moonlight shining on her hankerchief near her eyes. Daddy followed her and I went close to the screen door so I could hear what they were saying. He was pretty loud.

"Zettie Mae, you got me in this mess."

"It ain't no mess. We been underpaid and lynched if we speak up about it. At least you got the opportunity to pulls up with some money as you be the one who know the recipe. You know Chet Gunstein beholding to you and all them peckawoods like your white lightning. He ain't gonna let you loose from it even if one batch didn't brew up good. He making much too much money offa you to do that. He just trying to scare you up to make sure everything turns out all right. But you know just like I cook pies, they don't all come out. Most of them do, though."

Momma became startled.

"Althea, what you doing out here? If I hear you breathe one word about something you don't understand, that switch you see up there will shut your mouth."

No one had the nerve to say anything at the dinner table for the rest of the week as the tension was too thick between Momma and Daddy. Two nights during the week, Daddy didn't come home at all, even though June Bug was home and Mr. Dave and the others we saw behind the cornfield had been spotted on their wagons or wandering about. The next thing I knew was that one day Daddy asked me and Luella to ride along with him to a store. He told us that we would be near Olellean where the tall pine trees stood. We arrived at the Parson Spring Liquor Store where two white men came out to our car. One of them was Mr. Chet.

Peering into the window, he said "How y'all chillens? You get bigger and bigger every time I see you. Take these buffalo nickels and go inside and get some candy bars. We got some business here to do with your daddy."

"It's alright. Gone on," Daddy's eyes assured us.

Seeing the trunk of the Mercury fly up and the men dash in the back door of the liquor store, Luella and I dashed in the store and let the "candy bar" words overtake our inquisitiveness to try sneaking a look at what was in the car trunk. The sweet caramel-melting and nut-crunching layers could only be soothed with a cool-steamed belch-making Nehi fruit flavored soda water or an RC. Eyeing each other on the verge of a giggle, Luella and I spotted an old man without teeth buying Beech Nut chewing tobacco. He plopped it into the empty cavity and squenched his jaws up and down, smacking and then spitting it out in long brown squirts. Daddy Al had said for us to go, but our eyes stayed fixed on the old man's jaws until we heard a lot of clink-clink sounds as the trunk flew up. Daddy and some men put boxes of empty jars in the trunk. I heard one of them say, "that some really good whis-key."

"Did you hear that, Luella?"

"Yep. What's whis-key?"

"Don't y'all girls think about that word cause it's something only grown up folk doing."

"Yes sir, Daddy."

Daddy hummed all the way home. I thought about Momma and wished she could also feel happy this week.

Chapter 6

Fire

"**D**addy Al! Daddie!!!! FIR-E, FIRE, FIRRE"
"We are not ready to go to church yet, so be quiet."

"No, June Bug. No!! It's Mr. Jake's and Miz Iola's house on fire."

"WHAT??"

June Bug shook Daddy awake from his drunken Sunday morning stupor. Daddy groggily stumbled outside.

Luella and I were only pretending to be Noble Queens sitting on the hood of Daddy Al's '46 Mercury, our royal carriage. We were waiting for June Bug to escort us to Sunday School as Momma had to leave the house early to set up communion with the Missionary Society and meet with some church officers as she did every first Sunday of the month. Luella and I knew that our carriage ride was over as soon as he would walk out the door. Suddenly I turned to take a bow when my eyes caught a glimpse of the wigwam pole bean stakes that stood in the garden, and through its top was real, red, flamy smoke. Now jumping from the car hood, I slid and rolled in my regal cape, struggling to breathe. Pushing Luella down to the fender with my whirling motion, I was about to cry when I realized that my left shoe was caught in the bumper. I ran with one shoe on.

"THE BUCKETS!! Gotta get them old folks out of that house."

"They at church, Daddy Al, where they always go on Sunday morning."

Folks at the church meeting saw it too because Momma said she thought the Holy Ghost had hit Miz Siddie as she dropped the communion glasses, looked out the window and screamed "Holy Smoke." Most everyone in the church said they thought her nasally voice was sounding ... Holy Ghost. Dust flew down our road and across the path to the Barnes' place. Like a herd of stampeding cattle, all of Corn Hollow, except the hill folks on foot or in cars, stampeded to the burning house. Momma and the Barnes crammed in the bench seats of the Goodsons' truck bed and braced themselves as Mr. Daniel sped over the ruts and bumps.

"Oh Lord, no!! NOT OUR HOUSE. The chickens, oh Lord, what about my chickens? I gotsa show and trade some at the County Fair."

"I know you bellowing and stewing over them chickens, Miz Iola, but you get some more."

By the time folks showed up, Daddy Al and June Bug were just standing back. They couldn't make it to the priming pump as the fire was too hot. Pouring what water they could on the grass around the house, they were hoping the fields would not catch on fire. There wasn't a sound or movement by anyone. Folks just stood and watched.

The windows emerged as framed, dancing multi-colors of crimson and flickering twirls swayed back and forth. A deafening roar wailed like a thunderstorm from the house, and growled twice as if begging for release. Instantaneously, smoke burst forth and rushed heavenward as if it summoned the whole community to see its splendid, vaporous puffs. Surely enough, it signaled an alarming alertness. The Sunday drinkers, including Daddy Al, had risen like Lazarus from a tomb of paralysis. Suddenly the red and yellows leaped to the top of the sky, seeming to cry. Wait for Us!!

"Bucket!!"

"No use. It's gone."

The door frames seemed to be the last to fall in and flake to ashes. What used to be the Barnes' house was now an inferno of blistering, red-hot sizzle and burning embers. Momma stood to one side of Miz Iola and Cousin Hortense on the other, rubbing and patting her back and crying with her. Cousin Hortense looked up at Momma as if she knew what to do next.

"Let's back away from here, Iola. It's hard to tell whether your house burned up or burned down with folks looking up to the sky and then on the ground. Y'all be staying with Miz Siddie and Mr. Daniel tonight. 'Bout time Daniel convert to a do-gooder, even if it is a few days." Momma then started talking to the crowd.

"It's okay now ain't it? All y'all come to my front yard. We get down pallets and food and then we pray."

In our kitchen, Miz Quintilla and Verdie started opening up canning jars and heating things up. Meanwhile,

Cousin Hortense and Momma asked me to help pull out old quilts for pallets and we also used our after church, already cooked and ready-to-eat Sunday dinner. Momma seemed to be calm in commandeering the fateful event. Daddy Al had gone to the smokehouse and pulled a ham down. The frying pans came out so the ham would be ready quickly.

"One of y'all take them fried chicken legs down to Siddie's, that sure to relieve poor Iola's mind."

The Reverend Stokes and Reverend Tate prayed. The smoke had not only drawn out the two church memberships, it aroused Miz Attie. I recalled at the Circle meeting her being called a whore and devil-sinning. As she stood outside our gate, no one asked her to enter. Most of the men froze with their mouths either stuck or flying quietly open. I ran to get Momma.

"We got more company."

Simultaneously, the ladies started walling their eyes at each other as Momma spoke. "Come in the yard, Attie."

Pointing and shaking her head to the others, Momma put her pointing finger to her mouth and said… "Not now! Attie, can you lend a helping hand and make ar-the-ritis salve for them skin singes and overdoing by them fellows who gonna sort through them ashes and silty embers?"

"Yes, Zettie Mae. I also bought you over some ingradients just for that there rubbing salve. Gonna need two more lady's hands to help me, though."

"Loo-ok!" Thea's crackled voice got full attention. A tall, skinny man stood up and spoke.

"I ain't no lady but can I, Miz Zettie?"

"Why, ain't you one of the Fairly boys?"

"Yes, ma'am."

Pastor Tate began to stutter a singing sermon under our sycamore. "Let-let me tell you as we ga-ga gathered here to help them Barnes and got to-to pray together, there's an old sermon that you don-don heard before. *OF ALL pl-pl-PLACES you spec-ex-pect you might meet up with the Devil, you never figure to see him in church not, do you? But the Devil have a lot of spherience-ex-perience, and he say you got to fight f-f fire with fire, water with water, and wind with wh, wi-wind. Well youuuu know-oooh. He does not have to hang around places like Sodom an gah-ga Gomorrah 'cause he ain't needed there. Folks in those pl-pl-places already doin' his work for him. 'Nother thing, the Devil de-Devvvil can't always go around lookin' like the Davel-Devil. If he did that, he ain't goin' to get no-where. He got-got to pass himself off like ordinary people. Sometimes he even got to pray and shout like he had been saved-d-d-d. Now there-there ain't nothin' more against the Devil's nature than that, is there-there? I'll t-t-tell you what I mean.*

Our Methodist Reverend Stokes softly spoke up, "Now Pastor Tate, let's come on back here away from the devil and go to Saint Matthew 14:15-21 verse."

And when it was evening, his disciples came to him, saying, this is a desert place, and the time is now past; send the multitude away, that they may go into the villages, and buy themselves victuals. But Jesus said unto them. They need not depart; give ye them to eat. And they say unto him. We have here but five loaves, and two fishes. He said bring them hither to me. And he commanded the multitude to sit down on the grass, and took the five loaves, and the two fishes, and looking up to heaven, he blessed and broke, and gave the loaves to his disciples, and the disciples to the multitude. And they did all eat, and were filled: and they took up of the fragments that remained twelve baskets full. And that they had eaten and were about five thousand men, beside women and children.

So now let's take this all to the Lord in prayer that we gathered here on account of the burned down house of Brother Jake and Sister Iola Barnes and we take care of them and we asked the Lord to bless them. And we thank you Sister Zettie Mae for your quick and willing act of kindness and Brother Alfonso for sharing y'all's provisions with us.

There was a simultaneously "Amen" from the crowd. We all ate real quietly and several of the ladies pitched in and cleaned up after everyone. Folks went home after a lot of handholding and tears. Momma stirred around in the house. That's when Thea and I went to the front porch swing.

Chapter 7

Fiery Moments

S winging in the front porch swing with Thea, I confided in her what I heard Daddy say about Clifford and what he knows about white folks. Thea responded to me like I was joking.

"And I know about that fire too, Tamara. Get up."

Then Thea took the peach tree and pretended to hit me on the leg because I couldn't stop talking.

"Tamara, what if we start talking like we wear the boots, not like Clifford by repeating what they say?"

"Yeah, saying that only we can wear these boots."

The front door slammed. It was Momma with something in her hand.

"Who in the hell saying that there is a fire and you all just playing?"

"How come everybody pretending that fire started with a bad chimney flue? Daddy and Mr. Leo helped Mr. Jake fix it last summer."

"Girl, you run your black mouth too much. I got to shut your mouth. You gone get us all up in trouble before you don't hush your mouth. Hush. I tell you!"

"Daddy Al, help me. Momma's hitting me hard."

"Ain't no use in you calling out to him. He's busy going through those ashes and embers. The things you say don' help us none. You gotta stop."

"Yes ma'am, Momma!!"

"No you ain't."

"Think back on those flames, Momma. It's because that foreman accused Mr. Jake of telling his nephew, Sid, that it's alright to move to Olellean because they were hiring coloreds to work in the John Deere factory to do heavy lifting and paid good wages. That slime ball did it because Sid no longer help at the cotton gin so he got even know he feels like Mr. Jake and Miz Iola his daddy and momma."

Althea looked up with nervously broken-up speech. "Mom-a ma ma what you doing? Oww!! Oww!! That hurts. Somebody stop this crazy woman. My back is burning in pain."

"Girl, you the one who crazy. You so black, you run your mouth too much and you gonna gets that foreman to light us up in the night."

"Stop, Momma. Stop. You been hitting us on the back of our legs and bottom. Now you hurting Althea's back and that ain't no peach tree switch. It's too big, Momma. Stop! Please stop! Momma … Mom-ma."

"You think you bettern us Althea? You worse. You blacker."

Althea let out one more scream. "I know you wish I

was dead." But as Althea started guarding her body with where the big stick switch was coming down she hollered.

"Owww! You hit my finger. You so mean, sniff, sniff … She cried and screamed, HELP SOMEBODY. HELP!! I REALLY KNOW THE HOUSE WAS SET ON FIRE CAUSE … I asked Mr. Jake if he had a fire in his fireplace all this week and he said no, so why you beating me for somebody else's crime?"

"Keep your hand out of the way or I hit another one."

Seeing Althea's body go into tremors as she tripped to the ground, and hearing her beg Momma to stop got me real mad. I said to Momma to pull back a bit and that's when I jumped in front of her. "Don't kill my sister." I was then struck on my arm.

"Git back, Tamara."

"No." Momma was about to hit me again and she raised her head after I said, "You told us to tell the truth like in Sunday School lessons when someone asks you a question." Momma was shaking and she just dropped that stick and ran towards the backyard breathing heavily.

Verdie stood shyly and upset outside the front screen door and would only enter when the commotion stopped.

"Hey, Thea. Let me have a look. Your finger is not broken, only struck hard like when that timber log rolled on your Daddy Al's hand."

After a couple of hours, both Verdie and I soothed Althea's deep pain with kind words about the truth telling and even held a hankie to her nose to blow. Then Thea let out a grin and a sniff and stopped crying.

"Let's go down to my house."

"Good idea, Verdie. Cousin Hortense can salve my back."

It wasn't long after the quiet salving by Cousin Hortense

that she left the house in a rush.

"Girls, keep rubbing the salve in. I gotta go talk with Zettie Mae."

"I'm going with you, Cousin Hortense, to get Thea's favorite book for her so Verdie can read something to her."

After going into our room for Thea's book I couldn't help but overhear Cousin Hortense and Momma talking.

"If only I hada the nerve like they say to do away with that man."

"Ah girl, 1 done heard all of that before and I lived it with old Charlie before the 'berculosis done took him in to God. Git that stuff outa yow head. And if you have it on your mind, then no wonder you kept beating and that ain't right. And then what happens if you rot in a jail cell over a cheatin' man and you lose everything and every famlee you thought you had, even me. You gotta get real right with God, Zettie Mae. I ain't saying this to you no more. You gotta stop taking out yow stuff on that gal. You know she real smart and you hold it 'gainst, her that she real black. But she your girl, Zettie, and you ain't have no business letting on like you thought up that quilt sample for the County Fair either when you know Althea the one who done it. Let alone when you and Alfonso done got mad with yourselves, you ain't suppose to take it out on your chiren."

"I'm sorry. I am so sorry I did that."

"Tell her!"

"I can't." Momma tried to slam the kitchen door when Cousin Hortense caught it.

"Hey, Zettie! We gotta put our mind somewheres else. Hows 'bout them stored away fruit jars and picking out the ones to stir-lize and can in 'em for the County Fair?"

"Sounds lika good idea, but you know Hortense there

70

be a Creole saying about that."

"You can throw them Creole sayings out the windo but it is my business if them gals come hollering in pain when you mad at Al. I'se your friend and I say, you gotta get a hold of yourself."

Momma's head leaned forward as some of her Creole hair ringlets had pulled away from her loose headscarf covering most of her face. Tears started dropping on her dress as she repetitively opened and closed her clinched fist, huffing big sighs with fixated eyes as Cousin Hortense patted her on the back.

Chapter 8

Too Wet

The sky was changing from the billowy white fluffs to gray and black in places. It was a rain-drenched five weeks since Momma had her Community Circle meeting and a new building was being nailed together by all of Corn Hollow's colored men for Mr. Jake and Miz Iola.

"Just make sure, Thea, that Momma don't know what I told you. You know why. Gotta find Luella and we going to walk somewhere."

"Can I go?"

"You never wanna go with me and Luella."

"I don't want to be alone with Momma."

"You don't have to."

"Isn't it funny to look down there and only a partial

73

chimney stack in view? Why are you crying, Tamara?"

"It's just a tear, Thea. You and Luella don't have to worry about me. Sniff, sniff."

"Here. Wipe your arms and hands. There's snot and tears all about."

"Hey."

"What, Luella?"

"It's raining. Let's go in the house and sit in the kitchen under the table"

"We haven't done that in a long time, besides the others are in the corner of the living room or by the dining room table waiting for the rain to blow over."

"Shut that window."

"Yes ma'am, Momma."

"You gonna do that, Thea?"

"Yeah, maybe Momma start looking at me in the eyes and say thanks."

Just then Daddy Al walked into the house. June Bug and Isom were not far behind. Daddy Al's eyelids dropped on Thea like he was so sad that he could cry. He slowly pulled a half-eaten candy bar out of his pocket and tried to hide the fact that he was sneaking it to Thea. This made Thea laugh and Daddy seemed pleased.

Daddy Al just turned and left for the back door as Tamara just stared at Althea's back and finally said something.

"Thea, your blouse sticky and a little bloody."

"Yeah my back is still sore. The skin just broke and need more salve."

Luella pointed to the curtains. "You shouldn't have reached so far to pull those curtains in when you shut the window. We'll get more salve for you."

"Oh yeah, I have some. Cousin Hortense gave me a

portion to keep in case of any pus or blood. And let's keep our voices down."

Staring at the others sitting in the dining room, I scooted further under the table. Somehow we all knew it might be anytime before we would be commanded to move from under the metal-legged dinette table. It was so close to the newly waxed linoleum surrounded by a procession of chrome and torn flaps of thick vinyl that occasionally scalloped around the horizontal edges.

"So Tamara, when you told me about Daddy making that whiskey, we have to think that he was smart like a chemist (like we read about Dr. George Washington Carver who make things from peanuts). Daddy makes things from corn for those men to drink."

"You sound coo-coo, Thea."

"Now Daddy can't tell anybody, because Mr. Chet is a bootlegger and he sells Daddy's whiskey and Mr. Chet don't have to pay bunches of taxes. It's about Prohibition so says the 18th Amendment of the United States Constitution."

"Well, when I go out, I will put boots on my legs because it has been raining. And why are you laughing, Thea?"

"It's funny, baby sister. Ever give any thought to talking with Mr. Daniel and ask him your questions?"

"What? I don't want to talk about asking anybody anything anymore."

"You said, Tamara, that Daddy blasted his mouth about Mr. Daniel knowing a lot about Mr. Clifford. Maybe Mr. Daniel can answer that question of yours. Plus, I would love to know what that man Clifford gets away with."

"Well, Miz Siddie didn't answer me at the Circle meeting and she talks like she hates other folk. Nobody listens to me but Cousin Delmar and he didn't answer my question either."

"Is that what you want, Tamara, to be listened to?"

"Just be still, Thea, so I can rub this salve on your sore. There's not much room under this table. Just keep sniffing, seeing that I know it hurts. Stop crying so hard, Thea."

"Okay"

"Is your arm alright, Thea?"

"It was a teenie tiny bruise and is now a healed-over scar. Cousin Hortense tended to me very well. It really doesn't hurt anymore. It's why Momma did it in the first place that hurt me so much."

The bubbled up part of the linoleum was walked over and we both turned at the same times hearing sort of a squeak.

"The rain has let up and I'm going over to the Goodsons to check on Miz Iola, so crawl out from under that dinette."

"Yes ma'am."

"Luella and Tamara, now that Momma is gone, put on your rubber boots. I'll show you all what Miz Siddie meant when she talked about them other folk. We're going where the river levee ends and bogs of gumbo mud begins. It will take your rubber boots about three to four days of soaking before the sticky mud comes off."

As we approached what seemed like a home, Thea made us take a close look at Shad and Bernicia Hall's house that Thea called a 'shack.'

"We can't go inside, Althea. It looks like nobody's home."

"We don't have to go inside and it's okay. I know the Halls are over in Olellean paying a fine for peace disturbance. Daddy said so this morning. Sit right here on this log and just look."

With all the previous rain, I had to admit to Thea that both front and backyard were comparable to our hog lot with missing pig poop.

"Yeah the Halls throw feed out to the chickens right off the front porch where they cluster for table scraps while scratching their beaks, not like Momma have us do in the chicken yard. Right here, the chickens generously leave their plops of charcoal grey and off, white digested waste curled and squeezed out like toothpaste."

At another glance, I noticed a deserted washing machine, a tin tub and tin buckets against the side of the house. My eyes then fell on the cantilevered and loose porch steps that lead to a series of planks that were boarded to an old, rotten joist. It was uplifted with triangular, crop-topped cement blocks to give the porch support in hopes that no one would fall through a loose, half-nailed or decaying board. Looking to the left side of the porch, rot had already taken over. Two of the end planks were like a bit-off, chewed, and crinkled fire stove mishap that got too close to the burning embers that later became building material.

"Don't go up on that porch. You could fall in or it could come down on you."

Somehow temptation got the best of me. Luella was right behind me waiting until I did it first. The step boards bounced as I slowly walked across the warped, nail-rotted boards. Looking at the porch hole, a big crack in the wood exposed itself to me. It was like a broken pencil that impossibly propped up a book. My stomach crackled and moisture was drenching my face. I lowered to all fours and trembled.

"Luella back away. Tamara, back down, one step at a time and move slowly-slow-slow."

I was like our dog Pluto being sneered by a wild boar.

"You don't have to say anything, Althea. So how is the wringer washing machine held up on that porch?"

"Now baby sister, you know what kind of house these folks live in. As for the other folks up the road a bit, they are an odd bunch and very superstitious people."

"What's super-stitch-on?"

"People that are quiet for ten minutes before answering a knock on their door or upon hearing a car sound outside their house. They are afraid to mingle for fear of walking across the path of one of their seven cats, especially avoiding where a black fur had trampled."

She continued to talk.

"Their other neighbor over there, Miss Attie, got a reputation. And I know you don't know what that means, and trust me you will find out soon enough. Well, the Halls here have to live in this lowland because they got run out of Olellean for their anywhere, anytime, fighting and threats. You remember the time at the Methodist and Baptist meet together day when you were with Verdie and me and we got scared half to death when the Hall couple brawled and pummeled in the churchyard with sticks at each other? I thought they were killing each other with all that blood coming from their heads. The stewards and deacons had to ask them to settle up in another place, and better yet, another town. They straightened up a little and got to stay around for another year. Shad Hall has the opportunity to work the soggy, mosquito-ridden cotton patch surrounding his shack. Last year he even made a decent boll yield out of them stalks so they let them stay even another cotton season."

"I want to hear about them other folks the ones that you say really make Miz Siddie so mad."

"You mean the outcasts? The ones that came from the white folk hills, well I told you a little about them already, Fairly Farrow and her family. Behind the white school, much further back in the hills, many white families live, mostly poor and they work in the sorghum fields for Clifford and Jeffers, but not the cotton fields like us coloreds. No one knows why and don't seem to care to find out. It is just that their strange ways fell from the back hills onto our community. Rumors of inbreeding spread in the air, which meant acceptance of Fairly's entwined cesspool of commingled genetics that was generally forbidden. The lower status of a Corn Hollow whore ranks higher than Fairly's."

"What are those words, whore, inbreed, and com-mingled?"

"I thought you wanted to hear about the Farrows."

"I do."

"You know, Tamara, that Cousin Hortense keep telling us that's the way they are and its God's business, not ours. They are human people so that means they are God's children."

"I think differently and have heard it said many times that Fairly Farrow's family must have made a mistake by throwing their own out the door. The servant helpers of Cliffords, Mr. Matt and Miz Effie Mae knew. Said that Miz Fairly Farrow's pa brought her to Clifford's house as a baby because the baby came out with dark hands and feet and said, 'if he doesn't take of it he was going to put it in the ditch to die.' Y'all keep squirming. Now I'm telling you and Luella to go play boggy sog in your rubber boots after I finish."

"Okay, Thea."

"To continue, Clifford told Miz Effie Mae that since she tends to all the children anyways, folks wouldn't know if she was babysitting one of his. If it turns colored, then she had to take the baby home and he would help with food and clothes. The funny thing about it is that she was a white girl. Miz Effie Mae told Momma that Miz Clifford was not partial to the baby's presence in her house. She chided the child with such rude tongue-lashings that a child should ever hear so Clifford deduced at the age of fifteen that the fair girl had to work the fields until she could somehow be pawned off to some man for a wife. What those hill folks didn't know was that the baby's feet got caught up in the umbilical, that babies are attached to during delivery."

"You mean the baby tripped and got tied up?"

"Well, not exactly, except not enough blood could 'sap' through Fairly's hands and feet as they were corded off, as I learned as I eavedropped on Momma and Cousin Hortense. Fairly asked Mr. Clifford for a house of her own in the fields and to teach her to shoot a gun for her protection. Even though Fairly talked like a colored person, and seemed tougher than she was, behind her coy and demure personality she prided in taking care of herself. Miz Effie Mae had taught her to help her to cook and clean. Mr. Clifford was always taking Miz Effie Mae for visits to Fairly's with boxes of food and old clothes and threw dollars on the young lady's porch when they departed. It was also on church community day that Miz Effie Mae prayed … 'Lord please help that fair gal I raised.' This incidently became her name, Fairly."

"I don't remember that, Althea."

"On the other hand, that family living next to them is the Dewitt family and they are colored. Old 'Snake' Dewitt kills and skins river snakes for food. He and his mentally delayed wife, Pecola, would pride themselves on catch-

80

ing and frying up the fattest possums in Corn Hollow. I'm telling you this because Fairly ended up with child and later children of various shades and colors. She had three boys, two that looked like Snake and one that was surely all white. Three and four years later she gave birth respectively to two girls. Fairly's daughters birthed five children mostly in the month of April that caused coloreds to talk and question who the fathers were since they resembled their own uncles. They got suspicious because every 4th of July, Fairly Farrow would go off somewhere with some favorite fellow for a couple of days and her sons had to watch over the bunch. With such a big family, Clifford and his brother Jeffers were happy to assign one hundred acres of cotton for them to sharecrop. Fairly never worked the fields."

"Let's go home, Althea. I just don't know why you seem so mad when you talk about those folks."

Before we left, however, my eyes fell to the strongest part of the house, which was the rusty tin roof. This shimmy-shack, as Thea also called it, seemed to goggle back at me with its tarpaper siding and windtorn, gritty red covering that imitated brick patterns. Underneath the red coverings were some more bits of tarpaper showing wood cracks leading into Shad and Bernicia Hall's bedroom. I could see a sinkhole in the bubbled up linoleum where water had leaked a small puddle onto the floor.

"I thought you wanted to go home, Tamara. You just staring back at that shack."

"I'm coming." A mop that was resting in the corrugated grooves of tin also caught my eye.

"I can out-run you, Luella."

"No you can't."

"No fair, Thea. You let us catch up with you."

"Hey baby sister, someday you can ask your question and nobody will get mad."

"I don't want to talk about questions anymore." Althea took our hands and we sang, 'I can wear these boots. You can wear those boots.' Wait a minute, Thea, Momma got mad when we said this before."

"We'll stop singing it when we get to the house. Besides, she got the County Fair to think about."

We skipped and continued singing through the sloppy dirt as plops of mud kicked up on our boots and some on our clothes.

Chapter 9

The Bus

There was hardly any time of the year when I didn't hear continual squawking of one sort or the other about the upcoming County Fair. Earlier in the year, however, there was a time they stopped talking about it.

It was near the end of cotton chopping season in late May when Claude, "the main" colored cotton ginner, drove to the fields to find us. Claude got his name for holding the cotton gin blowers real steady while standing in the cotton wagons, thus sucking up more cotton quicker than any of the other ginners. He did odd jobs for Jeffers and Clifford when it was not harvest time. His presence made us all curious. He parked at the edge of the cotton patch with a message from the general store for Momma Zettie Mae. Her grand niece, Miz Etheline Hollis, as the note said, "been crying out on her death bed, Zettie's name."

"Alfonso, I gots to go. I'll take one of you with me."

"I'll be the one."

"Thea, this ain't no pleasure trip. This just three days of saying farewell to Etheline."

"You be worrying me about going here and doing that. It ain't your time. A seven year older give me less trouble than a twelve year one. Tamara, you be coming with yow Momma."

I tried holding my tongue as Momma puts it. My left hand covered my mouth. June Bug looked at me and I tried changing my mind.

"But still Momma, why come …?" Now June Bug gave me a cold stare that pierced through my head. His lips were clenched and his chest was raised. Momma had frozen and I thought had stopped breathing.

"Why come Miss Etheline dying?"

June Bug's stare seemed a bit kinder and he lowered his chest at the same time, Momma let out a sigh.

"Guess it is her time Tamara. She been sick for years."

"Maybe you make Thea feel better if she goes."

"What?"

"Yes ma'am."

"Wh-i-te, col-o-re-d." I pronounced syllabically over and over as I was learning to read. It was so chilly. The wind felt like it was blowing needles into my shins as I stood motionless in front of the bus station wall. I couldn't figure out why there were two ladies' restrooms. As I turned my head looking at the two room doors, I felt my headscarf blow backwards where the glimmering spring sun peeped in from the wide-opened garage-type doors of the hound station. Greyhound it was.

I phonetically pronounced the same words and then closed my eyes and tried to spell them out loud. In my mind, spelling was really like some sort of spell when you shut everything else off and somehow start remembering how some words would go together. It was a pleasurable pastime for me; my own private game and I was always the winner. I made up the rule of standing still while I closed my eyes. They stayed closed even longer if I opened them and missed a letter. The spell was literally broken when I felt a big warm hand clutch my pinkie, which slowly took me out of my trance without frightening me.

I knew it was Momma as she softly whistled like a sweet Tennessee chirper, as she was happy to go visit Etheline in St. Louis. Since last year did yield a gain by paying off all the sharecropping debts, there was a little extra money. Therefore, a short trip to St. Louis was okay before the next bout of hard work had ended.

"All aboard. The hound is about to roll."

"Let's go, Momma!!" I called out as I pulled Momma's hand and her arm pulled me back.

"Not yet. We've got to wait our turn."

"One, two, three, we're next Momma!!"

"Do what I say!"

I knew from the snapping scowl, which was not at all the mood she was in that day, that I had better do exactly what she said and keep my mouth shut. I watched people walk by us and board the bus first while me and Momma stood to the side. There was one other real old colored lady who stood behind us and was obviously not from Corn Hollow or even here in Olellean, where Daddy Al had dropped us off to catch the bus.

"Guess she transferred from another bus and is traveling real far today," Momma whispered to me.

When the bus was loaded with the other people, the three of us were left. Momma and the old lady waited for the bus driver to beckon for us to get on. She even had me to help her board the old lady.

"Tam, you help her and put her hand on the rail as I'll get behind her to make sure she doesn't fall backwards."

I whispered. "But Momma! Why don't the bus driver help her and why didn't she get to board first like you say we do for elders?"

Then I noticed how the driver looked upset. His face had turned from a bumpy pink to a slight tomato red. With his squinting eyes and elastic-wrinkled lips shut tight, there was something going on that I did not understand. Since Momma didn't respond, I sensed that I had better not say another word. Instead, she held her head high as if I hadn't said a thing.

Again I tried to control my tongue when the sound of "wh" turned into a muted clearing of my throat as Momma looked down at me with her eyes bucked, her mouth clinched, her head nodding, and her hand giving me a tight squeeze that felt it was almost ready to jerk me. A sombering mood came over me as my arm seemed tensely stiff and my belly wanted to ache. Momma nodded and smiled at the other passengers until she and I reached our seat all the way back, in the very far back of the bus where there was one long seat under the back window.

I had noticed enroute to my seat as Momma pulled me along, that a lady had some colorful yarns of red, yellow, and green which turned my head as I walked until I had to turn around and be seated. I also noticed that there were empty seats in the middle of the bus. As I tried to pull Momma into one of them, I was met with such a strong grip that I thought my wrist was about to separate from my arm. I was like a wagon being pulled by a team of self-controlled mules and it had to follow.

Momma's good mood came back again and I even heard the sweet, kind, Tennessee bird voice as she released a little hum from her mouth. I leaned against her warm arm and chest and started to rest. When I felt Momma's fingers lose the grip on my hand, I explored. I looked up and saw the old, colored lady napping in the seat directly in front of us to the right. I also saw Momma's head weave back and forth as she caught it when she attempted to go into a deep sleep. Momma finally leaned against the window and seemed more comfortable. I felt it was safe to make my move. My mind sprung into colors of the rainbow as I pranced up towards the front of the bus.

I felt all of the other passengers noticing me. Ignoring the stares and even the old, colored lady beckoning me to come on back to my seat, I made my way to the old white woman's seat with the yarns. The yarn woman was wrapping yarn around one big wood stick and crossing it over with the other. She was a very, very, old white lady who didn't seem to mind me standing and staring at her. The old lady gave me instructions.

"Pull on this while I wind this red skein up."

Again, I was spellbound for the old lady was kind enough to let me help touch the yarns. I was mesmerized from the zigzaggy twisting of color as my eyes followed every movement of the yarn lady's hand. Not a second later did the old, colored lady call out to Momma Zettie.

"Woman, go get that gal 'fore she ruins our day and wese end up to walk a hundred miles!!!"

I looked up and Momma's eyes were red and her hand looked like she was going to slap me on the spot. I noticed a gloomy frown of panic over Momma's brow that I had never, ever seen before. And never hearing Momma's voice become so threatened and full of terror except when she beat Thea, made me confused. I remembered that it was like old Top that started foaming at the mouth when he went mad with rabies and his low growls started folks to running.

I shook and cried on the spot as I ran back to my seat, hearing the menacing low-toned rage in Momma's voice.

"And don't you move from that seat. Mighty sorry ma'am. Mighty sorry, sir," Momma repeated over and over as she went to her seat.

Several of the women just turned their chins up and looked out the window, accepting Momma's anger toward me as teaching me something, which meant they accepted her apologies. But what was this something? Soon the bus driver called out very loudly.

"Well its 'bout time she learns her place."

I wanted to say, "What place?" I breathed deeply and spasmodically cried softly for the next fifty miles until I cried myself to sleep.

For days and days to come, my spontaneity and free, happy, high-spirited nature was repressed. Every time that I thought of the bus ride, I went into a dead-like trace. I kept mumbling under my breath, "How could watching an old lady with pretty yarns and wooden sticks be bad?"

Momma would say to me, "Ain't nobody stuck pins in you, cause yew act like pins been pierced in your young heart."

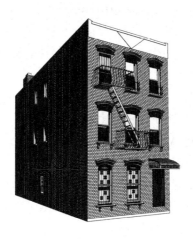

Chapter 10

St. Louis & Back

I thought it was real strange eyeing colored men bowing and running rags over white men's shoes as they sat up in big high chairs like kings I saw on television.

"Why are the black men dressed alike in dark maroon pants with lightly colored stripes up the side of their pants? And they only carry the white folks' suitcases and not yours!"

Momma did not answer me and I was thankful that she had stopped pulling my arm. I could still hear the loud speaker voices as we left the inside of the big, bus station that opened up into a series of other loud noises.

"St. Lu Saint Lu-ee!"

"Ex-tree! X-tre! Read all about it!! Only one nickel!"

Horns were honking and so many cars piled one behind the other. Police were using whistles and car brakes were screeching. "Hot Dogs!! Peanuts!! Get em right here!!"

"We gotta stand over here, darling, and wait for your Cousin Denton."

"Cousin who, Momma?"

"They'se be the ones that picks us up. Now I see that old lady riding with us been picked up by her peoples so we can go and wait for Denton."

I sorta smiled at the sight of Cousin Denton's automobile. He had the same kind of Plymouth Belvedere like our Reverend Stokes.

"What you think of my fine car, Tammy?"

"My name is not Tammy. It's Tamara and my Daddy Al says these cars are no good cause the radiator and the motors are weak."

"Why, Tamara, you were rude with your Cousin Denton."

"I learned somthin' from her, Zettie Mae. It's okay. Bus rides can make you tired."

As I looked out the car window, I saw a man wobbling and fall down. Every street started to look the same for me. I could see red brick three story buildings that Cousin Denton called some "fine homes for coloreds."

"I don't see a crack between the houses. Where can kids play hide and seek?"

No one answered me.

After a few salutations and hugs from strangers, Momma took a short nap as Etheline was asleep. While she was resting, I stood on the second floor apartment balcony and looked down to the street. I couldn't hear any birds singing in the trees. Kids were on the sidewalks riding bicycles and disregarding an elderly man by not letting him pass first.

A woman was switching and using vulgar language while in the alley across the street a man was leaning against a building with wet pants. He was advancing towards the front steps of that apartment building where others were sharing a drink that was covered with a paper sack. A teenager about the same age as June Bug looked up and started eye-walling me with ravish eyes. I didn't understand and turned away quickly. Feeling more comfortable inside the apartment, I tagged closely to Momma. I had no feelings for my Aunt Etheline, even though I had to force myself to hug this very sick lady. It must have been the right thing, as Momma Zettie cried like a baby and all the strangers patted me and called me a sweet and honorable young lady.

On one of the days, Cousin Denton and three other friends of Aunt Etheline's took Momma and me on a fun ride. I was not much in the mood to expect anything but I became astonished at viewing the clean neighborhoods with new brick houses and big front lawns.

"Where is this?"

"It's St. Louis County. These the suburbs where white folks live and this is the only street we coloreds can drive down before violating property rules."

"What you talking about, Cousin Denton?"

"Talk 'bout other stuff, Dent." Momma insisted.

"Well, I know a colored fella who works three blocks over and says there is a big locked gate and thersa big lake, and boat houses all round it. Idse don't need three jobs, otherwise ids go to work out yonder wit' him."

"Momma!! Cousin Denton!! Stop the car for a second. I see a squirrel and some dogs."

"Where that gal going?"

I leaped out of the car and started to ask a white girl the name of her dogs. Next thing I knew Cousin Denton had me lifted up in the air across his shoulders and placed me back into the car. Etheline's friends were calming Momma down.

Denton got her back in the car.

"She didn't know no better, Zettie Mae. Don't say anything to her. You say she been through that stuff on the bus. All she wants to do is run free like any child. And it will be good to get her back to the farm to clear her mind from such things and start doing things like she is used to doing."

I leaned my head against the car door and just looked at the treetops as Cousin Denton drove his car. I only wish I could close my eyes all the way back to Corn Hollow. But before I knew it, my eyes saw tall brick apartment buildings and Cousin Denton opening the car door. Helping Momma pack our things was the only thing on my mind.

Chapter 11

Home

Happiness was turning my head out of the car window this Saturday morning. The push of the wind was blowing on my face, as I was looking behind Daddy's car to see the dust kick up from the wheels. Looking in front of the car I could see our house, yard, hanging swing, the sun and dustier road.

Althea approached me immediately. My sister's constant begging to tell her something was becoming annoying.

"Did you hear them talk about Miz Etheline? Did you hear them say... I want you to tell me, Tamara. Tell me more. I heard about these stories but I know something more happened with that woman because she was such a special lady that Momma and Cousin Hortense, and even Miz Iola said that she endured some stuff."

"Stuff?"

I refused to listen and walked away to find Luella to jump rope with. Trying to go to bed earlier than usual, I felt bothered when Momma came into the bedroom asking us to lay our socks and church things out for tomorrow. It became a chance for Althea to ask me more.

"She wouldn't even let me finish holding that white lady's big thread. I wanted to see more on how she made those long sticks roll over with all those colors. And when Momma saw us, she got real mad. It looked like folks on the bus got glad when Momma snatched me to my seat. She acted scared and got quiet."

"I'm not surprised at her actions, Tamara. Time I told you about Miss Rosa. She was a tired colored lady who refused to sit in the back of the bus in Alabama. It was in 1955 and everybody is still stirred up here in Tennessee and in other states like Arkansas and Missouri. Anyways, I'll tell you more about it. I learned about this on WBIA radio. Are you listening to me, Tamara?"

"Folks were spitting on the sidewalks. They say nasty things and kids don't help the old folks."

"You are saying a lot of things for a young girl."

"The only clean part of the city is the superbs."

"You mean suburbs."

"And only white folks can live there."

Meanwhile, in church the next day, my mind wandered to the yarns I saw on the bus. I studied the deep colors of the women's church hats: purple feathers, green felt, and straw with red bows. The yarns, the hats, and now the colorful flower arrangement sitting in front of the pulpit, took preference over Reverend Stokes' sermon.

"If I could only hear one of the chirens, like Tamara say, Aman. This young lady bravely said farewell to her Aunt Etheline along with Sister Zettie last week."

The whole church looked at me, but my gaze was transfixed with shades and colors.

"Child, what is wrong with you? That preacher looked right at you and you didn't even know he had called your name."

"I was looking at the colors in the flowers and ..."

"See if next weekend you can let your mind stay on them taters, onions, peas, and other things we gotta do next Saturday. Otherwise, I wake you up with a peach tree switch."

"Yes m'am," I dryly mumbled, and was glad for church to be over.

Knock! Knock! "Mr. Daniel Goodson is at the door Momma."

"What brings you here at this time of day? Let's go talk on the porch."

"I'll be straight. Zettie Mae, some white folks don't want Raymond Delmar and Miss Fruke to meet up again."

"But Daniel, Miss Fruke helping our kids with books and delivers em to Raymond and ain't nothing more to it. Just go and tell 'em that, Dan'l."

"I hope they be convinced of that, Zettie Mae." Daniel scratched his head. Althea overheard this and started talking to me.

"Tamara, it's that kind of stuff that I have been trying to tell you about because Mr. Daniel's secret job is just like Etheline's, being Tom. Well, did you know that when she was a young girl, she was a sl-ave!!?"

"Oh!! Don't talk to me like that, Thea."

"No, it wasn't her. It was really her Momma that was a

slave and everybody says she passed her ways on to Etheline."

"Why they say that, Althea? What ways? What you talking bout? I don't know what you are talking about."

"Well, you know her father was a plantation owner and his name was Mr. Hudsley and he liked her much, but you know what? He let her get whipped right in front of him. Then he was real kind to her like Mr. Daniel when he tells the white folks everything that we colored folks do. And there's more."

"Well, she was their house servant, and Miz Hudsley was there too and that she was her stepmomma, but nobody could say anything. Miz Hudsley was always real mean to her. She was even so mean that she tried to pull her arms off one day in an old wringer-type washing machine. Miz Etheline's momma looked exactly like Mr. Hudsley, more so like him than his own kids. Then, Miz Etheline ran off with a colored man and they tried to find her but she couldn't be found. She got tired of the bad treatment by Miz Hudsley. Anyway, no one knew where she was and eventually she showed up in St. Louis. She came into a lot of money because she helped tell the whites about what the colored folk were doing when they worked in the factories and what they were planning. She was allowed to work in the back office as a yellow woman who could shuffle some papers, mingle with the blacks and snitch. You must have heard that, Tamara. You went all the way to St. Louis and you can't say anything?"

Althea kept bothering me.

"Come on, Sis. Did you hear them say why Etheline's Ma ran away from the Hudsleys? Well, the story goes that Mr. Hudsley entered the plantation house one day and saw Miz Etheline's ma taking a bath and looking real pretty.

He had been drinking a lot of booze. 'You ain't no more my daughter than anybody' and that is all she told others about it. Miz Etheline was born shortly there afterwards. She had to run away when she knew she couldn't bear anymore of the pain in her belly as well as looking at that man. The colored man she ran away with died by some accident but someone told that he was found hanging from a sycamore. Then Miz Etheline, she was the brave one left behind and now she's dead."

"Althea!! I'm not in the mood for this. Sometimes I don't know what you say is true or not. And I don't believe that!!"

Chapter 12

Truck Patches and Canning

During crop lay-by season, school was back in session from late spring through late August. Not only were our minds at work through the week, our hands were free to work on weekends.

Truck patch planting time for us Banks was bigger than most other family gardens in Corn Hollow. Besides mouths to feed, Momma would grow for communal events, and grow string beans and onion braids for the County Fair. Potatoes, tomatoes, onions, pole beans, peas, lettuce, squash, beets, carrots, and other vegetables had to be rooted either from starts, slips, or seeds.

Although other weekends were spent picking and canning blackberries, picking peaches and digging up the root

99

crops, Daddy could be counted on to take over the "Dixie Queen" watermelon planting, the cantaloupes, and the corn patch. However, an exceptional amount of corn was used for corn meal, canning, and summer eating on the cob.

Althea and I thought that we would have a head start on school in late August by writing what Althea called "prose" about all the work that we did. Althea did the writing and I threw in the names of vegetables and the fun parts. We also thought that we would give it to our teacher, Cousin Delmar, in hopes that he would feel sorry for us. He could then talk to Momma Zettie and Daddy Al about stopping the laborious drudgery. We called it:

"Work, Work, and More Work"

*Truck patches are not a place for driving trucks
to be patched up.
It's a way to feed a family throughout the year -
A source of trade and swapping to pay off debts
of labor, extra nails, a car tire, and things we don't
have money to buy.
After the frost, the decomposed barn waste,
chicken manure, ashes, and lime are plowed in
Mixed & ready to be fed seeds and starts surrounded
by earthworms playing tag around its roots.*

*Each of us with a task,
Even Grandma, who has since passed on,
with her flour sack-patched apron pockets
Filled with radish seeds as she would sprinkle,
sprinkle, & sow the seeds*

The sun is hot and it's only morning time.
The birds are singing and waiting for
us to end the day
In hopes of retrieving dropped seeds
or a very slow-pokey dirtworm.
Daddy Al having slivered bucket upon bucket of
Irish potato parts with eyes that will bud
Roots and stems and germinate under
the covered ground.

The excitement of making a scarecrow before
the day would end
Made us kiddies overjoyed.

Within a few weeks,
like the laces lined on the shelves
of Momma Zettie's sewing corner.
It was rows of ups and downs
Of the hues of green
With protruding root purples of the turnips
And maroon topped beets
And green, round, red dangles on the tomato vines.
The tee-pee bean poles with their wigwam shapes
Lodging coils of curly strings and beans
Growing in viney fashion
Leaping from one pole to the other.

The occasional chrysanthemum or zinnia
at the end of a row
Decorating the garden with yellowish-red jeweled
laughter.

And then there was last summer

When we picked, gathered, strung, and peeled.
One of those days when we couldn't hold it together
Throwing just happened.
Tiny potatoes lurched across the potato patch.
Fast-flying potatoes that felt like a hot
straightening comb
That melted with a bundle of grease on your neck.
That sudden burn the yells the screaming
squalls of anger.
It was a time for retaliating from the direction
from whence it came.
One of us and then another was lifted out of
the thought of being uninvolved
And all plunged into the deep and unexpected demise
of releasing on an otherwise perfectly productive day.
Some sweet potatoes that had been hit
by Daddy Al's plow
Showed up as droplets shining in the sun
from its cut-through veins like unearthed
precious gold nuggets.

All hell broke loose for the only chore was revenge.
A time to expell the frustration of puberty, of structure,
Of a hot summer day's crop output.
Everyone remained rude, rough, and abrupt until...
A fine pitched yet loud voice seemed to
Penetrate through the big walnut tree
And bounced off the wire fence.
Quickly brushing the dirt off our clothes,
Wiping the tears,
And asking each other if they were hurt ...
And running to pick up the tossed-about taters
That ended up on the other side of the fence.

Uprighting the now empty lard buckets
and rushing to fill them
So we could quietly eat lunch.
With our breathing held in semi-suspense
Hoping the two tattlers did not utter the tale.
The onions had to be pulled and washed
Revealing their many thinned brushy legs
And the green blades in preparation
Of becoming a Kool Aid straw.
And the rest to later be braided and hung to dry
In the shed with the sweet potatoes, Irish potatoes,
And hanging garlic braids, and red peppers.

Labor, labor, seemed to never end for there was canning.
The jars being re-sterilized and the pressure
cooker made ready
Only new lids to buy that seals up a-new as
No one, not a soul broke a jar last year.

The peach barrel now emptied into the big
enameled dish pan.
After the peeling that leaves juices of pulp
oozing through fingers
And the big inlayed oval nugget of a seed to suck
off the tentacle-
attached fruit with its yellow and red fronds of nectar
That puts us kids into a slurping trance
That makes us wonder if it was the juice or
the heaviness of the seed
That made a thud on my head
When a naughty one of us prematurely shook a limb
While someone was under the tree picking up fallen fruit.

We could suck and extract from the crevices of the seed
Leaving it with the effects of two weeks rather than
two hours exposed.
Slurping and sloshing from this point on as we watched
Momma Zettie and Cousin Hortense take over from here.
The hot steamy vapors would flare up
to the kitchen ceiling
As the big, thick, pot holders lifted the jar holders up
And the jar lids sinking down with the seal
sound of "pop"
And the seal of contentment by all
For its contents would be devoured as a
wintertime peach cobbler.

This went on for a few weeks
Sometimes during the weekdays when we were at school
But mostly on weekends when we could help.

The string beans lifted from the pressure cooker
With their haughty stance.
The quartered cabbage with their unperforated leaves
Where worms did not tread.
The yellow cucumbers and the briny cucumbers
A pickle delight
The gush of the clear blood okra
Willing to slip through my teeth
Finally dissolving its seeds and skin into my throat
After a bite of a crispy fried drumstick and a piece of
crackling bread.
Jars of carrots, peppers, and tomatoes
Making its way for the best soups and stews
Reeking its savory odor all the way to the bottom end
Of the cotton wagon

At the end of a September afternoon.
All of which are like a Picasso ready for exhibition hall
At the next County Fair.

"Tamara!"

"Yes, Big Sis?"

"Are you thinking what I'm thinking?"

"What?"

"Did we see a vision of that boy named Till appear and duck from a flying sliced potato? Then he walked up to me and said, "Girl, that boy you eyeing is just a thief and a turn-coach. Let him outa yow mind."

"I think I saw him."

"Well, I also think that we don't have it too bad."

"If we didn't do these things, we wouldn't have anything good to eat at all."

"Maybe we could write a prose about picking cotton and Momma ..."

"Don't even think about it."

Chapter 13

Away

The following day I think that I had been hit in the head by one too many potatoes. All I could think about is that I really love my family and Momma hates me. I know that Althea understands me so I better talk to her.

"I told Momma who started that potato throwing. I know Luella and the rest will be mad at me. Momma needed to know that she can't just get mad at you, Thea. My tattling got us nowhere. Momma thought I did the right thing. And June Bug, you look like you want to holler at me."

"This is not like you, Tamara, telling on us and now we got more work to do because of you. Maybe it's about time I tell Momma Zettie what you drew and what you asked

Cousin Delmar at school."

I ran and cried uncontrollably. Slipping in the mud was like being at the Hall shack but I wasn't mad then. I quickly made another turn and made it to the Fairly Farrow house. I took a good look at her. She was white in every sense of the word but talked like us coloreds. There were black and white and yellow children in the yard. They stared at me as I approached and asked for Miz Fairly. The entire front porch was fixed and there was siding on the house. Out of Miz Fairly's mouth came, "They gonna be mad, girl, for you coming here."

"I want to be here."

"How come?"

"I never knew anybody white. Some say you are not white."

"Come on in the house. It's late to turn you back around now cause the sun is going down and I'll walk you near Miz Zetties's early tomorrow after we tend to Melviner Tate's sores."

"We? Take me home now."

"No. After what I heard how your Momma whipped your sister, serves her right to have to worry about you."

"She'll probably beat me now."

"I know things about your Momma that you don't and she ain't gonna beat you. Come."

Fairly led me to her hidden closet that had a secret door behind the wall-papered over area in her bedroom. She said that cornhusks were good for boiling and drinking for the whooping cough and the old dirt dobber nest for a paste that goes with vinegar for bee or wasp stings. If there is no brown chlorine in sight, then mix a spoon of dried, sweet-smelling rose petals for a rash, and the dried peach and walnut tree leaves were for anyone to put on the truck patch vegetables to turn away the insects. The bugs don't like the odor and it beats poisoning food that goes in our bellies. Your momma already knows these things. "So that's why Momma told us the Coloreds have a remedy judging of our own under the big elm outside the fairgrounds by the County Fair sign? Momma said you the best judge and can tell by looking at potions and curing salves and asking a few questions that you know which one would win." I started yawning and Fairly lead me to a pallet on the floor.

Awakening the next morning, I used the chamber pot that the others used in the corner. Mr. Snake Dewitt was in the kitchen talking to Fairly and they were laughing it up. Shortly after eating some scrambled eggs, Miz Fairly led me to the Tate house where she knew it was Momma's turn to tend to Miz Melviner's sores. Two of Fairly's boys followed us with shovels. Fairly gave them instructions where to dig the new toilet hole for the Tates, since Reverend Tate was getting older and too stricken with grief to do it himself. Reverend Tate saw me and said, "Your mamma is a saint." I stepped inside the house and looked at Momma. Her hands were covered with white gloves and waxed paper was tied over the gloves, which had blood and slime on it. She turned and saw me and then continued with her task. I watched. Blistery lesions with pus discharging from Miz Melviner's leg and side, instantly made me want to heave. I left and gave Reverend Tate a handkerchief that Momma told me to grab from the dressing table top. "Tam, she-she done gone blind an-and she gonna go on to Christ by-by next morning. Miz Fairly done made up so-so much curing balm for yow Momma to dress my lovely Melviner's wounds. Your Momma-Momma and Miz Fairly the only ones in Corn Hollow to see-sees after Melviner after them sores started busting. Folk say bad things about-bout that Fairly woman, but she ain't bad, just led to doing what-what she hafto to be alive and cast outa-out her own family."

"How come some of her children white and some of them colored?" Scratching his head, the Reverend stopped crying and told me that she is white, but it doesn't matter to anyone because the whites don't want her and the coloreds don't either. "So just colored folk come into her house like Mr. Snake Dewitt? I saw him."

"Now Mis-Miss Tamara, you done asked enough questions that a young lady ought not ask. I ain't saying n-no more." Just then Miz Fairly walked up to the steps.

Miz Fairly stood tall and erect. Her always-brushed, brown and sandy hair, that looked almost dirt-colored, hung just past her neck as she pulled it to the back of her ears with her unevenly cut bangs drooping from her forehead. Some of the bang ends rode closely to the tip of her wire-rimmed eyeglasses that folks said that Mr. Clifford gave to her. He gave her most of Miz Clifford's hand-me-downs that she seemed to always cover with a green and white flour-sack apron with two big rick-racked trimmed pockets. Her small, beady green eyes looked clearly at me down her pointed and slightly crooked nose and sorta fat bottom lip and you couldn't tell if she even had an upper one. This often made her look tough until she opened her mouth and smiled, showing her plump cheeks stretching diagonally over her deep dimples on her olive smooth skin.

"Okay, Tamara, I'll figure out a way to tell Zettie Mae something that will not let you get a beating."

"Can I come back some time and learn more about your curing stuff?"

"I'm counting on it, but let me make the moves with

your Momma after the County Fair. I'll be glad to pass this on to one of Zettie's kids. Now go on home now and start your chores and be working when your Momma gets home." We smiled at each other and I ran towards home, but only half-way.

Chapter 14

Cotton Picking

Spotting Mr. Dan'l Goodson's truck, I figured he might see me and take me home and make a fuss of things. I know he would love to see me sweat and cry with peach tree marks because he was mad at me when I asked his wife Siddie a question at Momma's Community Circle meeting. I hid behind the wild muscadine vines until his truck approached closer. Not having a choice, I had to run back to Fairly's and hide on her back porch. Luckily, her boys and two daughters were gone to Olellean for tools. I squatted behind an old barrel and my legs were about to pop from under me in pain. Not being able to move, I heard someone enter. I grabbed an old flour sack that blocked my view from an open window in the kitchen. Who was in there? I could see a hat and then I saw Miz Fairly walk and then stop. I could see her hip and the side of her underarm. Then I saw a big white hand all wide and moving around on her hips. Hearing giggles and a man's voice, I ran with the clenched flour sack, dodging Mr. Daniel's truck. I saw the cotton wagon, and afraid to move any further, I hid under it and fell asleep. Truck wheels came near the wagon and stopped slightly ahead of it. It was Mr. Daniel and his boss men, Mr. Jeffers and Mr. Clifford. I could hear Mr. Daniel speak.

"Well, Al doing his part with his people. We check on them other sharecroppers in a bit. Them field hands working good. Mr. Clifford and me saw to it that Fairly's kids started out real early this morning to get you some John Deere plow disc parts and other 'quipment you been talking about."

"Good, Dan'l."

Jeffers rolled his eyes and looked at his brother.

"Ah, I just went by and threw her some change. Yeah, one good thing about Fairly, she knows who she is and that's why I help her out."

A sneaky grin twisted from the side of Jeffer's lips.

"Oh, yeah!?"

Both brothers laughed. Mr. Daniel laughed with them too.

"You see, even Dan'l boy know she come to terms with who she is."

"Yes sir." The truck then drove away.

Now I gotta stay under this wagon and act like I've been here all the time when they weigh in them cotton sacks.

"Is that you under the wagon?"

"Why you ask, June Bug?"

"Cause there's better places to pout than under there. Try putting some cotton in that sack."

I stood up and felt the air had turned from a muggy breeze to crispy and clear whiffs of pleasure now that fall was approaching. What was once a big, luscious, bunch of green leaves now took on an astonishing radiance that amazed my eyes with a grand assembly of white fluff with brown and beige open thorny bolls drooping towards the earth.

Miz Melviner had passed away and was packed with ice. Her funeral and burial were two days after her death so her sister from Nashville could make it in.

"Remember what the Reverend said about Miz Melviner?"

"Yeah, I do. That poor lady has never, ever, been out of Corn Hollow and knew nothing more than what her husband had taught her."

"How old was she?"

"Thirty-seven and too young to die."

Cousin Hortense had pulled her cotton sack ahead to chat with us.

"It was so-so good of Zettie Mae tending Miz Melviner's sores. She just put-put on some old stewardess gloves that she had to burn up after and takes them patches of cloth off and swab-swab the sores with a soft balm to help her suage her miseree. Those sores had gone clean through-through her muscles and done infected clear down to her bones. Yeah! Yow Momma like a saint, cause no other woman including-cluding myself, not Met-dist and not even her Baptist sisters, would come in her house while she passed on-on to the Good Lord."

"Well, Miz Fairly helped Miz Melviner."

"Sometimes she did, Tamara."

"Hunh, if Momma such a saint, how come she can't deliver us from this slave work?"

Cousin Hortense looked sternly at Althea after sounding out. I noticed her continuous discounting of any reflection of Miz Melviner. Thea sulked and became more loud and aggravating.

Smooth twists and turns made by the extra-thick, natural-beige muslin cotton sacks tiered behind Daddy Al, Momma, Althea, June Bug and all of Cousin Hortense Ludgess' family. All of us were a sight to see. We swiveled from one row's end to the next only to lift our heads and rotate to the dominant hand which emptied the soft, lumpy cotton into the sack. Since the bottom of the receptacles were half adorned with plastic dots underneath to protect the muslin from the sticks, rocks, and unplowed clumps of vegetation, the cotton sacks made a sound which imitated the howling wind when it was filling up. Prolonged with wailing sounds, the sacks become full as they were dragged along the cotton row. Some of the dots were red and others were blue which resonated patriotism, but to whose cause?

Actually, us Banks and the Ludgess family continued to move simultaneous and faced yet another row of luscious bolls, like cotton sack trance dancers. The spell broke when Isom and June Bug started talking silly. Daddy actually ventured to talk.

"Bet you can't scale up 300 pounds by sundown 'tween the both of you."

June Bug and Isom moved swiftly, made wide turns and kicked up dust as they dug their heels in the ground and leaned forward. Their sack loads looked thick in the middle and seemed like the old encyclopedia pictures of big pre-historic creatures, and if silhouetted would look more like the ends of brontasuarus tails than long, cotton satchels for holding fluff. Of course this acceleration precipated an even louder thundering howl, maybe like a baby dinosaur, or was it the whispering growl of wind in the original hollow at the center of the Corn Hollow pasture?

All in all, the noisy rhythm of Isom and June Bug's sack bellies seemed to speed up the contest.

"I know I can get about twenty-five more pounds in if I pack it down some more." Isom stopped to shake his sack down and compress his load.

I did not understand this type of competition. It was hard enough just trying to follow the flow of picking, turning, placing, shaking down, and repeating the action. And there were those of us who were inexperienced and would have to take it a lot easier. It was enough just trying to pace ourselves as long as possible before getting tired and asking Momma or Cousin Horetense if we could rest and play. Watching Cousin Hortense and Momma, who were fast cotton pickers, could make my head swim. And continually smelling those new sacks, a cross between a hay barn and smoked cotton seeds, took some getting used to.

"Hide and seek anyone?"

"No. Rest and seek, is what I'm going to do. I'll tell Momma that I am going to watch you little ones for a bit."

Althea then pulled a book out of her cotton sack and stretched out on it near a sunny, hot rock. She started reading something aloud to me:

"Certainly, she had ways that most everybody never say a child take up before, and she put all of us past our patience fifty times and oftener in a day: from the hour she came downstairs, till the ... "

Althea stopped reading and started panting with fear. Her actions were so strange that I slowly peered off the end row and observed that Althea was eyeball to eyeball with a variegated, scaly-patterned, black and tawny-brown snake. Making a disgustingly angry, hissy sound like knotty pebbles shaking in an old gourd, it couldn't be ignored. I started to panic. Surely if Althea could have crawled out of her skin, she would have. Her shoulders had risen five inches high and her body was dripping sweat. The hisser's red, fork-like tongue was all ready for the wrong move to complete its vaulting thrust. Out of nowhere Momma appeared and held a hoe arched in a ready-to-chop position. Althea looked up at the hoe and screamed as Momma killed the snake.

Althea said, "Thank God. I thought it was real."

Cousin Hortense signaled with her hand for us kids to be quiet and told us to get back to what we were doing. Somehow we were not tired anymore. Momma and I just shook our heads at Althea's comment.

Without any forewarning, Daddy Al let out an unrecognizable sound. Althea squealed with laughter.

"Could that be a guttural jungle song from the slaves and now Daddy is passing it on to us in the fields?"

Isom and June Bug didn't know whether to join in or start sniggering with laughter. Soon enough, June Bug lost it and started to giggle. He shook all over, fell to his knees and held his mouth while tears came to his eyes.

"Oh, wow-wow, et ke mo to yahh ke mo."

The sounds then changed to a chant. As if caught by a spell, June Bug transformed his giggling into a high tenor sound.

Daddy Al howled loudly as if in a trance with his words: *"Wacuma,* wacuma, ho ya, wacuma-a."

Althea rambled, "It's a spiritual cantata, a song of torture, or it's too much sun beaming through Daddy Al's hat down to his head." Both Althea and Verdie were baffled.

Mr. Leo and Miz Quintilla, whose family picked in the adjoining twenty acres, heard the harmony and their voices flowed back and forth from one field to the other.

"Bet if we went up and down all of Corn Hollow's turning rows, folks would be singing. Maybe it has something to do with Miz Melviner."

"You mean spirits, Verdie?"

"I don't know what it means."

I stood still, trying not to listen to Thea and Verdie. I looked behind me towards the cotton wagon. All young heads were standing up in the wagon on the cotton piles. Bodies were turning in all directions to hear sounds from one field to another as their straw hats wobbled while chanting and picking cotton. Clapping, humming, and more repetitious sounds resonated. A big clap and one lasting deep hum completed the sonance.

Everyone seemed to be at such peace that it would have been dishonorable for anyone to ask questions. Even Althea managed to keep her mouth shut, until she whispered:

September 16, 1954, Miss Melviner is no more than age 36, known to be a good wife and church-goer, very good with canning and field hand work, barren of child, taken by serious pox in her body, rest in peace our Sister Melviner.

Daddy Al, Isom and all packed their sacks and threw them across their strongest shoulder. They were very quiet as they anxiously waited to place their sacks on the cotton scale to see which one weighed the most.

The silence broke when a sudden breeze blew an appetitious delight over everyone's olfactories. Stomachs began to growl as the food smells emitted hefty aromas. Isom caught a gust of peppery-flavored frying chicken that took him out of focus.

"Oh Lord, heaven for the belly. I know there's those bittery collard greens and grand hoecakes just for me."

Momma had left the field an hour prior to finish up in the kitchen, as she had prepped dinner directly after lunch before rejoining us in the field.

The sun was an hour from going down and almost everyone had already made their way near the back porch to prime the water pump and wash faces and hands.

As the family chowed down after the supper prayer, Daddy was notably preoccupied in thought.

Chapter 15

The County Fair

Waking up in a daze from some kitchen noises, I immediately fell back asleep, not sure if it was a dream or just my thoughts. But my mind was fixed. Somehow after the snake experience I gave up pouting about what Momma did to Althea and how she wanted me to stop asking questions. Instead, I decided then and there before a hoe-chopped snake that I will ask questions, even if it takes me many years to find an answer.

We had to get up so early on Fair morning. There was so much hustling and bustling. I had to get out of the way many times because I thought I was gonna have some sort of fit just hearing Momma move around so nervously with excitement. Mr. Snake Dewitt, along with Mr. Shad and Bernicia Hall, had driven to our place with those squealing hogs in the truck and that woke me up so early. I heard Daddy's voice, and then a woman's voice that I thought was no doubt Miz Bernicia. She was telling the guys what to do and they were telling her to sit down and to count which animal goes where, and to what hog lot. That morning was awfully busy.

Daddy and June Bug argued. "On them female gilts and brood sows, they look at how far the ridge is from the withers to the loin."

The chatter continued. "No, back 'em in. No sit 'em sideways. You gotta put that in because you got all that other stuff of Leo Hickles in there. You've got those Herefords in there. You know those heffas and those pigs just don't work out well together. Now we gotta separate em. And then there's that goat. A near screaming snort came out. And Lord knows where in the world we gonna put a small lot of Miz Iola's chickens."

"Aw, yeah. That's right!!"

"Well Bernicia, maybe you hold them chicken cages on your lap."

"I'll be chicken -- if I do."

Momma kept banging on our door.

"Git up. It's time to git up and git yow stuff ready. I got yow stuff ready for the talent show. The livestock truck come around and it's time for us to git ourselves out of bed now."

And every year I wondered what this is all about ... The County Fair, The County Fair. Everybody is making such a big deal out of it. When we get settled at the fairgrounds, that is when I feel really happy. I see something everywhere I turn or something to do "from food to fertilizer." Maybe it should have been called that instead of the Grentwood County Fair or even "cotton candy to Ferris wheels." And would there be a county fair without cotton candy? Seems like one of the biggest things that folks were trying to get together that morning were the hogs, the cows, the chickens and the goats. Heaven knows everything else that crawled or walked-in, that they had in that fair. They called it the agriculture department. When Luella and I looked to see if Daddy and June Bug's hog was in the hog lot, some guys said, "they look like winners." They were feeding slop to them and we could tell Daddy they were taken care of. Now Daddy Al could help put things up at the colored 4-H booth and in the colored canning and quilting area next to it.

"Get this information! Gypsy moss!!"

An auctioneer voice spoke over the loud speaker. It was the pre-fair sale.

"Long horn beetle!! Get your pesticides now so you have a better yield of crops. Get one of these here applications. There is a way you can store it right here on your farms and yow families don has to smell all that stink. Get it right now. Come on extree."

My mind flew back to St. Louis, hearing "extra" where guys were selling newspapers. Then the big voice came up again. "Had a bob, a $1, $2, $30. Going once, going twice, sold." It was where I stopped and heard lots of car motors starting and stopping.

Leaving the agriculture department, Luella and I went to the bumper cars. I couldn't wait to get in one of those later on, if Momma would let us. I saw approved youth with pretend sheriff stars on green shirts directing with their hands and arms as folks crossed the road and unloaded things. Meanwhile, others in real sheriff clothing were taking tickets at the gate and saying to "have a nice day." Althea, Verdie, and all the Ludgess and our family were just roaming over the place and still trying to stay close to Momma and see all the stuff going up that day. I saw a big stage over to the side for entertainment. Then Momma threw the word out to us really hard. "You know that song you all sang, you and Luella? That song you all sang about *Who Got the Ding Dong, Who Got the Bell.* Well, I'm gonna give yowall these outfits here and you all going sing it up there on that stage so proud."

I lost touch of my feelings and couldn't respond. I glazed at the big Ferris wheel with my eyes, saw the fun house going up, the whirly bird seats being attached, and the bottle-throwing counter. My stomach boiled in fear and I started breathing hard and short. I had waited all this time for a day of great fun and now it's all ruined every time I think about the talent show. Luella was not overjoyed at all. I had to put it out of my mind and say to myself that Momma was just joking in order that I could have a little fun.

"She ain't gonna let us do that. I can't and ain't gonna or I'll be sick. So that's it!"

"You gonna be sick. Ha!! You know our Momma is not going to stand for that even if you are sick."

"Why don't you just hush, Althea?"

"No, why don't you just sing, *Who Got the* …?"

"All right, just cut it out, gals. Cut it out. Where yow Momma sets up them jars?"

"Over there, Daddy. She's in there. We'll be right behind you."

"Hey, Luella, there's a big sledge hammer that hits that target when men pound to make that rod hit the target and get prizes. Food vendors are getting ready to cook hot dogs and other stuff." My eyes passed another area that was near the agriculture barn.

"Let's go to the Farm Yard Friends area." Over there were the goats and the chickens. The smells of wet dirt and freshly cleared out manure came my way. A pen filled with corn kernals instead of sand was a play area for the kids when they need to do something else. They entered the pen with no shoes and troweled corn kernels into toy trailers and small tin buckets. The little pony rides where the kids could ride a real pony also joined some milk cows for a cow milking contest. How cute, I thought, but I decided to stay away from this area after I looked at Miz Iola's chickens.

Miz Iola was up real early as she and Mr. Jake rode in with Miz Siddie and Mr. Daniel because they live close to one another. I thought she would be at home because she's been moaning more about her chickens than other stuff she lost in the fire. She did have two guinea fowls that were not burned and a pearl with a mixed variety of pear and lavender keets as well as a full-grown white guinea chicken. She kept her word.

"Them folks 'spect me to be here with my chickens and I gonna have what I have. Gonna tell them 'bout my house and we do more trading in other ways. I gotta be here to get more chickens and tell some of these other folks coming up here with these chickens what to do for them. Some of these colored ladies think they know everything 'bout them. Som don knows them birds need to be scrubbed with warm water for showin. Got put som of this here oil on the legs cause they gots scales on 'em. How they think I won all of them blue ribbons over the years? Hopefully they washed the chickens a week fore the show so that them natural oils don't return to the feathers and they gotta be here early to start settling down fore folks be round saying look at them cute hens and all that has to happen fore them judges come round. On a hankie I put a little oil to shine up them feathers so they look good and make sure they water 'em."

"You can't tell people what to do about they own chickens, Iola," Mr. Jake snapped.

"Well, they better do this and I sure hope they dusted 'em with some powders so them fleas don git on everybody. If them judges start scratching their hands, the chickens outa the contest."

"Iola, come on now. You kant mope 'bout them chickens all the time. Know what, Iola, you talk that out with Miz Zettie Mae and Miz Hortense. I ain't here today to talk about them fowls."

The goat area looked inviting as Luella and I, totally adapted to so many barnyard smells by now, went to "Come Meet the Meat Goats." Entering a barnyard gate, an antelope, looking goat met us with a sagging udder. It was tan with dark streaks of hair on the spine all the way to its short outpointed tail as it moved to a stall with nudging, and butting motion to find its way to his hay stall. Some of the other goats had long ears with markings like a paint pony with hooves and feet standing like stout, furry boots as they made their goat sounds. Through screen door pens we could see other goats with green stamped tags stapled in their ears to show their prize winnings of a most elegant breed that seemed shy and were real pretty. And then I looked up and believed that I saw a goat that was most possibly sired from a donkey and took every bit the head of a billy goat. What I didn't like were the posters on the goat stalls showing drawings and illustrations of eatable cuts of goat meat for the doe and buck.

"Let's look at the steer, Luella."

A sign read, "Please Pet Us, We Like It."

Somehow we didn't think that was such a good idea. It was funny that the prize cows and bulls looked like they were on some of Miz Fairly's sleep medicine as they were bedded off their feet and onto floors of oat straw, some nodding away in crotched positions as their ropes kept their heads up so folks could see them and take pictures. Oops. The rope got tight as the head of the one named "Dirty Martin" had to be untangled. It read under his name: DOB-November 16, 1953. The remarkable thing is that these sorrel brown creatures were so clean-sheared and calm. Do they know the signs above their heads read: "The Bluford Beef Masters," not knowing their imminent fate as steaks and burgers?

I noticed Daddy waving his arms up in the air, beckoning us to come in and not wanting to shout because there were so many people around. And surely he didn't want to make the white folks think we couldn't do our thing. We wanna go in the FHA (Future Homemakers of America) booth now. Daddy's movements got sterner.

"Now kids, yowall got all day and now we gotta get these things together for yow Momma and Hortense. So go over there and help 'em out any way you can."

"Daddy, we really want to see the flowers and the vegetable part. They call it flora bin or flors something Flora cul-ture."

Heads turned as I was reading aloud. And June Bug said that he and Isom wanted to go over to the agriculture mechanics parts and see the demos of the big tractors and plows.

"Now look, Tamara, I can talk for myself, okay. I'm going to do my work and then I get to do that. But don't you even tell my Daddy what you want him to tell me what I can do. Git it little girl, lil sis?"

Anyways, I ignored June Bug.

"Hey Momma, there's the Home Arts."

"Don' be fussing wit yow Momma. Don' be talking to her now. She be setting up for these things and she be in bad shape."

"But they show people how to make corn husk dolls. We got lots of corn … can make lots of dolls."

"Momma, I'll lay out the salves." I thought of Miz Fairly's secret door behind a wallpapered-over area in her house and what she told me about dried corn husks also being used for whooping cough.

"Wese all knowd, Miz Fairly, as yellow as can be and fair-skinned for a colored woman, they say. Well, she done turned to be the judge. She can tell by looking at the texture, smellin' and asking questions which one of us will win. Yow Big Sis will only pitch them remedies out the doe cause she ain't together with anything 'bout Corn Hollow. It's good, Tamara, that you know sumthing 'bout remedies so you can help folk."

Shaken out of my daze of this early morning, I then heard Momma talk. "Go spread them salves out on a box and put some lace fabric over it fore puttin' down the lace and take 'em out there to Fairly."

Mr. Jake and Miz Iola did their trading and it was no surprise to see them walk around with their big, brown clutch bag. Althea and Verdie were up on the Ferris wheel screaming about something and stopping people dead in their tracks.

"He snatched the bag from Mr. Jake's arm. He's over there hiding behind that stack of crates."

Confusion, cuss words and hollering went on.

"We got you, boy."

The Ferris wheel stopped and Mr. Jake, out of breath, said, "Thank you Sheriff."

"You mean I did all that for a colored."

"Thank you sir. Thank you, sir."

"Git on outa here, boy, and don't make no more trouble."

"Ain't nobody gonna do nothing bout it." Verdie became frantic.

Looking back at Verdie, the Sheriff groaned. "What did you say, gal?"

"Nuthing."

"Better be nuthin'."

Sheriff took a bite of chewing tobacco, frowned and walked away, shaking his head.

Daddy mumbled, "Tomorrow, I gots a dig them folks a hiding hole for that satchel 'fore someone takes off with it for shore."

"It was that boy from the school yard named Trig Alvin who was nice to me and now he lowered himself to a mere thief. How come he had to be the one? I sorta liked him."

"Don't you ever let your Momma hear that."

"I won't."

Miz Fairly wiped the sweat off her eyeglasses with her apron and gave me a break from the salve area and told me to enjoy myself because there had been enough excitement already and to forget about it. This made Luella and me happy as I entered the canning area where Luella was helping her mom, Cousin Hortense.

"Go on you gals and have some fun, but check in here every hour on the hour."

"Yes ma'am."

We had to see most of the farm stuff before making our

way to the noisy side where the fun rides were.

The Petting Farm was where most parents with little toddlers roamed. It consisted of chickens, rabbits, piglets eating shoat and lots of screaming mothers saying, "Real cute" to their young ones and, "Wash your hands at the pump."

Over near those animals were advertisers who parked their big, new John Deere and Farmall tractors where the overalled farmers looked under, over and around them. A couple of big Ford trucks sat near them as well.

Colored folks and white folks grouped with their own color. But it was a good feeling for me to see all on one fairground. Some of the white folks and their kids wore wide cowboy hats, cowboy boots, Western snapped shirts and tight jeans. And how could anyone miss those big, shiny belt buckles embossed with horns and ornamentations?

An open arch area displayed a half-folded, semi-circled, political style banner of red, white, and blue that indicated: Livestock Display. As we walked under the arch, pure stinky stench from the pig pens reeked out to us. The FFA (Future Farmers of America) sheep were sheared down to their boot fur. Kids were struggling to get their goats and steers to cooperate for show time as muzzles and cinches were tightened as the goaties objected to having their heads put into a metal stand where they could be held still and seen.

"We've had enough of this stinking stuff. Let's see what ribbons Momma and Cousin Hortense have won at the homemakers area and the 4-H Booth and see if Althea and Verdie got something for their green flour sack skirts they sewed up. That way Momma and Cousin Hortense can see that we checked in with them. Now we can get some fair coins that they saved up for us for some rides and cotton candy."

"Let the fun begin, Tamara."

"Okay, Luella. The rides are over there."

"This side of the fairgrounds is so noisy and seems to be the most fun."

"It was you who wanted to see all those cows and goats and things."

"That sign reads five cents for Cotton Candy, Yeah!"

Apple, popcorn, soft drinks and brown hushpuppies were peering and rotating through semi-steamy glass. The sweet smell of the cotton candy hit the top of my head, sorta like a quick shot of gulped ice on a hot day, causing my head a feeling of change. I could taste it before it actually left the tub with a fan in it blowing angel-type hair that came in blue or baby pink. A flat stick was placed inside the fanned tub that was rolled around as we and many other young kids tip-toed in wonder to see the cotton candy being made.

There were so many things to do and we had to choose because we only had enough money for four rides. We knew the Ferris wheel was one of them but had to get Althea and Verdie to ride with us because of our size. I remembered Momma talking to us at the dinner table about the Ferris wheel being the centerpiece of every County Fair, with its spokes that circled high above the treetops to be seen in the daylight and and at night with its twinkling lights from afar. We counted fifteen carriage seats and room for two couples or eight tiny kids facing each other.

The Rocket Cars would be passed up as they spun around in the air that made it hard to catch your breath. Momma warned us to not go into that Haunted House because she was tired of calming us down from our nightmares in the middle of the night. It wouldn't have been our choice because the growls sounded like fighting dogs, and claws and scary eyes seemed stupid. The rocking horses and other rides seemed to be more fun. Making our way back to where Momma Zettie and Cousin Hortense were, we came upon a wool show. Bags of sheared and labeled lambs' wool were everywhere. Local wool spinners with their big spinning wheels were demonstrating their craft. Knitted and crocheted caps and sweaters hung from the walls.

The food smells started to take our breath away. It was like a whop of sudden wind that blew smoky sausage, sizzling chicken, searing burgers, popcorn and fried potatoes sticks. We made it back to the Home Arts area and you never saw two colored women so excited, for they won a blue ribbon for their standing, up green beans. Not to mention, the quilt that got a blue ribbon, which was Althea's idea. On the other side of the Home Arts area was all sorts of breads, cakes and pies that took their assortment of the ribbons by other Grentwood County folks. We saw so many things, like the water bath method of canning pickles and peaches and also many types of jams and jellies. The sewing area was dominated by quilts, while it also included the Christmas pillows, various placemats, hooked rugs, vests, dresses, skirts, and other sewn goods.

The daytime was a delight and at sundown the talent show passed like a flicker. It blurred by me as the strain of the torturing lights made me want to shut my eyes and run. All I remember was my legs were wobbling and our voices were wavy when we had to stop and say "Somebody bad stole the wedding bell," and we rang some tiny bells that Momma got from somewhere.

"I'll never, ever do that again no matter how Momma

thinks it was so lovely to do. Whew."

We did manage to get a second place ribbon for our skirts that we decided to wear on stage. The peach and dirt dobber salve that Momma made was judged by Miz Fairly to be the one. June Bug had a blue ribbon for his fat sow. Althea had her first place ribbon for a 4-H blouse and skirt set that she commented on.

"Of course, what else would I get? And what do you think about that quilt? That was really good, didn't you think?"

My eyes rolled over to where Momma was standing.

"Did you see Miz Iola get real cheery when Mr. Jake outright bought her a rooster and hen of each variety stock? Thank God them folks got their money sack back. I think it was a new type of Cornish and Buckeye breed that an Olellean man brought down from the north on a train."

"My stomach aches," Luella cried out.

"It ought to. Everytime I turned a corner there were little girls stuffing cotton candy in their jaws trying to eave drop on me. Got any idea who I'm talking about?"

I couldn't help but lash out to June Bug.

"Well, who was that fuzzy haired gal?"

"Momma Zet-tie!! Got some chores for these bony leg girls?"

"Come here, Tamara."

"Yes, Momma."

"Fairly and me been talking and she thinks you ready to learn more about them salves and curing and I do want someone in this family to know about it. We both will let you come with us to a place in the woods where a lot of healing herbs grow and teach you something about them. I'll let you know when. Is that something you wanna do?"

"Yes, ma'am, Momma."

"Good."

In a rush the front room was cleared. Althea perched herself in the front porch swing and asked me if I really heard Till tell me what I thought I heard in the potato patch. I confirmed it and she sat swinging and staring into space. "How could Till have known what he did about the Barnes' bag snatching?"

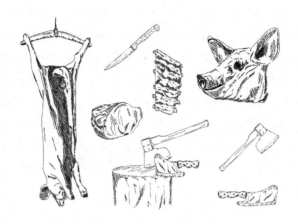

Chapter 16

Slaughtering Time

Four and a half years passed like the blink of an eye and the same things kept happening over and over in our family as we aged. With it came either a growing tolerance for the way things were, or a simmering impatience. Our looks were in flux as I was getting more conscious of my physical features while Althea started looking like a young lady as her bosoms were snugly uplifting the darts in her blouses and dresses. By now, Thea was almost hopelessly uncontrollable with her explosive sayings. Tension grew in the past as in 1957, when Central High School in Little Rock, Arkansas, had to comply with integration. Guess it was Miss Rosa Parks who started it all when she appealed the segregation law to sit where she wanted to on the Montgomery, Alabama, busses. School kids have to be out on the front line, like a war, to make things change. Or at least that is what the radio said.

"Thea, do you ever think we will have to go to an all-white school and be spit on?" There was silence. "Who knows, with the way things are so slow-moving in Corn Hollow. Speaking of slow-moving, Momma is still talking to me about me helping grind sausage real soon. I can't bear the thought of doing what Daddy Al does to those hogs. How can I get out of this?"

"Good question, Baby Sis."

Anyhow, the name Melba Beales stayed on my mind. Not sure it was the complexity or the bravery, but it meant everything to me. I just didn't want to have to go through this type of treatment in Corn Hollow. The radio gave us an earful. Now it was the clanking pots and pans in our kitchen making a racket.

I had awakened early due to the sound of footsteps on the squeaky kitchen floor. Momma was prancing and humming spirituals ... *Amazing Grace* and *Glory Hallelujah*. Metal was clanking on metal. The sound of pans coming apart and falling down as Momma cleaned the biggest pot that I had ever laid eyes on. It was big enough to fit a doubled-up, seven-foot-long cotton sack holding eighty pounds of cotton. I walked by the kitchen door several times and tip-toed away. Just then all racket and tumult broke loose. Bang! Clank! Habunk! Clang! Jingle! Then all the pots fell from the table onto the floor as Momma had caught an open safety pin from her apron and dragged the pans to the floor when she squatted to pull out more from the bottom cabinets.

"Hey, Althea, have you ever seen Momma so relaxed?

She didn't get ruffled over those fallen pans."

"You're right. It's not like the way she got when we rode the bus to St. Louis. Let's not jinx it."

"I notice you look a little gloomed over, Tamara."

"I don't like it ever since I heard Momma say that Thanksgiving is over and it's cold enough and not yet freezing, which tells that its hog-killing and the County Fair winner will be the first one to go. The salt can now dissolve and cure the meat."

"The bar, the sow, I keep hearing. Who gives a hoot?"

Bar, sow, kept ringing through my head no matter how hard I tried to push it out. I heard Momma chattering again and again.

"Those shoes cost too much for you to ruin them. Put them on right so I don't have to cut your back to pieces." No one ever believed a back was cut as Momma used a peach tree switch on the lower back legs and the hiney.

"It's just an old saying, Tamara, like when the slaves were whipped in those days to a point of having a leather whip cut through the skin."

"Oh, nobody would stand for that."

"Believe as you wish. You did it to my back. Someday you will wake up," Althea whispered under her breath.

Instantly, Momma was far removed from what she had even said. Being so happy and expressing such genuine jubilance, June Bug and Isom felt it very pleasant to be around her. It was a day that Luella and I could have gotten away with "holy hell" except that I was feeling sick about it. I did not wear the anxious glee June Bug was showing as a proud yard peacock ready to show his manhood. Momma was beaming with a haughty attitude throughout the day.

"Last Sunday, her five-foot height rose to about eight

feet with tilted chin and long straight neck when the congregation stood and sang *Amazing Grace how sweet it is to save a wretch like me.* She is more than my Momma this week."

"Huhn, Momma is getting a little hard to understand," Althea chirped.

"Where is our sweet, down-home, cuddable Momma Zettie?"

"Speak those words for yourself, Baby Sister, because she is acting like the Czar of Agriculture is coming to visit us tomorrow and gracing your highness with a bucket of emeralds and gold."

"Althea, maybe if she could just help me clean this chicken poop under my shoe, I would feel better. How can hog killing make someone feel so happy?"

"Superior is the word, young sister. Yeah! Superior?"

I felt a sickness in my gut and wanted to heave up and couldn't. I wanted to cry and wouldn't. So much preparation was underway. I went inside the house to cut myself off from this frenzy. As I walked past the living room window, the wind blew the fine sheer curtains back and seemed to set a theatrical stage for Daddy and June Bug.

I could see a few sycamore leaves trying to shed their deciduous frock as one dropped on Daddy Al's pukish-gray, beaten up, suede work hat. It fell to the ground as he turned his head to look up from his stump throne to talk to June Bug. I had never seen June Bug look more like a man than now. He stared and nodded as Daddy would often do when he was figuring out things, not his usual jumpy self. His head sit right atop his neck rather than the forward slump like when he was picking cotton in his six-foot-tall walk stance. And I know that Momma Zettie didn't iron his dark navy denim overalls this morning, but

I could swear there was a crease down the front lanky legs, sorta like in Mr. Daniel's pressed khakis.

June Bug was sitting on the broken fence with his left foot picking at a nearly loose gatepost. He was so content and had Daddy Al's doubly undivided attention. This mostly unconversational man was seen moving his lips. He was gesturing to June Bug with the pointed butcher knife in one hand and his file in the other. His motions indicated through the flickery, fan-blown curtain, to cut and then to pierce it. I realized in a flash that Daddy and June Bug were referring to the hog's throat and piercing the juggler so the poor critter would bleed profusely. Inside my head I could hear Momma's voice. "The pork be purer when yow daddy get through with them hogs so we don't have blood-sopped meat."

I readjusted the head of the fan so I couldn't see them from behind the curtain. The whole thing made me queasy and nauseous.

"Sis, I feel a cold, steel ball inside my head pushing against the walls of my brain trying to get out. It seems to be talking to me."

"What is it saying?"

"It is saying, let me out of here!"

Althea just looked impassively. She pulled me to her and whispered, "One day this will end."

My head continued to ache with excruciating pain, so I held my palms against my ears.

"I hope she doesn't expect me to give him a hug. I'll have to pretend to Daddy that I fell asleep real early from playing so hard. I've got to pretend I don't have time for him."

"You're putting up an invisible hate wall for what he does to those swine."

139

"What?"

"You are protecting yourself, Lil Sis. It's a lot for someone your age."

Althea sat down and started to rock me and I squeezed close to her. I wished that I was in the cotton fields, even though it was Saturday.

"You know, Althea, in the cotton fields I can work when I feel like it and play when I want to. I could scale my way up from the wagon tongue, up the splintery wagon side and carefully drop my body into the wagon and feel free as a wild bird. Luella would follow behind me and we could squint at the sun."

Instantaneously, Momma called out, thus removing me from my dazed, dream state.

"Get yourself busy and help your sister do more cleaning to all them parts of that meat grinder. No need of pouting and sulking during this blessed time. At least we've got hogs to kill and can send your Aunt Lucelia in California a cured ham for all she's done for us."

Big Sis gave me three discs to clean: one with big holes and the other two with jiggered and curvy small holes.

"Let's clean them and then get out of here."

"Don't tell!"

"I won't."

I then walked to the hog lot and just looked at what would soon be our day after tomorrow's breakfast sausage. The air smelled of sour hog slop and pig poop as I gazed at the sow who had weaned her piglets. "Sorry you won't see your piglets grow up, Momma Sow." And you, Big Bar, would probably be the last, loudest squealer, trying to hold on to dear life in a strong masculine protest of having a stuck juggler.

Meanwhile, tomorrow came and I was up early. I could

hardly open my mouth for my nervous system needed to be quieted. There was a high order from Momma that dictated:

"All kids stay in the house after breakfast and I will tell you when to go outside."

I did not obey this command last season, nor did I have the intention of doing so this season. Momma was so busy in the kitchen that she hardly knew that any of us kids were watching a cartoon, which was most unusual and never ever done except on very cold winter Saturday mornings after doing all the house chores. I made my move when all eyes were engrossed in the loud sounding, suspenseful, "Superman" rescues, and the goofy laughter towards "Mr. Magoo." Yes, Big Sis knew to muffle out the background sound in the hog lot and its adjoining stockyard as Momma had instructed.

I found myself sitting on a fence half-hidden by an overhanging walnut tree branch watching the movements of Daddy, June Bug, Isom and Mr. Dave. At the end of the day Mr. Dave knew that he'd take home a good part of the pork. All were so preoccupied that they did not see me. They really must have gotten up early. After all, the stock was set up in stations.

Noticing the big, huge pot that Momma was washing out the previous day made me feel uneasy. It was boiling over as the fire was twinkling embers under it. Beside it was a big half-barrel with a lid on it. It was partially filled with hot grease; it was so bubbly hot that it looked like it could fricassee the skin of a yam by merely holding it over the ebullient, popping pot.

A crossbar stood on the far end of the lot similar to the cross of Jesus Christ himself dying to save others. Beneath the crossbar was a barrel that was propped at a 45-degree angle against a steel beam. Fire was under the barrel and I saw a steamy mist blow to the left and then to the right, sorta like when Daddy made whiskey.

And there were, of course, cutting boards, meat cleavers, a meat maul hammer and the sausage grinder set up on the kitchen table that I spotted as I sneaked out.

While counting the number of leaves growing from a single walnut tree stem and looking out onto the scene, I envisioned the whole process.

I heard a thud and instantly lifted my shoulders and momentarily closed my eyes. I saw Daddy lean over and saw that piercing gesture with his right hand that he and June Bug had rehearsed in the yard.

THE SCREAMS CAME AND THE SCREAMS CAME.

It jarred my body, spirit, and soul as my inner core was called into a more primordial time, somehow giving me the strength to accept the ways of family so that all could be fed.

THE SCREAMS WERE SO PIERCING THAT THEY WOULD PUNCTURE MY HEART FOR YEARS TO COME.

Alas, June Bug repeated the act with the sow and they all, including Isom, did the misdeeds to the porks.

A dead silence, almost catatonic-like, filled my space which seemed to take the air out of my lungs as I struggled to breathe. It all happened in slow motion, one hog after another until four of them were slaughtered, each going through the same procedure.

The hogs were dipped into the cocked barrel of hot water and their hair was pulled and scraped out of their pores. Mr. Dave loved this process and I overheard Isom call him the hog barber. Then, the hogs were hung upside down on a crossbar. Only Daddy Al took a special knife and with the skill of a surgeon, carefully ripped open the underside of the hanging hog.

It was a true anatomy lesson within itself. The flesh separated like taut silk fabric being cut with the highest quality of shears. In this case, it was a very small, yet sharp, butcher knife. The kidneys, liver, lungs, and heart were all intact without traces of blood disrupting its view. The body heat could be seen as mist and the organs just smelled raw and fresh.

Momma moved in with a big vat as Daddy pulled out the intestine. He used slats or small boards to prop open the cut carcass, while strategically placing organs in certain other pans that Momma handed to him. One long intestine at a time, known as chittlings, was placed over the half barrel with a lid.

Momma took the end of the intestine and squeezed out the hog shit without touching it as it dropped into the barrel that had a lid top. It was like being around dug-through cow manure, horse manure, and old chicken manure all in one pungent gust. Anyone around the chittlings for more than five minutes would surely have their olfactories anesthetized.

The hot grease pots were later layered with hunks of fat, meat and skin. The fat would then melt down and the skin was left to cook in hot oil and curl up.

"We're gonna have some nice pork rings to chew on," Isom bragged.

"No man, Momma gotta make some crackling bread soon as those skins crinkle from the lard ends."

"You wish so, huhuh."

"You know that sow head is the one your daddy'll have Momma Zettie cook up for him for New Year's Day. Why he so superstitious?"

"Don't know. By the time them girls stop giggling at him, he throws the rest to the dogs. That's the one time I see my Momma act like she is a child and she sniggers with them gals."

I really couldn't get out of helping Big Sis and Momma. Sis had to press clumps of fresh, undesirable pork into the sausage mill with a sausage spoon. I mumbled to Big Sis. "Smelling this slippery gush sounds like a cawing crow in the distance is just a big mistake we all made. Animals should not have to be killed so we can eat 'em. When I get grown up, I don't have to eat pork and any red animal stuff. I don't ever want to see a big butcher knife in my kitchen."

Althea looked up at me. "It sounds like something that I might say."

"Then why didn't you?"

"Are you alright, Tamara?"

I just walked away.

Chapter 17

Miss Attie

Times were visually changing. Our black and white television and our radio kept blasting out the news. "Out in the open, in Little Rock, Arkansas, nine black students have enrolled in the all-white Central High School this September, 1957. The 1954 U.S. Supreme Court ruling has declared segregation in public schools as unconstitutional." Folks were holding their breaths thinking the children might be killed.

Nevertheless, Corn Hollow school children had not experienced this. Things were spinning similar to the Ferris wheel we all loved at the County Fair. Folks finally calmed as the winter season was changing and their attention focused elsewhere. In the same way, Althea started to notice

Verdie's very rapid, eruptive changes.

The sprinkles of rain that softly pounded the tin roof left Thea half roused from her sleep and yet still restful as I observed her tossing and turning, trying not to open her eyes for fear that she might not get back to sleep.

Althea mumbled to herself, "Another April shower and another vomiting spell with Verdie. I've got to talk with her when we chop cotton this morning."

At the fields, Althea didn't hold back.

"Verdie! How come you so slow with keeping up with me? You always pass by me and then slow down until I catch up with you."

"I can't hide it any longer Thea. It hurts when I chop and I'm so dizzy right now, I can hardly stand up."

"Them sausage cakes that Momma Hortense fried this morning nearly ran me out of the house, cause all I want to do is heave."

"Verdie, you sound like Miz Quintilla when she started growing Esther's baby sister."

In an instant, Althea dropped her hoe, pushed her right hand tightly over her left, which sealed her mouth. Tears swelled in both Althea's and Verdie's eyes.

"Just tell Momma Zettie. She can help quiet down my Momma."

"I'll say you got female cramp sickness. Go home now."

After Thea told Momma the news, dismaying jolts seemed to alter both Momma's and Althea's personalities.

"I'll handle this. Just keep your mouth. I've gotta go to that God-awful place of favors," Momma Zettie disgustingly announced.

Favors seemed to be one way of getting what was wanted. And such generosity was extended as a way of life for some. Althea had told me that it was what some men of Corn Hollow expected from Miss Attie Cole who lived in a well fixed-up shack on the back road of town. Miss Cole expected pure money in return.

Men had been seen driving their mules or walking themselves past everybody else's place before they made it to Attie's. It became really easy for them to sneak off and end up at Miss Attie's. All they had to do was go to their back crop row and cut down by the river bank and hop on over into Miss Attie's yard.

Miss Attie Cole was betrayed by her fiancé, whose gang of friends boozed up and gang raped Attie as he watched. She seemed so lost and was still on the search for a man who would love her and become her husband.

She turned to this man and that man, not knowing how to control her liquor. She ended up as a female drunkard who accepted money for sex. Some of her patrons told her that she could get lots more money if once a week she would be available to them.

It was old man Dan'l's daddy, a widower, that gave her the old shack and fixed it up for her. Attie was indebted to him whenever he visited. When the old coot died after three years of this, Mr. Jeffers allowed her to keep the place.

Most of Corn Hollow's men stayed away during fishing season as that was when she made most of her money, money that the Corn Hollow fellows just didn't have.

Then there was all the catfish that the men had given her as a tip. Miss Attie had her half-baby sister, Clarise, fry up some for Saturday night stayovers. Clarise, who lived in Olellean County, only visited her sister during the summer months when the fishermen could be expected to visit at anytime of the day or night. This all depended upon where they conveniently docked their boats.

One of Attie's river friends brought her an old phonogragh and two honky-tonk records. Clarise was the big attraction, however. She would bring her friend, Imogene to help out. The three of them cut up some and drained the fellow's pockets dry.

The rivermen were friends of Chet Gunstein, the Parson Springs Liquor Store owner. Mr. Chet allowed these men to buy their corn whiskey direct from Daddy Al in exchange for fish for himself. Daddy Al was more than content to exchange some of his jars of white lightning for some real money.

On one odd, hot, muggy, and overwhelming even when you step outside in the yard, summer day, an uninvited guest came to see Miss Attie. The rare thing then was for any visitor to approach Miss Cole's house except her customers. I followed Momma and hid far behind in the bushes and heard and saw everything. Out of nowhere, Till, Miss Attie's son, stopped in the middle of the road in front of Momma. This startled her a little bit. Then they started talking.

"Till, you done started to read? I bet you can."

"I don' hafta, ma'am. I know things not with them words. I know my real momma tis a special lady with a lots respect and it ain't Attie."

"Stop it, boy. You can't talk like that. Attie your momma."

"And I problee won' be in this here world a long time like most folk. God wants me."

Till ran towards the house as Momma stood with her mouth wide open.

Momma acted spooked and started talking to herself.

"Reckon Attie think she dreaming as she is after a long

night's work. Is she stirring now and then to put her head back on her pillow?"

Then the voice got closer and closer as the road twisted and unwound at her house. Momma was calling.

"Miz At-tie, Miz Attie. I need to talk with yu."

Miss Attie Cole flew out of her bed and stood in her front door frame as a summer breeze blew her torn lace curtain that was apparently a screen to deter the mosquitos. The curtain blew up just enough to reveal the shiny, greasy legs that Miss Attie had rubbed Vaseline on to look good to the men. She wore some run-over sling shoes that her heels had crushed down the backs. She was buttoning up a white blouse over a pleated red skirt as she was about to address Momma. While standing, she was fanning, of all things, with a Pack's Funeral Home fan that were given to the African Methodist and the General Baptist churches of Corn Hollow.

"Have Mr. Pack's, Momma Zettie mumbled, been served by Miss Attie? Oh Lord, let me get this out of my mind and finish up what I came here for."

"What in the Sam-he I mean, what brought you back here, Zettie Mae?"

"I am so sorry."

"Anybody in a family way?"

"Yes Attie. It's my Cuzin Verdie."

"It's the only thing any woman sets foot in my yard for."

"We don't know if it was Mr. Daniel who overtook her, but me and Hortense can't make any sense out of what she's saying. Whenever we mention going to visit Miz Siddie to help her can, she always has an excuse to not do it. We know she loves Miz Siddie but she hides out from her under the saw horses when she comes over to quilt with us."

"How far along is she?"

"Reckon two to three months."

"Another weeping willow." Miss Attie's voice then got lower and she murmured, "I'm going to fix that Daniel Goodson so he ain't wanna stick it anywhere else 'cept up Miz Siddie."

"What?"

"Just something that I say. Don't mind my sayings."

"So why didn't Hortense come here herself being since Verdie her daughter? Never mind, Zettie. Tis better that you came on account of me and Hortense go a long way back. We bound to get into an argument and she storm away and that wouldn't help Verdie. Zettie, you the only nice lady to me in Corn Hollow."

Momma started to breathe real hard. "Now, Attie, don't start letting out foul words 'bout other folk."

"Say, you know me well enough, huhn."

"I'll spare you have to stand there and listen to me."

"I'll make Clarise and Imogene mind the place tomorrow. Just do what I tell you, Zettie Mae. Go gather me a pint of turpentine, some real clean, untainted wires so I can hook the end of it, some real clean sterilized cloths, lots of old rags for soaking up the blood, have a pot of boiling water on, and make sure Verdie is real comfortable and not scared-like."

"Maybe that shed out back of your house be the perfect place while the chirens at school, and she can rest up for the rest of the day and moan and sleep in case someone comes up to youall's front porch."

Momma answered hurriedly. "There's still a bed in there where Cuzin Claude stayed before Mr. Jeffers decided to keep him on at the cotton gin. I'll get rid of the cobwebs and cushion the bed and set it up comfortable for a day."

"We are goin' start real early in the morning, the minute after them children about a mile up the road to the school-house. Go to one of Alfonso's hiding places in youall's house and get a pint of 'white lightning.' Maybe Verdie and certainly me gonna need it."

At that moment, it looked like ripples of hate and bitterness crumpled over Momma's face.

"How do you ..."

And it seemed that Momma changed her mind about speaking. Momma took a few deep breaths and started to mumble under her breath. "I gotta put this stuff way away in my mind. It's Verdie that needs the help and Miss Attie the only one in Corn Hollow who had the record for careful bilities in this way. She never lost a gal yet."

As each day passed, Verdie got stronger and stronger. Cousin Hortense and Momma began to stop fretting over her.

A month later after the deed was done, Verdie was able to walk around the yard and not have to have the excuse that her female days were getting her down.

"Did you hear Iola that Mr. Daniel, the widow Dan'l's son, had a spell put on him and he wears a rabbit's foot around his neck every single day?"

"Some say he done changed his ways."

"Guess Miz Siddie is powerful grateful cause Mr. Daniel put all his faith, hope, trust, and charity into her now."

"Tee hee. Giggle-giggle. Miz Siddie say they got a bit more spending change now."

Then one morning Cousin Hortense was listening to Momma sob when I ran up on them and they didn't know that I was near.

"I told Al before we fell asleep that Miss Attie was by here last week. He asked what for? I didn't answer him. When he started snoring and sleep talking … Attie move on over and keep doing it like that. Yeah Honey, Yeah Honey."

"He could have been talking about you Zettie Mae."

"He never called me "honey" in our years and I never heard that word come from his mouth, ever."

After all these alterations, Momma Zettie Mae started showing change herself, the General Baptist way.

The Reverend Stokes' wife relayed to Cousin Hortense, "Zettie been telling me some strange stuff 'bout her morning."

"Yes ma'am, I know what that's 'bout and she gone get better."

At the General Baptist revival, I saw Momma roll and lap in the Holy Ghost until it went straight out through the top of her head. She toppled and flopped like the walleye did in the fields after an overflow.

Some early mornings, before she cooked breakfast, consisted of a walk to the watermelon patch and putting two canning jars of beans, beets, peaches, or whatever there was an excess of at the end of the field plot. I would stare at her out our bedroom window and she would return empty-handed.

Daddy got real curious about her behavior.

"What you walking down to the patch for every morning, Momma Zettie?"

"They'll be picked up by someone me and Hortense are indebted to."

Daddy Al knew to leave this matter alone. It was as if he knew about the whole incident with Verdie and the repayment, or at least he acted like he didn't.

Chapter 18

Christmas

Less than a month passed. Daddy gave a big stretch
before he came to the kitchen table to eat pork sausage, eggs, biscuits, and gravy for breakfast. There
was an icy breeze in the air that felt like needles prick-
ing my cheekbones and made my eyes water. Overhead,
clouds hung in a dark hue and seemed to speak of pulling down aqueous vapors that would have the atmosphere
filled with snow in a matter of hours. This was acceptable
for the holidays; however, the bulletin that was posted on
a paper in Olellean made its way to our mail and that was
when Momma seemed to panic.

I heard her talk with Cousin Hortense. "Why did Odes-
sa from the Olellean Baptist Church think I want to read

some mess like this as a 'noucement to our congregation? The church a house of God, not for devil work. Says that nobody better even think of sending they kin folk over to that thare lumber mill 'spectin work. Better off with the cotton sacks than a tightn rope."

"You mean they talking 'bout hangin folk like them years ago ifen they try to make bettern for themselves?"

"Sound like it to me. I been at peace knosen we gots plente to eat and like doin' them Christmas programs. Now this done spolt my speret."

"We just tell Mr. Daniel and he spread tha word."

"He even tell Mr. Clifford & Jeffers, w'out a doubt."

"That stir up things then."

"Bettern him then us."

"Yu right, girl. I ask Alfonso to daliver to 'em and we do way with this on our minds."

"Al-fonso!! Tell them kids 'bout fetchin' a cedar tree to decorate for Christmas. Then thare sumthin' else I gots ask you a do."

All I could think of was the tree already decorated, our hair, new clothes, the good food, the Christmas program, and our Santa Claus gifts. Then I noticed Momma not looking too good.

"Are you alright? You so bent over and holding your belly."

"Gone on now with June Bug and the rest and gets a nice tree. It's indegestion cause thangs on my mind."

With an expedition led by June Bug and Isom, two trees were felled, one for us and the other for Cousin Hortense Ludgess' house along with some mistletoe. This arduous event occurred without mishap. The table was filled with thick, glass-scarred light bulbs of red, green, blue, and white that Momma had painted two years ago, two fat and long silver garlands, old package bows handed down from Mr. Clifford's wife, a box of saved tinsel string icicles, and remnants of itchy angel hair balled up in wax paper inside a paper bag.

In the same way, the tree wasn't the only thing that had to be dressed. Every family in Corn Hollow was spruced out from head to toe for the Christmas church programs. Althea got her hair straightening wishes. I often wondered if that was more important to her than having a pair of shoes in the snow.

The thick, brass, metal-toothed hot comb was placed on the top of a good stove fire in the cold months while during summers, a small campfire under the walnut tree winded soot in my eyes. In either season, emotional eruptions were inevitable.

"I am so happy, Momma."

"Thea, hold still."

"Can you not pull on my clean hair so hard, Momma?"

"Look, girl. I gotta comb the knots out and then put on the hair grease."

Out came the red and green cardboardish can with a silver colored top and a crown embossed on it.

"I'll open it, Momma."

"Just look at those hard bubbles of compressed hair petroleum ready to be applied to my hair roots. It contains balm and fragrance."

"Shut yow mouth, gal, and let me sop my fingers in that grease."

The hair grease melted into Althea's hair as the hot comb stretched and pulled it straight with its heat. Unlike Momma's usual charades of love at Christmastime, she was snappy, moody, and unfocused. Come to think of it, I saw her pass the door frame in the middle of the night when I used the porcelain chamber.

"Hey, Momma! Don't let the comb get too much hair dressing or those hot droplets could ruin my week. You know a drop could create a sore in my scalp that pulls out plugs of my hair. That would be so painful, Momma."

"Girl, that might be true 'bout that. Just don't let go of your ear and don't jerk."

Ironically, from personal experience, the scalp could feel the heat before the straightening comb was actually placed on the hair. That was most unnerving. Big Sis knew, however, not to jerk or be nervous. I could tell by her smirk that she was thinking of her beautiful hair, thus taking her mind off the hot comb dilemma. When Momma's attention drifted during Luella's turn, a melted grease glob got her.

Althea had something to say about it. "Another Saturday tragedy has occurred with the straightening comb. Stay tuned for more episodes, particularly if you have a cold or any head congestion and your hair must be cleaned. In that case, fluids and I did say *fluids* will do the trick. Puffs of cotton are pushed on the regular, cold, plastic hair comb end and down the entire row of teeth, like white clouds hung in mid air. Having a jar of coal oil nearby, the comb was dipped into it and then combed through the hair. Nevermind the awful chemical smell that stenched danger and sent odors up the nasal cavity. The smell is unpleasant to say the least. The fluids have to dry for two hours or so to avoid combustion in the coif, especially if the hot comb hadn't cooled off much."

"Stop your noise and call your daddy, ask if he heard a word from them Hickles."

It happened that WBIA, as Momma called the colored radio station in Memphis, clicked on. Since Momma called the hair grease "Coyal" instead of "Royal," we seemed to hear it as Momma phrased it. "Coyal Crown, the Petroleum Jelly for your hair."

Althea couldn't resist putting in her remarks. "Why can't we buy skin lightner? You got real light skin, Momma, and you a pretty woman and your hair bourn of soft fuzzy curls."

"I warned you before to stop talking about me like that. I'm gonna whip you if I ever hear that again. Ain't nobody gonna use those lye creams on they face. Folks just have to accept my straight hair and my pretty smile. I don't think the Good Lord intend for us to act like we some kind of bad defect that all us Mommas done give birth to."

"But Brer Block whistled and hollered about how the French invented a safe and quick way to whiten skin."

"Yeah, I know Cotillion's nephew's wife, Miz Flora, come visiting from Chicago and had spots in her face. She showed me the package with a colored face, one side was pure black with 'see how sad' and the other side was bleached white with 'see how happy' and you know that's the devil at work, gal. Now turns that rad-e-o off."

Although personal appearances were extremely valued during the holidays, the heart and spirit of Christmas season was set with gloom. For two Sundays in a row now Miz Quintilla Hickle shouted over missing her eight-year-old, Esther. No one would openly talk about it as her husband, Mr. Leo, argued with his hot-blooded, rageful, white foreman, Larry Moore, on a gin building project. A note had been left on the fence post of the Hickles'.

Ever want to see your chile whole bettern shut your mouth for ten days and she'll walk back in your yard.

Trying to quiet me and all of Corn Hollow's children was nearly impossible. At home, I questioned Momma right after church.

"This close to Christmas and her Auntie took her over to Olellean? She would have bragged about it at school."

Luella got her words in even though Momma couldn't speak. "Then why Miz Quintilla shout and says it's like in the old days and she look so sad when she should have the Holy Ghost?"

Gasp-yu-yu-gast! Momma held her mouth as pink sausage bits and spit oozed between her fingers. She flew out the back door, heaving on the ground.

Luella and Verdie were talking to each other.

"Hardest of all is hearing Miz Quintilla's morbid pain and seeing Mr. Leo walk around like a stunned corpse."

Momma stumbled in and calmly and emphatically spoke to us.

"We gotta brush this off our lips and keep praying for Esther to safely return home and we got to get on with our lives."

Lo and behold, divine intervention occurred on the tenth day of this peril. Esther had been placed in the Hickle's front yard before dawn on Christmas Eve morning. The veil of pain was lifted. Miz Siddie Goodson, somewhat skilled in midwifery, checked Esther over to insure no violations had taken place. All Esther told us was that a white woman fed her chicken and said she would go home in a few days. All in all, we could now focus on the Christmas program that was set for 4:00 o'clock that evening.

A hot fire built by June Bug an hour prior to the program roared and sparkled through the tin stove front where fire could be seen through the pinwheel damper openings. A couple of times the racy blue tin sides turned red hot and the damper was turned shut as Corn Hollow Methodist ladies shed their coats and wraps and revealed their

Christmas frocks, some made of starched flower sacks, others of handmade cottons from last year, and Momma in a turquoise second hand dress that Aunt Lucelia sent in our annual Christmas package. Miz Quintilla had a hard time letting Esther out of her sight as she stared over at the children's bench. I was having a lot of difficulty myself as my head started to pound. Cousin Hortense glared at me. She raised her big thighs from the pew as it sorta teetered down to the right when she lifted her 295 pounds. She pulled off my green plastic headband that was embedded in my straight, greasy hair, which left tiny imprinted teeth marks in my scalp.

"That's too tight for your head."

"Yes, ma'am."

After the program, all of us girls hung around Esther and talked about how glad we were that she was back and didn't miss much, like Isom and June Bug trying to frighten them with the wringing of the hen's neck trick. We told her that we falsified our reactions as the blood popped in tiny spurts and the neckless hen jumped and flopped.

That wasn't the only thing that was falsified. We faked the belief in Santa just to please Momma. It was clear, though, that our hearts did not fabricate what we felt for Esther's safe return home.

Chapter 19

Cotton Chopping

Before we knew it, springtime had rolled around and folks were not so tense as before Christmas. The inevitable task of chopping cotton was before us as soon as Daddy Al filed a hoe and handed them to each one of us. "You'all can put yow name of the hoe handle if you want to."

Althea was appalled at this type of identity and just shook her head. I had to jump into some old shoes and be prepared to let some of the drier dirt clogs in our cotton fields throw themselves on my legs. The soil was not at all comparable to the lowlands I visited, which never seemed to dry out. Thus, I was dirtied with dust that stuck to the Vaseline-greased glaze of my hairless legs. This protected my skin from drying out, whether the weather proved crispy cool, windy, warm or outright hot. It happened that this first day of cotton chopping was sunny, yet cool, as the April air still left biting, March-like chills on my face as a residual of the last bits of a cold spell.

To any colored person in Corn Hollow, just seeing some green, two-flocked leaves with their pink stems pressing up from the dry clods of dirt, and other green leaves trying to raise themselves from a partially covered dirt clod, meant Spring. For it was time a sharpened hoe had to methodically chop every other hoe length, thus killing and thinning out the cotton stalks so they could grow with room to breathe. A bit more of consideration had to also be taken for crab grass and Johnson grass as wild weeds also liked to grow in the fertilized soil.

The sky started to change. Daddy stressfully chided. "We'll go as far as we can 'cause that weather could put us further behind." But before the first row had completely been chopped, a crackling thunderbolt belched like falling timber from the sky. When the crashing and decrepitated burst shot off once more, it led us into a cantering gait, holding straw hats with one hand and dropping the metal end hoes on the spot.

Althea cried out, "Thank you, God! I hate working in dah blasted dirt fields chopping weeds."

Shirts flew as everyone ran in the direction of the wind like parachutes of air and ballooned backs withheld each person's every motion to half of its intended pace. I glanced at two light green straw hats and their big, painted, block-printed pink flowers soaring like hawks ascending and descending as if stalking prey. My face became soaked and I closed my eyes and opened my mouth to taste the rain and felt the cool drips of the fresh water.

At the house we looked out to observe the splendor. "It got the old oak!!! It's slivering and burning the limbs. There's a little fire and now smoke."

"Hey! Don't worry about the Lord's work. Draw them curtains together. They flying like heavenly wings. Now sit back down. Unplug that TV and the 'frigerator, and anything with a cord in the wall."

Although Momma kept insisting that we had better sit down, Althea looked right through her with cold eyes of disbelief. The next thing I knew, Thea had gathered Luella and Verdie in the dining room corner and was telling the real story about sharecropping. Of course, I had to hear it.

"What's sharecropping?"

"It's what poor black folk do. It started at a time after the Civil War when landowners needed their crops worked and the sharecroppers got part of the crop in return for labor. They didn't have to give us a place to stay because we already had our Banks house and Cousin Hortense has hers from her daddy. But some folk were given cabins, mules, feed, fuel, fertilizer and charged groceries at the general store. By the time for crop payoff, most of the sharecroppers had charged up their full wages or were cheated out of their share. Since they couldn't read, they couldn't argue. And even if they could, they knew better. The landowners took advantage of them because they made it nearly impossible to get out of debt. So there was just work and more work for us."

Momma crept in and stood over us. "Don't you have more to do than fill they heads wif yow ways?" I took Thea by the hand and led her outside to pout.

Chapter 20

The Big Hole

Four months passed by. Time seemed to be pacifying Momma's emotional wounds while unrest stirred with Althea. Cousin Hortense strolled up the cotton lane to visit Momma one morning as one eye of mine caught a glimpse of her stopped in her tracks upon hearing the flare-ups.

"But, Althea, how come you so down on Corn Hollow men?"

"Yes, Sis, and there are some fine men, not dirty teeth cotton pickers in patched up overalls."

In a snorting frenzy, Althea continued ranting.

"And I hear what you have said, little sister, about the city. You just haven't lived in the city and are too young to know everything you saw when you went to St. Louis with

Momma Zettie."

"But Big Sis! Did you ever like anything in Corn Hollow?"

As Althea's voice grew louder and louder, I didn't think she could hear me at all.

"No! Well, you and Verdie, cause you two listen to me, Cousin Delmar because he understands me. Oh Yeah, the vegetable garden and the berries. Not the hog killings and its brutish ways that boys think they become men around here and all that sliced up carnage we put in our mouths every day. You see, Lil Sis …"

"I'm not little."

"If only I lived in the city, I could do things like go to nightclubs, dances, see jazz musicians and look at the hottest fashions in town."

Althea wouldn't be quiet and started to appear strange and different. Her nose was wrinkled and her brows lowered. There were hardly any eyes to be seen as they were so narrowed. With her tongue protruded, my big sister resembled a baby who sampled lemonade for the first time. As she raised her cheeks up to speak, her upper lip curled with downturned corners. With her head shifting backwards, she spoke in a deep guttural and hysterical voice.

"I don't have to hide behind my two not good uncles."

Momma shed tears that fueled more anger as Althea had pushed her too far. The uncles, Momma's brothers, had not been seen by Momma since she was a young lady in her early twenties. A bit of family history indicates that Momma's grandfather was sired by one of Mr. Clifford's uncles. It happened that our family was the only colored one that ended up with a piece of land that was given to us with an understanding to button our lips concerning relative affiliations to its grantor. Momma's Pa busted up the spread to go around to two of her brothers, who squandered and sold forty acres cheaply back to Mr. Clifford's homestead to buy tickets to Chicago and have spending money. My uncles were last heard of twenty-five years ago on the run from their gambling debts. So what was left was the twenty acres that we Banks outrightly owned. The adjoining forty acres the family agreed to sharecrop for Mr. Jeffers. With Althea's knowledge of all this history of ours, Momma probably never thought that Thea would use it to turn on her whether she was present or not. This was forbidden ground that Thea had tread upon. Momma, unbeknown to Thea, just listened.

"I'm tired of it!!! Oh God! How did I ever end up here? And how did this dinky part of the woods ever get this ghastly name CORN HOLLOW? And they talk about that dent in the middle pasture like God Almighty put it there. It's nothing but a big damn hole. I bet Mr. Clifford, and Mr. Jeffers' families joke about us blackies to their friends and guests."

Tears were slowly dripping off Momma's face. Anger was fueling as Big Sis was slinging hurtful words. I stepped back, shaking my head, wanting to get her out of her self-absorbed state. Momma came forward and expressed herself in a triply enraged tongue.

"You the big hole … in my side for that matter… and always trying to punish your family on account of you think you bettern us. I'm plum fed up with your mess, girl, and your high falluting, stuck-up self. You don't even know what you talking 'bout."

With her head shaking from side to side, she paused to deeply breathe before pressing on.

"You better shut up and hear what I have to say. You don't step on my toes now. You sit yo butt right down here and let me tell you a thing or two. You putting down yo great, great, grand pappie."

It was as if Momma was calming down.

"There are thangs yu don' know and you need to know 'bout. I betya you didn't know that this here town, Corn Hollow, down here in Tennessee, is really ments to be called Cornallow. It happened when my great grand pappie on my Momma side of the famlee was just 'bout to be outs the shackles back in 'bout 1845. The hounds couldn't catch scent 'em since he knew the trick. He would find a pole cat, get'em fierce, shoot out the balm, and then kill it. Some say he took a rag, rubbed it in cloves and tied it around his neck 'fore the trick. Pappie would say that he heard them hounds howl and that he took the carcass and rold his sweat all over him."

Momma seemed captivated with her thoughts and shifted to a stiller and trancelike posture.

"I can hear him say clearly all 'bout it just like when I was a youngster."

Tis deff and like deff itselfs come through my head and my belly till the rank done got me like lepros. I know twas over when them houlds and them hosse huffs go nearer and nearer. Twas 'bout to meet my maker when I herd a call out. 'Get on here dogs, that damn ol polecat reaking all over them bushes.' The hounds and the hosses pulled off and sounds like Gabrell's loud horns and thunderbolts causa mine ears being right on the dirt like the dirt moving and shaking me inside. Maybe I be with my Maker. I turn my head and feeled my arms. They still be there. Lord Jesus the hoax workd!! When I done come to wheres the resta us been hid, theys a went-a-running and hold they face. Ise so beholden the Good Lord done sheeled me I forgets I stunk.

"No futter," them folks hollered. Them big bucks gone and tooken buckets of dirt and one ol shovel that one of em had and break up the groun' and tells me to git in.

"I ain't dead yet!!"

Then one them patted his bosom and hisa nape, meant git in up to here. I gots covered with dirt and pulls my arems out. Them ladies tip-toed sideways whila holden them face way from Ol Nig. Done jerked theys arms lika hissin serpant gona get em, and theys a runs way. Nother one giva me som corn. Ise pulled one arem out. Ise so starvn my belly done growled so bout ate the cob. Next monning them buck done dig me out and giva me rags, peels offa my pole-tainted garb ana puts them rite back in the hole ana buries the cobs wichin theys feet back down in thata hole. Nex un tekin a rock and pounding the mettle from thaten ther ankle. Them cherens and big boys come to where Ol Nig done been and saying 'corn ina hollow.' Twas outa harms way whensa I semettle broke loose.

"That spot real blessed and been known as Cornallow ever since. Someday you might really come to know what this big hole really means."

Althea only breathed deeply and stared while I hugged Momma and Cousin Hortense put her hands on Momma's shoulders.

"From then on, great grand pappie said," Us es loosen afta thata war and lots thems other wena back a Cornallow, first place back in them woods ever seem like home to me. Thems white folks heared us a say meants wheras the blackies live and wheras theys lots corn in the back part of the new groun."

As Althea started to walk away, Momma began to raise her hand to beckon her to return. Cousin Hortense whispered to Momma.

"Let her settle. We gotta go to Cotillion's to help her pack up."

Chapter 21

Changes

O ne of the saddest days of my life was when I found
out that Mr. Clarence and Miz Cotillion Parker had
to move to Chicago. Momma was busy trying to
ignore the situation by packing quilts and Daddy seemed
really strange as he was cleaning off his 1950 Belvedere
that Mr. Chet from the liquor store had sold to him at a
bargain. It didn't seem right, somehow, not right at all that
these two old people had to leave. Mr. Parker was well up
in his eighties and Miz Cotillion is trailing right behind
him, but I guessed it was like Momma say, it's something
that had to happen. Momma said that Mr. Clarence has
gotta get help for his emphysema and maybe lung cancer.

Cousin Hortense started mumbling.

"Hadsa been that smoke he sucked in his body from that pure bacca he growed and dried in his back yard. Bound to make Miz Cotillion sick just smellen that stuff. Come to mention it, I never ever seen Mr. Clarence without one them bacca smokes in tha corner of his mouth even whena he working and talking, but not in church, though."

That's when June Bug jumped into the conversation. "Can no colored man get them treatment in Grentwood County Hospital?"

"Stop this. Stop it. Stop it right now!!" Daddy bellowed.

"And can't the women folk in Corn Hollow give him 'is medicine? Cause Miz Cotillion could be so tired being old and that."

I had never seen my brother so frustrated. Yeah, he and my Daddy were attached to Mr. Clarence and I didn't know in what way or how. And I could feel the tears come to my face. All of us Banks loaded in the car and somehow squeezed in Cousin Hortense and Verdie to wish them well. Miz Cotillion came out in the yard and spoke to Althea first.

"Wipe them tears, Baby. Honey, I'm gonna give yu that Four Queens quilt because I never saw a youngen stare and admire a quilt before the way you fell in love with it when it hung up at the Countee Fare. I say one day it's yurs when it is time for you to catch a young man. So just use it now and later remember that is a wedding present from me 'cause I ain't gonna be roun' here on God's earf that long."

Althea wept like a baby as she hugged Miz Cotillion. She soon jumped back and composed herself. A procession of hugs then followed.

"So who you all going to stay with, Miz Cotillion?"

"Well! We gon stay with Henry and Flora. They want us up there. Says Clarence can get some curin at them horspitals. Can't talk him otta it and Lords knowed I tried. Says he wanna be able to make a yard of begonias and flat shrebry that looks like theys belong in a palace garden when they done pluckin on it. One of the good things is that old Doc Morris at Grentwood Countie Horspital says he spare one them oxgen tanks which he said might last for a week, since Clarence done such a good job working on the Platt's house, friends of them brothers Clifford and Jeffers. That doc said to Clarence that it's this or stay in Corn Hollow till its all ova. Yeah, Henry and Flora say my Clarence can get ample supplie of that oxgen often and can get to the doc offen and the doc in Shecago can drop in to the house when he felt he needs to. Good thing yow Daddy saw Clarence swerve that old truck when he overtook 'em and drove him to the hospital. We neva wooda founds out till its too late."

Mr. Clarence, through a cough and a panting chest, mumbled, "I never heard yow Daddy say so many pleases, mams, and sirs just to git that ol doc to come out to tha car.

Momma cushioned the car seat with one of her own old quilts for Mr. Clarence and said that Daddy could do the rest.

"Let's go hug Mr. Clarence because I can't stand no much more of this. Yow Daddy and June Bug can pack the rest of the trunks in the car and drive 'em off to the bus station house. We all gotta walk this off and pray as we walk."

And I knew when my daddy returned home with whiffs of whiskey on his breath, wiping his eyes, and blowing his nose on his hankie, that he felt something.

He spoke softly to Momma.

"There was another colored family going to Chicago who promised me that they would watch after the Parkers until they kin met up with them at the bus station. So I gave them that extra bag of chicken sandwich that you said give to someone who would help them out along their way. Lord know, Zettie Mae, I peeped at them waving to me at the back of that bus window and it nearly tore me up inside when I waved back at them. You know that Mr. Clarence taught me things that my own Pappy could nota teach me as death hit him young. Yeah, that big right hand of his done popped up in the tiny bus window. His head could barlee turn half way around and could see them tube stings tied round his ear so he could get some oxgen air. Miz Cotillion threw a kiss with her hand, the bus hit a bump and clouds of dirt come up from them wheels and all I could see was it make a turn and then they be gone."

"How come things had to be so sad this week? Our good friends are gone."

"Well, daughter child, nobody says we gotta perfect world. We just gotta do what the Lord has us da do. Someday we gonna be free from the pain of the Parkers on account of it be best for Mr. Clarence. It's justa one sad week, Tamara. Sorry 'bout that. But what we ain't sorry 'bout is that poster that we gotta deal with now."

Twas on the wall on the side of that cotton gin. Soon as Mr. Clarence got a whiff of that old way of frightening folk, he said he is too old and tired and can't stick round as he has been in Corn Hollow long as he could. Other than his lungs, that's why he done moved on."

"What poster, Momma?"

Althea had come out from behind a chair where she was standing.

"Sis, you are so naive."

Momma gave Thea a shoo-off with her hand and walked away.

"Now, Thea, it's not about you and your thoughts on thata poster. Think 'bout something better like the Parkers."

"Well, Thea and Momma, I don't know what you mean by the poster and Mr. Clarence. I just know that I miss the Parkers."

Chapter 22

The Decision

Not knowing everything that grown-ups knew or did not want me to know at my age, I peered through one of the window panes. How could we deal with the sadness of the Parkers' departure from Corn Hollow, and how could I get out of my head the dreams of two nights ago that I knew those two light–skinned, worn-out faced black men who I saw at the County Fair when I was a little girl. I could see glimpses of the moon that seemed to be coming up before the shadows of darkness had fallen on our farmhouse. It was so peaceful. Daddy Al rekindled the embers where a big, slow-burning log had kept the house warm all day. With nightfall, the air would be even cooler and the hot blazing fire was a perfect addition.

Momma had called me out of the bedroom to have dinner. Just as we finished with dinner she wanted everybody to listen to her. I blurted in the quiet moment, "Does anyone remember those two yellow skinned black men who worked at the County Fair in 1954?"

Daddy Al loudly cleared his throat. "Git ready to hear what yowr Momma has to say and don't think about stuff like that."

"Was I dreaming?" Althea and I just stared at one another. Momma started to speak about the moping we were doing about the Parkers and read a verse from the Bible which I didn' hear a word of. I whispered to Althea while Momma turned her back after explaining, "She got a way of putting things so anybody can understand them. So why was she so mad at me that time I traveled on the bus with her when I did nothing to deserve it and when you got beat up because you told the truth about the fire?"

"That's how she does it. Oh! I got something to tell you, Tamara, when I'm sure she's through talking to us."

"Well Tamara, I don't want to end up like Verdie here in the country. I'm seventeen and almost eighteen, graduated from Olellean's colored high school after riding every day in that old station wagon that Mr. Frank Kelly was given to drive us to school. And besides Momma and Daddy told me two days ago that I could go stay with Miz Flora and Mr. Henry Jenkins. They have room for another one in their big old house until I could pay my own rent and move out. Mr. Henry was trying to pull everybody out of the South and move up North. It was also good because I could keep everybody posted on Mr. Clarence and Miz Cotillion Parker. Momma and Daddy knows when I can afford it that I will send them some money on a regular basis. I learned about this about the same time we all found out about the Parkers leaving. They thought it would be good to have Miz Cotillion so closely tied in with Corn Hollow by my staying there. Tamara, I was so happy to buy my bus ticket. I did all I could to keep my mouth from spurting darts at that ticket agent. Maybe because that poster was up that he had the nerve to say something to me."

"Huh!! We need you to help yow daddy work crop, gal."

"Will you tell me why white folk won't come into our house?"

"Oh, that question. Yes, I promise you I will and I will not break that promise to you when I think it's time."

"You know you can't break a promise with me."

"Just wait until I tell you so you won't stir up the rest of the others when I'm gone and I will write you all the time and I'll come home to visit by Christmas."

"That's good, Thea, but it was just yesterday when Momma and Daddy made me feel really bad like I stirred up something and I didn't even ask that question. It was when we dropped off Mr. Frank at his cook job at the country club. It's that job he has when school is not in session and he's not driving the bus. Well, just as he was about to get out of the car, a white ball hit the fence where we were parked. Mr. Frank mentioned that it was one of those Hogan golf balls with its white dimples. He called out 'fore' and two white men came to the fence edge and grinned at him. They said they were looking forward to some of his barbecue spareribs after their round. I had no idea what Mr. Frank meant when he picked up that ball or called out. It just seemed to interest me. After Mr. Frank tipped his hat, he stuck his head inside the car window and said, 'A black man named Charlie Sifford can do that too but better. Some of them northerner visitors talk 'bout that Sifford being really good with his clubs. 'A fine colored golfer' is what they called Charlie."

"If a black man can do that up North then a black woman can, too."

Then I said, "Yeah! I wanna be a black golfer." Daddy's voice roared, "You wanna be a black what?" Then both Momma and Daddy turned at the same time and rolled their eyes down at me in the back seat.

Daddy smeared out, "We didn't hear that and you didn't either. Frank, quit feeding them things into her head."

"You knowdt I was just a joking 'round, Al."

"Well, that gal ain't maybe taking it as a joke."

"Well, Tamara, it sounds like what they did to me when I mentioned that someday I'll fly a crop duster. You know when we had to close up inside the house for two hot hours with all the windows and doors shut and we watched the airplanes out our windows spray the cotton crops?"

"How can I forget that, Big Sis."

"But know that someday I will also tell you more about them folks hitting balls with sticks."

"Sticks?"

"I mean clubs. I read about them folks and what they done with Charlie Sifford when he first started that game called golf."

"What did Mr. Frank mean by 'fore' and 'round?'

"Much later, Tamara."

"What?"

"Nevermind."

"Maybe it's better to be a woman golfer than a woman cotton chopper?"

"Now that's funny, baby sister."

The two sisters laughed uncontrollably. "Take this

Thea," as a pillow plopped into Althea's face, and this pillow slapping continued back and forth.

"You just gotta be you. Things are hard enough when you are trying to be honest and sincere like they tell us at Sunday school and then the grown ups get all huffed up when you do. I can't stand it any longer. I just don't want to leave you and I know it's my time to do something else." The pillows dropped.

With sniffles and tears we continued to say good-bye.

"I'm gonna miss you, Thea, more than anything."

Althea reached to hold me in her arms and we both cried and whimpered at the same time until we started laughing again and couldn't understand what the other was saying.

"Wanna help me pack, Tamara?"

Chapter 23

Moving Along

"Turn that darn TV off. Hear nothing but killing and jailings. You can't let that stir up our minds. Just gotta do what Clifford and Jeffers allows us to do, say 'thank you,' and praise the Lord."

"Momma, there's nothing good about this year. 1964 is like the devil came up here on earth to destroy Negroes."

"You got the point. Just don't mess around carrying them signs and marching. Thataway you won't get yourself in this mess."

"Things gonna change, Momma."

"Like been beat at Woolworth's, shooting Medgar Evers, them poor innocent kids getting blown up to bits in that Alabama churchhouse, and now they done kilt President Kennedy causing he want laws changed like them rebel black folks."

"He died for a good cause."

"Gal, you been brainwashed. No more TV for two weeks. Go git yow hat on and we meet up with Fairly and teach you some things about them medicine salves."

"Yippee! Thanks, Momma Zettie."

"Gotta get you doing something else so you won't mope bout Thea and git that TV stuff outta your mind. We walk over near where the old Harris house once stood before they got burnt out and they moved to St. Louie. Old Miz Harris' granma showed these plants to me and some of us who got interested in healing balms and herbs."

"You told us never to come over here."

"And you bettern not less you with me or Fairly fetching them herbs."

"No needen us telling Tamara 'bout more than two of them herbs now."

"Shore is right, Miz Zettie Mae, cause saying too much at once can confuse."

"You see over there, child, in that swampy area where you see them purple flower tops tangled up with them other vines, that there is what we wanna see. Old Betony called the one for almost everything. I got my boots on and I wade out through the soft swamp and watch out for them snakes and snip us up some."

"I know, Momma, cause June Bug and Isom done scared us up so much about them big black snakes near the old Harris place."

"Well it's now July and time for them to be picked and dried. You tell Tamara what it is used for whilst I get it."

"Surely, Zettie Mae. Remember when Miz Melviner was so sick. Well, I made up a salve by putting some of Mr.

Dave Dove's saved-up beeswax from them honey bees he tends to at Mr. Clifford's, and Jeffers' houses. Well, I mixed some of this special oil and put some dried and smashed up 'cure-all' adding some marjoram, some Florentine root and Eyebright and yow Momma tended Melviner's sores. Just remember that main herb, 'cure-alls' and you learn about the others when its time to pick them. It works better when you well nuff to hold the powder in your bottom lip and just let some of the juices trickle down the throat bit by bit and spit the rest out. I even boiled some up and when the juices cooled down, put it on clean soaking rags and laid on that poor woman's sores. Them juices can help heal yu when you accidently get cut from filing a hoe or chopping meat. That 'cure-all' can also be sniffed up the nose to heal the worse of headaches. We gonna go back to my back porch with yow Momma and we make up some salve for this summertime with some herbs we done picked in the Spring. We let you stir it around. Now the next thing we tell you about is that Camomile, that's good for picking under this summertime sun. We make a balm from the oil that is good for colic and cramps of the stomach."

"Like when Verdie had stomach cramps?"

"No, child, that was a different type of cramp. You will learn what cramp balm to use or not to use just by asking a person many questions 'bout their affliction. We teach you more when you get older about that."

"You say that boy babies get the colic a lot so is that why you are always giving Miz Quintilla that stuff, because she still has a baby boy?"

"Yes, and I used it for my boys when they were little."

"Did they just eat it?"

"No, when me made up the camo oil, we put in six tiny droplets of sugar water in the oil, then you drop a spoonful into the baby's mouth and they love sucking it down or if they are big enough to eat, pour it onto a small piece of biscuit and they seem to like it."

"Nows Fairly you know that there is so many things that Camo can be used for healing folk. Made into salve it feels good on the skin for them swollen joints, for foot callouses and the big foot of gout. Them flowers of the dried camo can be made into a tonic. If we were ever so lucky to buy some quinine water from those quacks over in Olellean, thens we add some dried flower camo to the tonic water."

Momma continued with her talking.

"And them river boat men get back to work real soon after being at Miss Attie's. Now I done said too much but anyhow its good for morning drunkness or hows a person feels after drinking lot of the sinful drink."

"Think we done taught little Tamara enough for today, Miz Zettie. Let's go and show her how we dry these cure herbs and make up some salve."

"Okay, Fairly. Tomorrow we be headed over to my boy's place."

While visiting June Bug with Momma Zettie, we had to listen to the TV news program of his new wife, Ruby Mae. In spite of cruel retaliation, and more protesting for Negro's Civil Rights, the movement for change was moving ahead. My brother June Bug, now 21 years old, had moved ahead as well, for Ruby Mae was bulging with child. He was now foreman to Clifford's friend in Olellean and could have cared less about the Civil Rights movement. His leased property was a sanctuary of its own and a definite escape for what was going on in neighboring states and cities surrounding us, even in our state of Tennessee, Memphis of course. It became hard to talk to June

Bug because he had the same belief as Momma Zettie and Daddy Al about one's place in the world. Momma and I had hitched a ride with Verdie and her new husband, a cotton ginner from Olellean, as they had just visited Cousin Hortense. June Bug and Ruby Mae were very proud to drive us home in their 1956 Chevy so he could talk with Daddy Al about under the hood stuff.

Part II

Post-Civil Rights Movement

Chapter 24

Althea in the City

Dear Tamara,
Here I am settling into Chicago. The houses and porches are glued along side each other attached to dark red bricks. The home of Henry and Flora Jenkins looks like the rest of the ten houses on the block. When I sit down on the concrete steps, I don't know which is more painful, my butt and backaches or staring at the dirty and trashy sidewalks. Despite that, when I step inside the Jenkins' house, my spirits are warmed up at the slightest thought of homesickness. Can you believe it that I can actually miss Corn Hollow a little bit?

The unpleasant part of being here is seeing Clarence and Cotillion Parker deteriorate right under my nose. Just falling to sleep is often hard as Mr. Clarence makes a rattling and crackling sound with every inhale and exhale that starts with a whiny wheeze sound that is heard throughout the house.

Mrs. Flora is real family-like. She tells me to be back from work early enough to watch the evening news with them. Once I am out the door, I walk my usual safe route that Mr. Henry Jenkins recommends. It is down the street, cut a left, walk two blocks, avoid the alley paths, and catch the street car going downtown. I know to avoid eye contact with men, keep my mouth shut, don't show my feelings, and act like I know where I'm going even if I miss pulling the cord at my stop.

It is so hot on the streetcar, even though little windows near the ceiling are open. Sometimes it is easier standing up than sitting on the hot vinyl seats. Flirting men have said, "hey pretty baby, you wanna hear some soul jams with me?" or "Stuck-up bitch!"

Ignoring the deviants, I would slide down into the empty vinyl seat and just stare ahead at the railroad type streetcar tracks, the dark oil spots in the pavement, the broken-down cars, and watch finger pointing and gestures of men and women cussing the other.

What distresses me is coming into the high rises and seeing in the distance very tall, steamy pipes coming out of factory rooftops that makes it appear like it is about to snow in August. It kind of chokes and gags me to breathe it.

One of the ladies working on the line at the sausage factory recognized me and we sat together on the streetcar. "Hey girl, you got it good, working in the front rooms with them papers. You even got fans in them rooms." I sorta smiled at the lady and inquired about her job. When she told me that she was on the big grinder, I couldn't say anything more. She kept talking. "Better seeing meat piece come out the other end than whensa I started and hadsa put them chittlings in a trough and pull back on some handles and you knowed what I seen and smelt all day. Musta been your relative, Mr. Henry, who spoke up for ya."

Tamara, my mind keep drifting to the many times Mr. Henry bragged on himself to Mrs. Flora. "Yeah, theysa respects me. I tolds my old foreman friend to not put her with the meat. She heapa smart and can work with filing them papers."

I could hardly eat lunch for thinking about that factory worker who reminded me of Momma and is so appreciative of her job. With dismay, I kept whispering under my breath whenever I sipped some coffee in the office or just thought about her. "That poor lady once cleaned chittlings, day in and out and now grinds sausage EV-ERY single work day?"

When the whistle blows, the workers leave the factory. Since I am an office personnel worker, I help close the front office after all laborers are off the premises. I then catch the street car and focus on the heat waves dancing like a mirage on the pavement. The cloudy smoke sometimes breaks away so the sun can shine on the approaching towers and the windows look like mirrors. The wired attachment follows the street car like a big fish line. Along side the slow streetcar, a perfect rhythm creeps at a certain speed on the tracks. Popping up on a billboard that I have seen many times:

Show your pride. Write a story about your childhood. $200 Grand Prize.

I often thought that this was not for me and on the other hand, I might give it a try, Sis.

Meanwhile, folks rush in all directions catching taxis, buses, or more streetcars. Finally, I reach up pulling the cord where I get off one half block from Clark's Clerical Training School where the sign reads, *From Here to Management*. After rushing in the bathroom to freshen up, I try being all smiles with a changed attitude. Mr. and Mrs. Desmond Clark do not care about race or nationality. Of their twenty-five students, fifteen class members have medium to dark skin tones. The others are white. They seem to care about their tuition payments and training their students to seek good paying jobs so they can brag and continue with their notable reputation.

When the two-hour clerical and etiquette class ends, I make it back home in time for the evening news. Mr. Clarence generally rests while the rest of us watch it. "And now for a live report on the Reverend Dr. Martin Luther King, Jr. with a speech that has rocked the nation, reported from Lincoln's Memorial, Washington, D.C."

Mrs. Flora always makes choking sounds, cries or hums as she repeats the words of Dr. King. She hopes to see the day that our skin color makes no difference and everbody thinks about freedom. I thought of my Saturday freedom to go to my first beauty salon appointment.

Mrs. Flora said that I would like Miss Mabel as she knew how to make a lady feel good when she is through dressing their hair. I told Mrs. Flora that I couldn't miss my appointment. Off to the streetcar I went. The ride seemed to take forever and the careful scrutiny to not get lost 'among that class of people' as Mrs. Flora would say, brought me to a barred up black door with a peep hole in the upper center area. I wondered if it really was Miss Mabel's Beauty Shop. And surely enough it had to be because up above the door the name "Mabel's House of Beauty" was written. So with a doubtful sigh I rang the doorbell beside the iron bar that showed my face at the keyhole while I shouted my name.

Once beyond the jail-type door that locked behind me, I heard a friendly voice. It came from a jolly, slightly plump, yet energetic and beautiful Negro lady with slick and wavy hair. "You must be my 2:00 o'clock. I dress Flora's hair about every holie day and when her A.M.E. Church Annual Conference tis in town. Just have yourself a seat young lady, and make yourself right cozy here at home. You next, when I'm done with this head."

Even before I could find a seat, clouds of hair pressing smoke, lye noxia and other fumes and perfumes passed by my nostrils. I stopped breathing for two exhales. Having inhaled, another client entered the door and a chemical gust was trying to escape. The big ceiling fan rotated its head right over my seat near the door. Out of the corner of my eye I glanced at a big, fat, snoring female with long, knappy, moppy-locked hair that leaped in front of her face each time she snorted. One of Mabel's helpers turned the music up which enabled me to talk through my teeth. I thought about what Momma Zettie or Cousin Hortense would say if they were here seeing a wide leg straddle, revealing that lady's dough puffs of fat and the tops of her elastic rolled stockings. They would clear their throats real loud or drop something so the lady would get startled into closing her legs.

With another snort, like one of Daddy Al's Corn Hollow hogs, I smelled something familiar. Ah yeah, Daddy Al would smell like this when I had to wake him up for Sunday afternoon dinners. Being repulsed by the lady, I looked elsewhere.

There were stall-like areas with carts that contained

hair rollers and other hair products. Beyond the carts and barbershop-type chairs were dirty plastered walls with remnants of hot spattered hair grease stains, hair dyes, and plain old gook. The ladies in the chairs were being styled with eye-popping varieties of hairdos. The press and curl method is what we only know in Corn Hollow.

I would just cough amidst the smoke, the loud music, the burnt hair fumes and the other smells. This is what I had to endure to make me look beautiful. I also had to pretend that I didn't hear the words coming from a skinny beauty queen's voice that the hairdressers were tiptoeing around. A total of six ladies pretended the same by looking at hairdo magazines without changing the pages as they just listened. "Awe yeah honey, his was so big I thought I was gonna burst wide open." She then threw more than enough money at Miss Mabel and left with an announcement, "I can find you'all some fine men and make some fi-n-n-n-e money."

Miss Mabel let out a big sigh of relief when she locked the big black door behind that customer. "What you gotta put up with to keep your business going is almost a sin," is all she could say.

"Uhn-hum," was what the other ladies expressed.

I chose the straight and wavy look like Miss Mabel. I asked her why she wanted to know if it burns because it was feeling cool on my scalp. After twenty minutes had passed, I understood what she meant. It felt like my brain was being pulled out through the top of my head. She instantly rinsed the mixture from my hair as I leaned my head back with a small towel over my eyes that faced upwards towards the ceiling. Finally, the conditioning, rolling, and drying were over.

Looking in a mirror, I discovered that my hair was

wavy and I loved touching the wavy curls. I then thanked Miss Mabel and I gave her money. She walked me to the door as she was talking. "Just wait 'til you through with that bookeeping or whatson ever school that is and them white folks gonna hire you. I'll see you in two months. Tell Flora how you do from Mabel."

Enroute home I got a lot of stares from men. I glared right through them and didn't blink.

There is one more thing, Tamara, and that is changing my speech to be ready for anybody's world. Guess I thought of taking one of those diction classes that Miss Potter keep trying to lure all the young Negroes into after church. I know the Jenkins won't mind because they just love Miss Potter.

I have to end this letter soon as I can hear Mr. Henry calling me. And you know, Tamara, Miss Potter can say things like those TV folks, and she isn't charging anything to help get rid of Southern talk. Mr. Henry said he would put in a good word for me.

For two hours I primped in the mirror and almost forgot supper. I thought that if I had $200 saved up, I could get my own apartment in the suburbs where it's quiet and real clean or some nearby country-like place.

Funny thing, Tamara, Mrs. Flora called me downstairs for supper tonight by saying, "Come on down here for supper, Miss Prettyhead Althea, so we can say grace." That made me feel so good.

Love,
Sis Althea

Chapter 25

Dreaming

I see June Bug grinning and being happy about cutting his first piece of wood; Luella, Isom, Verdie, Althea and I jumping in the low end of the river while June Bug is pushing me towards the bank and making each of us dog paddle; Daddy Al placing little old one-year-old me on the back of a mule as I felt the warm tickling hair against my bare legs; Momma letting me sit in a rain puddle as my diaper filled up with water and gritty dirt; and water gushing out the side of a red clay area behind Corn Hollow just as I pulled my spear stick out where Luella and I had been jabbing. As the water gushed out, I felt calmer and calmer like being physically moved somewhere else. Then I woke up.

I had fallen asleep in a big chair at the Big House of

Mr. & Mrs. Clifford last Saturday. Momma had asked me to help Miz Iola with Mr. Clifford's tending.

"Since you older and you kinda hushed on asking that fool darn question of yours, then I better give you the opportunitee to actually go inside that white folk house. Then maybe you shut your mouth about things."

Of course, I was anxious just to see the place and definitely to go inside that Big House, as everyone called it. With the exception of the big fireplace, I found myself liking the big yard more than the house that was filled with old antiques and whatnots, as Mrs. Clifford called them. The willow trees that leaned its boughs over to greet and touch you as you brushed by, the pottery sitting all around the porch, the red paper-like flowers called imported bougainvillea growing up trellises, and the big blooming magnolia tree were, by far, marks of beauty to set my eyes upon.

Mr. Clifford had some type of non-contagious fever that Miz Iola had nurse-tending experience with over the years. Since she might ask for certain herbs in her pouch to be boiled or wrapped up like Momma and Miz Fairly had taught me, that was my chore. Clifford had been talking out saying all sorts of stuff. Miz Iola warned me.

"Whatever he says ain't true so don't you get carried away with that talk. I gotta rest for fifteen minutes or so out on the back porch and you just keep putting that polstice on his forehead till I get back."

Delirium brewed as Mr. Clifford started talking.

"You know Lord that I give them orders for Larry Moore to stop any Corn Hollow coloreds from working in that John Deere factory as I needed them to work in my fields. I told Larry to don't get anybody hurt and you know your Paw and me rode a many nights together under them sheets. Forgive me Lord for what I done to them old folk's house. But don't let them take my boots. Old Morton gimme them things a day before he shot himself. One of his boys, Seth they call him, spilled red paint on 'em and he never got mad at that colored and I don't know why. Anyhow Lord, I want to be buried in 'em. They served nobody any good use. I did awful things in them."

I didn't hear Miz Iola come back in but she had apparently been standing in the doorway for some time and she looked dull and faint. Miz Iola grew quiet and she saw the sheets get wet and the smell got stronger. She started talking to Mr. Jeffers.

"Gotta ask Hortense to take over from here. I can't do no more for him. Come on, Tamara. Mighty sorry Mr. Jeffers."

"Iola you look like you saw a ghost. Has Mr. Clifford passed on?"

"Almost, Zettie Mae, it won't be long. I just realized that thngs I thought about him was what I have always known. His sins be suffered with him a lot on that sickbed. We gotta pray for all of God's children, even that sick Clifford."

Chapter 26

Integration

Momma seemed to make excuses for going to see Miz Siddie. She let me go with her and we found Mr. Daniel sweating and pulling himself up to a chair. His leg seemed to be troubling him with pain. When Momma went inside to talk with Miz Siddie, it was prime time for me to confront Mr. Daniel, who knows everything them white folks do.

"Yes I know more than most coloreds about them."

"What about them boots of Mr. Clifford? You know them boots, I can wear them boots."

"Where you hear that, gal?"

"Nowhere. Are you alright?"

"Yow Daddy Al knows what his Pappa done said 'bout

203

the man in the boot story. That old man Jambialiah told your daddy on his death bed. And you know."

"Why you stop talking, Mr. Dan'l?"

"Hey gal, don't you ever talk to me 'bout that again. Now gwone inside where your Momma and Miz Siddie is."

Enroute home I decided to stop thinking about Mr. Dan'l as he seemed scared of something when I talked about them boots. I got other things on my mind.

Mumble. Mumble. In-te-gra-tion Huhn!! The word "integration" was roaring from the tube box as Walter Cronlite, or however it is pronounced, so eloquently gave his news reports. Folks were talking about it all over Corn Hollow that kids would be going to an integrated school.

Concentrating on the fact that Cousin Delmar had been warned for pushing equal opportunities made days seem like murky water. Fear was beginning to cloud folks' hearts.

To say the least, the school year was climactic. Being future "guinea pigs," was how I thought of it. Having an opposite side were the Negro boys who thought it great as it meant more tender meat to the gazing eyes.

Hearing Obediah "Obe" Malachi say to me, "The itch done got me."

"You have an itch?"

"You're hopeless."

It would either be a doomsday or a better day. Moving from an all-Negro, one-room country schoolhouse with a total of thirty students for grades one through eighth was a comfortable, intimate pleasure. This made me think about something I got from one of Thea's books: "The ultimate childhood experience until the interruptions started coming like the New York Philharmonic playing a Tchaikovsky crescendo. The beat of the kettle-drums created a crescendo that evoked chills and interjected shocking terror into my veins."

"Oh God, what is happening to me, Luella? So much is going on. Is it more than the dizzy spells and the blemished gore that take most girls by surprise?"

"I think there is more to what we have to face at school."

At the church picnic, I noticed the glazing stares and the dropped jaws of the elderly, especially Miz Iola and Miz Siddie. This made me speechless and it seemed as if they had swallowed a dark gray cloud as I started to sweat.

"Do I eat another forkful of delicious salad or take another bite of chicken that I can no longer taste?"

Somehow as an adolescent, disclosing feelings out loud would be forbidden in this situation. On the other hand, we had to listen to our African Methodist Episcopalian minister, Reverend Stokes, as he geared his message to school children in his outdoor informal sermon on that church picnic day. This special event was held at no other place than the Corn Hollow hole pasture. Cousin Hortense had to be away with her niece in Olellean, so Luella stayed with us. Sticking together for the upcoming week was a blessing that started with a sermon.

With voluminous magnitude the Reverend preached.

"Keep your tongue, hold your temper, and swallow your pride. Some will make it a terrible road to climb."

Reverend preached, "Whites, just a few, will embrace the change."

Luella was really hoping that integration was a bad dream and she would wake up the next day and wouldn't have to go to school.

Neither Luella nor I could fall asleep easily that night. I focused my eyes on my yellow, ruffled dress that I had made on the old Singer treadle sewing machine for dress-up purposes. Momma said we had to look pretty and well-groomed.

My eyes closed slowly as I looked at the dart in the bodice of my dress hanging on the wall nail. "I can fit into this now, the only good reason to go to school tomorrow."

It was so strange to think this way as I loved school-books and learning, and yet utter dread entered my soul. Feeling my heart sink as my eyes filled with tears, I rolled over and covered my head with my plumaged pillow.

Next thing I knew, it was morning. I could hear muffled hums and see early morning light forming a perfect isosceles triangle on our streaky painted girls' bedroom wall that covered the maroon and gold paisley printed wallpaper that I always woke up to.

Was it really morning or a bad vision that I somehow conjured up but was never to be acted on?

"Rise and shine," a humming voice echoed from the kitchen.

I pushed my pillow into the headboard as I stretched. Luella was already up and helping Momma, who was high-pitched into "We Shall Overcome." I could hardly believe what I was hearing. Is she covering up pain with her sweet melodies like a motherless female who wanted to die as she watched her baby get auctioned off down the river? Or was she happy that all the public schools in the county will be mixed with both Negroes and Caucasians?

It was easy for time to pass for Momma's bacon, eggs, and hoecakes raised me up from bed quicker than Lazarus from the tomb. Every mouth-watering bite meant love.

"Everythings gonna be alright. Just hold your heads up girls and remember the Reverend's words, and eh listen to yow teachers."

With reluctance, Luella and I actually made it to the Turning Row Crossing bus stop, where dirt road converged with the black top. It was as if Frank, the bus driver, had announced "silent time." He was not the old Corn Hollow chatterbox that everyone was used to.

I heard a whisper.

"Is he afraid for us?"

"I don't know."

All of us kids seemed disgusted that 1964 had arrived and didn't want to go to a different school. Riding the fifteen miles to a consolidated school district was not a normal bus ride for us. The stares at the different neighborhoods and houses were stares of a new adventure for our eyes. However, I looked right through those houses reflecting my mind on the serenity of the old school days passed with the potbelly stove that was shared with family and friends of one color. Now I am saying goodbye to that world. I recalled the memory of an old newscast of that demure black woman in Alabama, with little status nor physical power, plopping herself into a seat that was meant for a white person on a city bus.

"Oh Lord, will we have to act bravely like little David slaying Goliath?"

"Is this good or is this bad?"

I mentally twirled. All I knew was that I didn't want to resist authority, brave-up to angry people, or hide my own panic button. I really wanted to run back home.

"Hey, Luella, I remember the newsman saying that her stunt helped to set in motion the whole Civil Rights movement."

"Just keep babbling, Tamara, I'll try to listen if I can."

"You are just scared?"

"You mean that you are not?"

"Keep talking and maybe we'll soon be to school."

I continued with my nervous chatter.

"Yeah, since Mrs. Rosa refused to pay a fine for sitting where she rightfully felt her tired bones should have been that day, it scared up the Negroes and the white folks."

"I'm listening, Tamara. Just keep talking."

"Then there was that Miss Melba Beals, one of the Little Rock Nine who integrated Central High School in Little Rock, Arkansas. Don't you feel nervous flip-flops in your gut? Are they going to curse at us, throw things at us and make us feel bad? They did have guards and we have nothing but our courage to shield us."

"And our legs to run," Luella marveled.

"I feel like there is no God, otherwise we wouldn't be in the company of what Althea would call 'pernicious folks' that want to rip our hearts out and curse our existence."

Laughter and chuckles poured from everyone as they continued to listen.

"And she would say that Miss Melba knows what humiliation is. Reverend Stokes spoke of this hundreds of times this year already. Yeah, yeah! A white student choked her and she didn't fight back. The ram was the military. The Reverend even said that Miss Melba was a spiritual soldier in a war to break down the barriers of segregation. She learned to stand tall, be strong and survive, which is not how we feel right now."

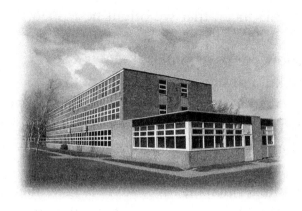

Chapter 27

The New School

Our fifteen-mile journey was up. I could see the tip of an American flag as our school bus meandered uphill to a tilt-top rectangular building perched on the top of Aikley's Ridge. Yep, an Ozark type setting it was with rippling hills, lush green lawn, and tall pines at the top edge of Grentwood County, almost touching the Olellean County line. Our arriving school bus was like the aftermath of a storm where the ship wrecked on an island and its passengers were disembarking. My brain was twining up like a gurgling gut that meant reform at my expense. I felt like a fettered outcast waiting to be run over by a locomotive. Simply put, today was that ill-fated and menacing presence of a curse. The sacrifice meant something that us new students had to walk through so others would have it easier after us. In an assured tone I evoked a question so everyone would hear it.

"Does this mean that we might be ripped right out of our high school experiences so that we can hold a torch of light to show our psychological blows?"

"What kind of blows?" Obe questioned.

No one responded, but rather stood up as our eyes were busy viewing this new territory. Our new school was now perched between Corn Hollow and Olellean with lots of newly built houses in the hills and on the roadside.

The white Principal, Mr. Floyd Slager, met the Corn Hollow school bus and handed out schedules to us. He wore a name tag that said, "Hi! I am Principal Slager."

"Welcome to Turkey Ridge High School."

Obe mumbled under his voice as he eye-scolded Mr. Slager.

"That's why they call this Turkey Ridge High."

Several kids quickly snickered as Mr. Slager slowly peeped from behind the schedule cards which served as his refuge to avoid looking at his new pupils. He stoically scanned all of us, one by one, perhaps looking for a prospective trouble maker. We bore expressionless faces as Principal Slager looked us over.

"Don't wait for your friends. Just take your schedules and go immediately to class. All hallways have girls and boys' bathrooms. Don't be late for class."

Pointing to the Vice-Principal, Mr. Arthur Simmons, the Negro Principal transplant from Olellean, Principal Slager continued.

"He will direct you to wing A, B, or C."

"Did you notice that he didn't smile either, nor say, 'Hello,' and certainly not a welcome?"

"Perhaps he was told not to show favoritism nor emotions, like a soldier."

This made me want to laugh.

At lunch, the cafeteria ladies acted like they wanted to break their serving spoons as they banged out scoops of macaroni and cheese onto our lunch trays.

It did break the tension for a good laugh. Luella and I stood with our trays, trying to find a seat. The white students were seated at all the tables, some two to a table, except the one in the very back of the cafeteria.

"It's saved!"

"It's saved."

"This seat is taken."

Seated at the back table were all Corn Hollow students except one.

"Where is Obe? He knows we gotta stick together." In deciding to find him, I walked past tables of blondes and brunettes looking at each other and their food and occasionally saying something.

"Pigs in the cafeteria. There is a pig in here and musta come from that hollow" A boisterous, shaggy-haired boy with chocolate or dirt around his mouth stood up on a chair and also bellowed: "Did they say Mud Gully or Hog Squalor?"

A seated voice hollered out.

"No man, Corn Hollow!!"

I looked back at our table, not knowing whether to go back to it or keep moving to find Obe. Luella beckoned me to come back. Mr. Bodine, my English teacher, had cafeteria duty and walked towards me with clenched teeth.

"Go take your seat. It's lunchtime."

I could all but feel the heat of his anger coming from his eyes. My stomach got hot and I could hardly breathe.

"Yes, sir."

I took two bites of macaroni and cheese and lost my appetite at the thought of going to my fifth period class taught by none other. Mr. Bodine explained to the class a few poetic terms and read some as examples and then gave the class some handout paradigms. The assignment was to write about one's feelings. I wrote:

"Crying Soul"

All I want is to be a teenage kid.
Rather, you look at me as if my presence is to forbid.
Is there a reason you hesitate?
Is there a time-period when this will abate?
My soul is crying for you to tolerate
Rather than hate.
I have a heart and my blood is red too.
I even have feelings just like you.

Arriving home, Luella and I saw the light of freedom, not from experiences at school but stepping into the kitchen at home. We caught scent of, while feasting our eyes upon, the sugary and yeasty dough on the rise. My mouth was wet with the thought of meeting Momma Zettie's cinnamon rolls and enjoying the creamy confectionery glaze that would disunite with my incisors while raisins burst open with their grapey nectar to mix with the delectable sweet bread.

"You are excused from your chores this whole week, but in an hour and a half we will eat supper."

"Thanks, Momma."

"Go rest up and I'll call you when it's ready."

Luella fled to the porch swing while I collapsed in my bed. Books and tablets went flying on the floor. I couldn't have cared less because I was as tired as a circus jack rabbit on a muggy day. My mind, heart, gut, and every muscle had surely lurched and lunged during the previous twenty-four hours. I heard snoring as the back of my mouth and my rear nasal area was vibrating. I couldn't tell if it was me, nor did I care if it was. K-z-zzzzzzzzz. When I woke up, I had a grand meal and told the family every detail of the day and Luella did the same.

Another day passed and I received my first academic grade. It was a D- from Mr. Bodine's class. There were so many hard-pressed marks of scolding and critical comments that the number two lead pencil poem was barely visible.

"I'm listening to the teacher, Momma. I'm really listening for the unspoken voice that echoes through the red ink strokes. The voice might be saying … 'I am an angry teacher who is using your good poem that deserves a B+ or above to chop through my unpleasant adventure of unification of schools. This tinted pen warms my rage and is my ammunition of diminution: I'm having so much fun'."

Momma Zettie just silently sat back as I rambled on.

"Does every teacher make you say things like that?"

"No, Momma."

I told Momma in simpler terms that luckily, every teacher's voice does not impersonate repulsion and insolence. There was profound genuineness in the speech and heart of Miss Hendy. Besides the play on her name by both black and white students, she, along with Mrs. Caldwell, were the only reasons I wanted to attend school without protest.

Miss Hendy and Mrs. Caldwell make me feel welcome. Miss Hendy teaches psychology and science and she seems to love all human students. Everyone thinks her grading is fair. She would give you C+s when you earned it and an A+ when you deserved it. Mrs. Caldwell teaches Home Economics and was re-assigned to the high school when segregation ceased. Thank God for miracles.

"Also, Momma, I won't forget that friendly white face of a student named Linda, who showed me where to find room B-12 as well as the cafeteria."

I did wonder if she was real or was she setting me up for something that hadn't unfolded?

Linda appeared again. Her pale white, friendly face seemed as innocuous as a fluffy white cloud in a cumulus sky.

"I know it's different for you. It's different for me, too, seeing a lot of colored faces here."

I shrugged at Linda's statement.

"I meant no harm by it, Tamara. Guess what?"

I didn't answer and hid my emotions. Linda proceeded to talk.

"Miss Hendy called all the white kids to the counselor's office and said she was re-arranging seats so we could all do more paired-peer learning. She asked if anyone would be your peer partner. The counselor made it real clear that we didn't have to do this and you would have to work by yourself if it came to it. I told Mr. Reed, the counselor, that I would sit near you and be your partner. I picked you because you don't seem to be walking around with what my folks call 'a chip on your shoulder,' all mad and upset. I know that neither one of our mommas would like it if we visited one another at our houses but can we be friends here at school?"

My heart lightened and I felt my shoulders relax as I let out a big sigh and managed to articulate.

"S-ure," and, gave a slight smile.

"There may be a time or two when I need to save my

hide from a neighborhood fight like when Esther and …"

"Big Ally."

We both spread arms out to continue the sentence and snickered with our hands covering our mouths.

Linda looked up and then whispered to me.

"There's Selene, the white supremacist queen we need to watch out for. Her momma died of cancer last year and she hates her brothers, her sisters, her daddy, and even her past best friend. She especially hates you all as she calls the "n" word. She would pin me to a bathroom stall and choke me till I turned pale as a piece of writing paper and leave me with one last breath to live and fear her forever."

"That sounds like Miss Melba Beals in a reverse situation."

"Miss who?"

"And, yeah, a Negro man named Mr. Oliver Brown had moved into an all-white neighborhood in Topeka, Kansas. Mr. Brown wanted his daughter to attend a school in the neighborhood but was told that she had to go to an all-colored school which was very far from where they lived. Mr. Brown sued the school board. From what I heard on the radio, he reminded me of my old teacher, Cousin Delmar, who had a lot to say about people's rights. "School segregation violated the equal protection clause of the Fourteenth Amendment or whatever he meant."

"So that's why last year my history teacher mentioned Brown vs. the Board of Education is why our schools will look different real soon. He wouldn't teach us anymore than that."

"Let's make a code for ourselves. This will let us know when we have to instantly stop acting like friends."

"How about us rubbing our pierced ear-hole whether or not we've got an earring in it?"

We were both nervous, excited and felt as cunning as two foxes when without warning, Selene was prancing towards us. Linda had her back turned. I saw a big white girl frowning and stuttering.

"Don't turn around." I reached my left hand to my left earlobe hole with my right index finger.

Linda froze. Selene puckered her chin as her top lip almost touched her nose and gave Linda a sign of approval. When she walked away, Linda and I were silent until we saw her actually leaving the building. When the outer door finally snapped shut in slow motion, we couldn't contain the laughter any longer. We laughed so hard that our eyes had tears in them. Miss Hendy was coming up the hall and we didn't see her in our amused frenzy. She definitely saw us happy, friendly, and sisterly. Miss Hendy smiled with approval and she briskly continued on her way. We knew that Miss Hendy was the most liberal and compassionate teacher at Turkey Ridge High School and that she was our ally.

"Broadway," Linda cried.

"Hollywood," I called out.

We skipped off in separate directions to exit the building from different doorways as we boarded our respective buses to our own communities.

Arriving home, I looked at Momma.

"I know you want me to read those words over yonder each day for strength that Miz Flora from Chicago sent you. Well, I am strong and I'll read them again if it makes you feel good."

Another school day arrived. We wouldn't know what might happen in the cafeteria at lunchtime. "Hope they didn't spit in it."

"sh-s—ss"

Before I could look Luella in the eyes, a loud squeal and screech roared through the cafeteria. It was two white boys trying to catch a loose gilt hog that they claimed ran from the agri-hog lot and into the cafeteria.

Chapter 28

Pluto

"That gal is wasting good money she could be sending home to me and her old Daddy Al."

Back in Tennessee, Momma Zettie was all in a knot after hearing of Althea's frequent visits to the beauty salon.

"All she gots to do is use that straightening comb and some hair grease herself. Since everybody wants to hear 'bout Thea, Luella, yew gone git Minter to come over here and tell y'all some stories. Tell him I just baked some pies."

"Whew!! These kids just going mad with them new words and now hearing Althea talk 'bout the city, Lord knows what's gonna happen to them. Dr. King now speaking speeches that they wanna kill him for."

"But, Momma, what he said 'bout all black kids not to be thought about as just black but consider their strength and qualities as good."

"Isn't it, Momma?"

"Huhn!"

Luella reported that tomorrow afternoon Minter would be coming over.

"Good! Then you can come with me and your Daddy to Olellean. After the supply shopping, the malt stand will be the last stop."

Daddy parked the Belvedere to the side even though there was plenty of parking spaces in the front of Frosty's Malts.

From the front seat I could hear a commanding tone.

"Hurry up and choose that ice cream flavor so we get home 'fore 'nother rain shower comes down … I can't see her over on the side. Turn your car lights over there. Looks like a big mud hole in front of the colored window."

"I'll go over to the other window."

With synchronicity to my sentence, the big white waitress glanced over from behind the screen and into the car, while both Momma and Daddy called out.

"No. No. Go to the other one."

I sorta got the hot shivers in spite of the fact that the late hot summer's edge of twilight added to the heat of the moment. So I straddled the mud puddle.

"Please, ma'am, can I buy two scoops of vanilla ice cream in the cone?"

Walking towards the car, I whispered to myself.

"Why is everyone being so strict? Every time our family is out in public, there's one time or the other for hunched up shoulders or they sound scared. They must all be crazy."

Ignoring them, I licked and slurped the cone. I swirled my tongue around the icy cold, sweet, vanilla ice cream and crunched down on the edges of the wafery perforations that sounded like swishing slurp that twittered and crackled between her teeth. Managing to very quickly finish the whole cone was like a magician's disappearing act. Suddenly a bumpy rush of cold ice hit inside my forehead. I started holding my head as I squinted my eyes and grit my teeth. The cold hurt slowly drifted away as I fell asleep in the back seat of the car next to a lot of crinkling bags. I could feel bumps in the road, thinking that we were nearly home but was too sleepy to raise my head.

"Oh God!!"

Momma's voice was so quivery. I suddenly lifted my head as I started wiping my sleepy eyes and saw that the car headlights were shining on Pluto, the family dog. Pluto looked as if he was leaping up at something. His front legs were pointing upward as they were caught in a wire and his head was leaning over. I couldn't see his eyes as an ear had flopped over them.

"He's not moving, Momma."

Pluto's hind legs were limp. Momma started moaning and this sent me in tears as I climbed over the car seat and sat next to her.

Daddy explained that Pluto got his collar caught in a wire and tried to keep pulling it loose and strangled himself.

"Musta been trying to jump over that fence."

Early the next morning, June Bug made a sling, put Pluto on it, and drug him off to the backwoods. As the vultures flew over, Luella, myself and everyone else decided to make prayers for him in Sunday school.

"Kids, that is all we can do for him now. We gotta let that old fuzz ball go."

Pluto was so hairy for a cocker spaniel and roamed the

fields and out of doors that Daddy nicknamed him "Ol Nappyhead." His curly black hair was one big mangle that matted itself with cuckle burrows.

"That dog been in ours familee since June Bug was a suckling baby."

"Who will bark the snakes away for us when we go berry picking?"

"Mr. Dave's boy is here. That's you, Minter, and you full of stories."

Without hesitation, Minter just started talking tales.

"That dog knows most everything about Corn Hollow's families. If only he could talk like when he got scared off and your Daddy Al found him running like a dying pup in the cornfields. Mr. Jeffer's pa done gone hunting with him and accidently grazed him. Did you know that Jeffer's told your daddy to heal him and keep him as he's a just a scardy cat? Now what poor puppy would want to hear a gunshot for the first time and then discover that his tail is burning fire? He had the best home that any family, rich or poor, could give to him."

Luella started questioning Minter.

"How come you know so much about Pluto?"

"Cause that dog done saved my life. I bet you never knew that."

"When?" A few voices uttered at the same time.

"Go fetch me some of your Momma Zettie's peach cobbler and a jar of ice cold water, little missy, and I'll tell you all about your own dog."

Minter sat down on a stump and Luella and I sat right in front of him. We were listening as we looked up at his teeth upon opening and closing his mouth to speak. Monitoring his proportioned hand gestures were of great interest to us also. Esther and Charlie had come from nowhere, as it always happened when Minter would tell his tales, and lay on the grass near Isom and June Bug. June Bug and Charlie were gnawing on a piece of semi-dry grass that took the place of chewing gum or tobacco as their elbows propped their heads inside their hands.

Reaching down and pulling off one shoe to shake a rock out of it, Minter continued.

"Y'all didn't know that Pluto had more than one life."

Most of us just rolled our eyes at each other in a pendulous swing of disbelief.

"You mean like a cat?"

"No, like a dog because cats don't bark."

Minter boasted and shoveled in three forkfuls of peach cobbler into his jaws.

"One day me and my Daddy Dave were digging a new toilet hole and we noticed that fuzz nap come snooping around. We didn't pay no more tention to him till after we done ate our lunch. Bleeping sounds came churning from the poo hole."

Lord, Lord, that dog done fell in there and done licked up some of that lime I had to soak in the bottom of the dirt hole with some water in it. I went down in there and put him in a looped belt as my daddy pulled him up. Since it hadn't been used for human waste yet, it was just cold up to my ankles. We reckon the dog done been poisoned from the lime and drowned. I got myself out with the help of a rope and some foothole prints that we always make when digging holes so I could put my toes in and mounted on up. My Daddy Dave done poured clean water over him now to get the lime water off. That dog did not move a muscle.

Since Daddy Al was back down in the north forty of Mr. Jeffers, we figured on taking him back home ourselves. Just as we had that dog in a sling and holding on to each end as we walked, Pluto took the load off of us and scrambled out of the hammock. He tried to stand up but couldn't. His muscles shivered like livestock shaking off horse flies. We tried to cover his back with the sling and he was cold. To our surprise, when he lurched right from under us, we had handfuls of hair that come clean off his back. Me and my pa thought it was real strange. We followed Pluto every step of the way back to here as he stammered and quivered and slowly got home. Luckily, Daddy Al was coming into the house for lunch when he saw us. We told him what had happened.

"No use of him shedding them naps against everything he rubs up against. Let's catch hold of him and scrape the rest of that rug. You should have seen the sight. It was like plucking the feathers out of a chicken's back 'cept they just come off without any pulling. That thing looked so spindly and awkward. It was like a pink pig. Pluto was the most pitiful-looking thing that looked like some cartoon on television. Those heavy doses of lime, and we later learned, strychnine, ate the hairs off that dog's back. Rather than have y'all little ones whooping and hollering over the dog, Daddy Al had a plan." We couldn't wait to hear what was next.

"Dave, put him up in that old hog pen that you don't use anymore, feed and water the thing and bring him back here when his hair grows back."

"Sure thing," Dave calmly agreed to.

June Bug spoke challengingly. "How come I never heard of this?"

"Because it was that time when you and Isom went to Olellean and when you got back they told you that the dog had run away or got in a tussle with a big coon."

"So how did Pluto save your life?" Verdie called out.

"I'll tell you when I finish these sweets."

After gulping down ice water, Minter carried on.

"You see, Pluto got real tached to me since I be the one to feed and water him in his pen. One day when I went out to slop the hogs in the next pen, I heard a moan that had me blowing off gas and choking up at the same time. I broke wind so loud that whatever it was, it probably scared that animal that makes that noise. I looked over in the pen and saw that Pluto had some blood on his fine, thin coat of black curls that had not yet been mangled in cuckle burrows and catchalls. I hollered out to Daddy Dave, 'How come he's not barking?' I had to then stop for a minute."

"Oh, Lord, he done died again by something fierce and now it's going to eat him. Being nervous and terrified, I took my hog bucket, slung it and ran. I fell down and jammed my foot into a wire fence. There I was on the ground knowing I was surely going to die as my right shoulder was stuck into the soft, reeking, putrid, and rancid pig poop and mud." Minter continued.

"So this is how it feels to be a hog. I rather die like a dog than a hog. My mind was going crazy with this hog-dog stuff. I had never heard this moaning, hollow growl that sounded all broked up and earsplitting at the same time. Of course, that is what Daddy Al said them hog bears sounded like when he would log in the back woods. I knew that I was dying like a hog and I can't bear it any more. I was so scared that I couldn't talk or holler. The biggest sound that I could drawl out sounded like squeaks. Pluto was 'parently not dead 'cause he came to and started barking in circles. The noise alerted Daddy Dave and he come out of the house with a double-barrel shot gun and shot the damn bear in his heart. The boom sound of the gun and the thud sound of the bear hitting the ground made my foot shake loose from the crossed-up wires. My daddy wiped his forehead and pulled me up out of the sh--'.

'Hadn't been for that chicken dog, you might have been mauled by that thing,' he said.

"So that's what a hog bear sounds like," I said.

"Yes, my Daddy Dave told me, and it was a sick one."

"Now I see on its underside that its had a really bad infection from a hunter's wound. It was about to die anyway. Me and my daddy pulled this d'seased thing out of the hog lot with the help of our mule and took it far off in the backwoods for the buzzards. We let Pluto out of that pen to see if he would go on back here or stay with us. That dog stayed with us for two days now that it was free and then headed on home. He was always good and friendly to us but once he set sight on you little ones, he knew where his real home was."

Isom spoke up. "I got to hand it to you, man. You can tell some tall ones."

"Reckon Miz Zettie got some more pie that I can have?"

Momma was pleased and smiled as she started off to get Minter his sweet pie.

"Someday them storytelling 'bilities be put to good use. Took them minds off that North stuff that scare me do deff. It seems to be the Good Lord's will for Minter to open his mouth and talk."

Before everyone scattered, I stood up and made a declaration.

"I told you that I had the best dog in Corn Hollow."

Chapter 29

New Words & More Changes

No matter how Momma tried to shut down the new words, a year later they were eventuating more and more. She even tried to shut them down as she spoke at the African Methodist Episcopal Missionary Society meeting.

"Let us pray they don't let them new ideas 'bout Civil Rights let them walk right into a hornet's nest and sting 'em for life. You know if they done shot down that good white president in November, Lord knows what they do to us folks. Let them know their place. In God's name. Amen."

Nevertheless, things had changed. Most colored folks were calling themselves "Negroes." Momma Zettie and a few others refused to make the switch. The political views in *Brown vs Board of Education* called for more educational freedom for black school kids. Ambiguity was the mood and stress was worn on most adult faces in Corn Hollow. It was like a two-edged sword. Folks didn't know whether to shout for joy or flee from problems when their new rights were tested.

"There's more of them new words blurted on the black and white tube box," Momma would say.

"You mean like *terrorizing, racism, justice, boycott, riots,* and *integration?*"

As the sound in the newsmen's voices seemingly gloated dangerous delights, these changes were also overloading onto our daily life. Now that Mr. Clifford had died, his brother Jeffers sold parts of their two thousand acres to rich white folks who began to build fine mansion-type houses at the edge of Corn Hollow fields. Jeffers complained that cotton picker machines grabbed their profits. He further grumbled about there not being enough field hands, as they are all leaving Corn Hollow. Therefore, he couldn't compete in the cotton market. Jeffers stuck to raising soy beans, rice and Angus cattle. House after house went up. Momma and cousin Hortense would comment about this every day.

"There's another one going up. What's gonna happen to our houses 'cause now them big houses make us coloreds' places look like shimmy-shacks."

The elders even started making their predictions.

"Before long, colored folks want to live better than they think they do now. They go try out the meaning behind them words with the building of a big bank and a big, new high school 'tween here and Olellean."

On the other hand, lifestyles and cycles in Corn Hollow continued in the same fashion for Daddy, Momma, and most folks their age. The growth spurts and hormones did its toll, for Corn Hollow children were growing older and budding into young men and women.

June Bug had fallen in love with the young lady that Luella and I referred to as "Miss Ponytail Frizz" from the County Fair.

It was right at this time that he wanted to be called by his real name, James, rather than June Bug.

He married Patricia, called by many as "Miss Tricia," in the A.M.E. Church where Momma Zettie could organize the whole affair.

James and Tricia Banks then headed off to Olellean County for his life as an agricultural straw boss on the Big O Farmstead where the land owner calls him the best "colored boy" worker he ever had. James just did his work and was not at all offended by his boss' bragging comments.

Having James Banks living in Olellean made it convenient for Corn Hollow folks to enjoy a taste of life that they had never experienced.

Whenever anyone from Corn Hollow would have business to do in Olellean, they knew that they were welcome at the James and Patricia Banks' home.

Momma would tell everybody about her new daughter-in-law. She boasted so much in a letter to Althea, even before the wedding, that Thea mailed a wedding gift and said she had to work.

"My son and new daughter show their Christanity and Miss Tricia taken after my own heart with the way she keeps up her yard and house and take special care of them babies. Yeah, honey, when you 'proach June Bug and Tricia's, them yard bouquets of hydrangea, chrysanthemums, spikes of foxgloves, and gladiolas just leap out and smile at you. Look like they pour out spirits of joy and love from above. Sweet Miss Tricia be up on the porch rocking one of her babies in the front porch swing. And when she ain't cooking, cleaning the house, eating meals, or out at church or town, her swaying and fluttering in the front porch swing like a big girl herself. Ah yeah! Corn Hollow folks feel like theys going to a royal bath or somethang when they stop by they house in Olellean."

James had made it clear that no wife of his would work in the fields. Cousin Hortense reminded Momma Zettie of the time when she had to stay over in Olellean.

"I wents into their guest room and Miss Tricia uplifted a window that held up by a wood slat so it could blow in calm streams of fresh air that pushed them lacy ruffled curtains out. And you knowd the guest room provided the scents to get one's tiredness to melt away with them bunches of dried lavender. Lord Almighty, that inside bathtub that James rigged up make you feel mighty special."

"Yeah, Hortense, he tooken a big, new, long feed tub and cut a small hole in the bottom so the water would drain out onto a flower bed in the yard. He also built that wooden platform round it so you can just step over in it without slopping water on the linoleum. And Miss Tricia stoutly prime that pump and fill it up half way. Then added in three boiling hot tea kettles of water that she always keeps ready on the stove to fix the water to the right temp. If her hog jowls, mustard greens, sweet potatoes, and blackberry pie don' pease you, James' jokes will. Best part 'bout Miss Tricia, she not wants any of them new words in her house."

Although Momma felt differently about Althea, she didn't fail to get excited when Thea mailed her an occasional five-dollar bill, accompanied with stories of the Parkers, the Jenkins, and updates on Miss Quintilla's niece, Dora.

Meanwhile on the home front, Verdie decided to catch

a young man who had worked with James in Olellean and they later moved to Corn Hollow.

Isom also stayed in Corn Hollow, busting dirt clods with Mr. Jeffer's tractors. On the other hand, Mr. Dave Dove's boys, Charlie and Minter, took opposite paths. Charlie took up with Imogene and Clarise in Olellean's backfield hunky, tonk hall getting into more scrapes and scams than any rabble-rouser youth should bring down on himself.

And Minter heard the Holy Ghost call him to preach the word of the Lord. I witnessed him mesmerizing his pew with Biblical stories while mixing in a few of his own. Becoming known as "Reverend Minter Dove, who speaks from Heaven Above," seemed to fit him.

As soon as Thea's next letter came to Momma's hands, news from Chicago revealed the death of Clarence and Cotillion Parker.

Mrs. Cotillion willed herself to death. She didn't want to be left behind. When Mr. Clarence's lungs gave out, she flirted with a series of strokes one week after we buried him. Mr. Clarence went peacefully on his deathbed. Mrs. Cotillion muttered a song that her grandpa taught her. 'Mo te' ne. Mote'ne. Sun mom mi, we mo mi. sun mo in, fa mo mi.' It was in a foreign tongue that sounded something like we heard Daddy sang when Mrs. Melviner Tate passed on.

"Mr. Clarence's eulogy said that he shined shoes with his oxygen tank next to him in that Chicago hotel lobby. It was like folks feeling sorry and giving him extra work and money to pay for his ills. His last words also read that Roy Rogers and Jimmy Cagney would ask for him to shine their boots each time they stayed at the Palmer House Hotel. He always added that special touch to those rhinestone and alligator snake skins."

"And, Momma, here are some special words that I put together after hearing all the special things being said about Mr. Clarence and Mrs. Cotillion at the wake. So until I can visit home, I just want you to know that all of us here in Chicago want everybody in Corn Hollow to read it."

CYCLES

"Having experienced all the cycles,
 When the death cycle knocks on our family door,
We are touched with a deep sense of remorse,
  Of shock.
It is a time to LET GO with tears, heartache
  and pain and time to be connected with the spirit
  that echoes from the core of our being.
We empty our grief by saying 'WE LOVE YOU'
For being, even though we won't be able to talk or
  touch in our usual way.
We will connect with you in the quiet stillness of the
  moon, the flickering wing of a bird, in listening to
  others around us that tell stories of you, times of
  you, and who you meant to them.
We connect with you through the passing of a
  thought, through what you left behind, for you
  Moved On....
Forward into Light, where darkness will be no more---
  into a transfiguration, a transformation, that
  keeps us emptying our tears, dispensing our
  fears... for we know our Beloved that we can
  someday dance to your peace...
  for you are released and WE LOVE YOU SO."

Momma made sure that this was read at the A.M.E. and the General Baptist churches. All of Corn Hollow prayed

232

and cried for two weeks, and lamented stories of Clarence and Cotillion Parker.

"They was like our flesh and blood kinfolks," cried Momma.

I had never heard the word *love* spoken so freshly, so sincerely, nor so many times. Living with the Parkers in spirit was such a change for Corn Hollow. I mostly occupied my thoughts with the season's upcoming walnut nuggets and waiting for Althea to come home for a visit.

Chapter 30

The Rape

In preparation for Thea's home visit, I started drying walnuts by placing them in the undulated ridges of a piece of old tin roofing. It was the chartreuse nectar that oozed from the crushed, thick walnut hull as I hammered and kept thinking about Thea. I could listen to her city stories and make pillow fights. I surely wanted to see her after the sluggishness I felt about the Parkers deaths.

Shortly after her arrival, I finally got some time alone with her when Momma and Daddy were in another room. Thea asked me if I had read her last letter. I told her that I was waiting for her to arrive so she could explain every detail, which would make it more interesting. With a serious look on Thea's face, she insisted that I go read it real soon. I didn't understand but knew I had to secretly read it right away, so I did.

"The door wouldn't open. I started crying and feeling helpless. I looked frantically for another way out and saw nothing. Even the phone cord plug was detached from the phone. 'Don't try screaming because I sent the staff out to a free lecture and lunch on the company. After that they were told to go home and not come back to the office until tomorrow. And sweetie, I told them you would be going home early because you have a toothache' as I wept."

After reading this in Althea's letter, I glared through the old scratched window pane beyond the thick, rust-webbed screen wire to a beautiful rosebud. I stood by the window and wanted to shed a tear as everything about me wanted to freeze.

Momma had the table set up with a faded, red, starch-torn table cloth, her flower sack dinner napkins, and corn-meal collected plates that were the outside trim for the pork chops, sweet potatoes, string beans, and buttermilk cornbread hoecakes.

Althea talked all about the Jenkins and Clark's Clerical Training School. She was reluctant to say much about her three-month practicum, or intern experience, with Chicago National Company that sells typewriters and all sorts of office equipment.

"Mr. and Mrs. Clark were so pleased with my eagerness, quickness of learning, my new appearance, and my voice elocution lessons, that they recommended me to a job at a subsidiary or affiliate company of Chicago National."

Momma Zettie and Daddy Al expressionlessly turned their heads with hearing 'el-o-cution and af-fil-iate.' There was also talk of her winning a writing contest at the dinner

236

table using one of June Bug's, or rather James', tales.

"What was it about?"

"That story was 'bout me, Verdie, Luella, and Tamara trying to catch some fuzzy baby chicks and about how Mr. Leo Hickle's pa murdered somebody and stuffed him in a cotton sack with blood dripping, and women bellowing, and how the men picked out blocks of ice on that hot day to set around him before his body went into rigor mortis."

Momma and Daddy again turned and looked at each other.

"I also told about how the law doesn't do anything when Negroes kill other Negroes. Also, I wrote about when Old Man Fenton got poisoned by Miss Attie's momma and Mrs. Lizzie married the widower Baptist preacher. Also, how that white sheriff took away Mr. Hall's property for shooting up his own wife in that honky-tonk because he was hot for Miss Bernicia himself."

Daddy started to mutter.

"All this time them thangs been goin' on 'rounds here and you hate 'em so and now you done took up writing 'bout em. Damn, gal, you 'prises me."

"Well, when Mrs. Clark reminded us students to brush up on our writing skills, I took a chance."

"You know yow brother got married to a real nice lady."

"Sorry I missed his special day, Momma, but I needed to work to pay for my apartment rent."

Then Momma went and got more hoecakes.

"When we gonna talk, Thea? Luella is going to be at her house tomorrow and I hope that we can talk then."

The next day it so happened that Momma was at church planning a program with the A.M.E. Stewardesses. The fateful hour had finally struck.

"Tamara, can you keep a secret that I think will help

you someday when you get out in the world?"

"Yes. I will not tell a soul. It's about where you work?"

"Yeah."

"Now you have to remember that these things are hard to say."

I waited as Althea gulped.

"Well, Lil Sis. You have to be aware of men. One day when I went to turn in my floor report my boss looked at me with passion and ravishment. He said, "Let's lock the door and have some fun.""

"He wanted you to do it with him?"

"You know about that?"

"I learned about it when someone drew a picture on the toilet wall before a tattler told Cousin Delmar that it was there and I read as much of your letter that I could stand reading."

"Well, I am surprised you know what you know. What you don't know is that some men will overtake you and take what they want. I told him that even though I thought he was a nice man that my body can't make way for him. He scowled when I said that and I told him that my heart is not open to him so my will is not dampening up to him. All sorts of soft-spoken bull—words came out of his mouth." He kept muttering.

'I've been turned on to you ever since you walked your pretty ass into this building. I was glad you got hired because you are not just beautiful. You are smart and I like that in a woman. If you were a white girl, I would divorce my wife and marry you. Since it ain't goin' to happen like that, since you are colored and all, I'll ask you to let me get closer.'

"He then staggered his non-rhythmic hips that were too stiff to actually wiggle. I called out, 'You are crazy or real sick, Mr. Woods' as I moved backwards with one hand behind me to reach for the door handle."

"Thea, I can't take too much more of this talk."

"Tamara, you the only one I can trust."

"But, Thea?"

"Please let me talk."

It couldn't be any worse so I let her finish. I saw myself being present with another red rosebud that I had been transfixed on after hearing the first part of this horrible story.

"Tamara, his imposition clouded my thoughts. I remember feeling like I was boiling and sweating over a canning pressure cooker as he came closer and closer. I started to push myself into the door. He put his nervously shaking hands on my blouse and started unbuttoning as an ill-wind blew a blast of peppery-garlic foulness from his breath." He then said, 'Don't cry. It hurts my feeling to see you in tears pretty girl' as nothing but tears poured out."

"At that point I almost heaved and wish that I could have. I became dizzy with disbelief and promptly blacked out. I don't recall anything except waking up with a crumpled piece of paper that said 'Thanks' near my chest. Tears flooded down my cheeks and Althea began to cry through her words. In an enraged instance, I tore it up. I then noticed that my pantyhose and panties were next to me, my skirt twisted up around my waist, and I felt an overly-sensitive energy of having been forcefully penetrated and invaded. I quivered as I jumped up nervously looking for the phone cord so I could call the police. What was I going to say, that my supervisor raped me and I didn't put up a fight because I was taken by surprise? Who would believe that anyway?"

Althea continued, "As I looked down at the desk I

caught a reflection of myself in the brightly waxed mahogany finish and ran furiously to the bathroom. I stayed in the company athletic shower room crying and scrubbing for two hours, a place that I didn't have the rank to ever enter. I had to suppress my anger every few minutes so that I could actually make it home. I put my clothes, even my secondhand tweed suit, in a plastic bag. I grabbed from a guest locker an exercise pant and jacket, some tennis shoes and a pair of sunglasses. I took my mind off myself and thought how I could clean and return the athletic wear by giving it to Amos, one of the security guards, and telling him that some company visitor had left them downstairs."

Althea paused. I left the building from the company backdoor when I knew that security would be in the north wing before their shift ended. I would normally have taken a cab or a street bus back to my place. The outside air, though smoggy as it was, felt better than riding. It was a dazed five-mile walk. I pitched the plastic bag into the next convenient garbage can. When I made it back to my door, I drew a tub of hot water and dashed in some rose bubbly bath and fell asleep in the tub. I still felt soiled and vile even after all the cleaning. I thought that something like this could never happen to me. It happens to those homely, verbally abused girls who need positive and kind words and are tricked by silver-tongued slimeballs who are nothing more than con artists who rape and pimps their prey."

"Since I am too ashamed to tell any family member, except you, I have decided to not allow this evil man ruin who I am.

Tamara, I can't give his actions towards me the power to overtake my senses. I feel that I am driven from God to be where I am and have to pass the test of pitfalls like that of Ralph Woods."

I even took my problem to a Negro social service office where they recommended a free course with facilitators to help me speak what's on my mind. One of these ladies helped me unlatch the numbness of my blacking out during that bad experience. She helped me to say 'NO' with intent, have it be okay to become angry and to let that stuff out. She encouraged me to keep going forward in life. Now, let me not just talk about me. What about you?"

"Well, the integrated school, the new changes in Corn Hollow but I told you when I wrote back to you. I wanna help you if I can."

"You already have. You listened to me. Now I'm listening to you."

All I could do was be still and silent for a moment.

"What if this happens again? Or what if someone else he has told tries it? Or what if you have to look for work somewhere else?"

"I've thought about the course I took. I am not running away to another office. I have called upon the Holy Creator for strength. It is what some folk say when they keep the faith and I have authorized myself to not be violated. Through a self-defense course, I am capable of knocking out any physical violator and call for help."

"You mean you take your high heels off and hit him on the head?"

"No, silly! It is not my intent to kill someone, just knock them out and get out of the way."

A pillow flew into Althea's face. "Like this!"

"No, like this!"

I looked up and saw three pillows coming towards my head. We laughed, giggled, and screamed and laughed some more.

"Let's go check on those walnuts to see when they will be ready to bust."

Leaping off the bed we strolled to the black walnut tree.

Chapter 31

Mistreatment

With Big Sis home, my mind was comforted just because she could share with me. What did concern me most was the irritability and the emotional states of Momma and Daddy. Of course, Thea and I reflected on this.

"Momma Zettie and Daddy Al are angry at everyone except June Bug for wanting to leave the farm life."

Althea was so kind to me and we seemed to grow closer and closer as best friends. It was also that time when Luella and I spent less time with each other.

A few days before Althea's departure, she pulled me aside. "Momma just walked down the lane to Cousin Hortenses' so let's go to the front porch swing. I got a little more to tell you."

"What?"

"It's about Momma and Daddy. It's time you straighten up this slanted way we've been living and start thinking for yourself."

"You mean it's hard to tell Momma and Daddy about the rape?"

"I'll never tell them that because when they choose to get mad at me they would make me feel like I caused it, and would put me down. It's like what happened to Verdie a few years ago when she had all those female aches which was her being pregnant by that flirty Mr. Daniel."

"You are saying that Verdie was raped by Mr. Daniel?"

Nobody believes that it was a shocking, violent rape, but that he befriended her and then overpowered her. Momma and Daddy always hinted to Verdie whenever Cousin Hortense was upset with her. They seemed to add into the drama which wore on Verdie like guilty heaps of gumbo mud that she could never wash away. I don't want this to happen to me. And furthermore, to tell Momma and Daddy would be like giving a weapon to a revengeful street gangster. When he feels enough confused misgivings, he will use it.

"And also Sis, I have confided in you because I know that you would not expose my pain. I surely am not willing to see their possible attacks on my unfortunate tragedy and squirt slander on my job training and educational classes."

I reached over and hugged Althea and shortly after a long syncopated sigh, Althea continued speaking.

"I'm talking about things such as jealousy and misunderstanding that hurt you inside, even more than rape."

"What?"

"More so because you love these people and respect

244

them highly."

"What are you talking about, Sis?"

It's the kind of mistreatment when other family members want you to give up on being who you are, speak incorrectly, be poor, and agree with everything they say. Otherwise, they think you are insulting them. They feel insecure about their own failures. It is so miserable to be around Momma and Daddy when either of them are in that mood with me.

"It's like their morals for living and their hard times give them permission to scapegoat when I come to visit. I never know if it will be a good visit or if they are in one of those begrudging ones."

Althea paused and started breathing quickly and heavily.

"It seems to always, more than often, happen when I'm in a need to just be around them and feel nourished and nurtured by their presence."

"Bet you that's what happened after you were violated."

"Oh yeah, and leaving Corn Hollow my eyes would water up. I would have to go into a bathroom at the bus station, put a handkerchief over my mouth and try to scream when I thought no one else was in there and then slowly cry until I could compose myself."

I clutched my arms around the waist of my sister and locked my fingers of both hands so she could feel that I was there and would always be there for her as I leaned into her arms.

"Give me some other examples, Thea."

"You know that we just can't keep talking about this, Tamara. Let's just say that I have been damaged and giving Momma and Daddy this information would hurt me more.

I have to get this toxicity out so it will not spread further and deeper like a blood-sucking leech. I cannot dedicate myself to this and somehow I must become unaffected by all of this."

The two of us held onto each other even harder and we squeezed tighter as if to guard the other and keep the demons out.

A few days after Althea returned to Chicago, I became extremely pensive.

Thinking about Althea's secret, Verdie's predicament, and how Momma and Daddy could switch their feelings on and off to Althea, quieted me by the day. I would race to finish my chores in order to have time for the two news broadcasts on television. One thing led to another as I looked at some folks in the news and wanted to be like them, feeling free and seeming happy and not burdened with thoughts.

I used our Singer treadle sewing machine and sewed in flared flour sack samples to make bell bottom pants and used shoe polish to make a big peace sign on the back of my school blouse. Momma found out.

"What's happening to my baby, Hortense? I had to burn up them freak clothes, which you know I would use for quilt patches but rather git rid of 'em than have Tamara ruined on foolish ideas. Her butt is even burning as I gave her the peach tree switch. I thought I never had to do that no more since she getting up in age. She done been putting elderberry juice on lots of her things that messed up her clothes. My kid ain't no clown freak. All my kids decent Christians like I raised 'em."

Chapter 32

The K Club

Reluctant to open another letter from Althea, I knew that I would have to because I thought it couldn't get any worse around here. With Momma being so tense with me most of the time, a diversion wouldn't hurt, so I opened it and started reading.

"You have to know what's going on. You can tell Luella and others when you are able to. Tamara, you can't go on like an innocent child not knowing the truth. Consider this letter is about Known Key Killers. You know that quiet fear you kept mentioning when you first rode a bus to see Aunt Etheline, and you kept saying that Momma was acting different. And also when you were telling me about those certain windows that Momma and Daddy hollered at you at the malt stand?"

"…Well, those folks against Negro people progressing and they really think we are not equal to them. If you do things the way they don't want it, you could be hurt or killed. I mean that those folks on the bus without color and the lady at the ice cream stand. Those white folks scare Momma and Daddy so they act that way when they don't want to."

I moved my lips without a voice as if Althea was in the room.

"They just folks like everybody else 'cept their nose is pointed, the hair slick and the skin got no tone." I then continued to read the letter.

"So the answer to your question: why white folks don't come into our house is because they think we are inferior to them. It's the way most of those folk think at this time. They think we are a lesser status or lower-ranking and they properly socialize with folk of their own rank."

I thought about Fairly's family, Shad and Bernicia Hall and Miss Attie.

"Listen up, Tamara! When Momma and Daddy were your age and even long after that, they say white folks in sheets burn down Negro field crops, beat folks, and bones started breaking. Those spooks would take a black man and hang him if he tried to do good for his family and even plant crimes on them to say they did it, then kill them right before their family's eyes. I know you remember Momma always telling the story her Momma told her about Miss Iola and her husband. Don't erase what she says about those stories."

I thought to myself if I was erasing Till, Miss Attie's boy, who got killed by a car when he was out walking one night from Corn Hollow to Olellean. Mr. Daniel Goodson

248

told us all that "nobody should think otherwise of his death as he smelled of whiskey when they found him." This was the message he brought from Mr. Jeffers.

Trembling by now, I had a hard time believing anything was true and yet I knew Althea was not telling lies. As I breathed shallowly and started to panic, I literally backed into the wallpapered corner and smoothly slid my buttocks against it and made it to the floor. My hands propped up my head as my left elbow braced against my knee.

Even though shattered, my otherwise foggy world was now clear. Associating this quiet fear to a horrifying distress that bled from one generation to the next, the echo of this painful experience struck chords in my old memory bank. The tied feeling and to the choking asphyxiation of the yoke around the neck that lead into a seasickening voyage. Or had I heard someone tell me this?

After crying and sobbing for about twenty minutes, I felt peaceful. At least I heard it from my sister and not Momma, because she would demand that I stop crying without a chance of letting me think.

Tamara, I am sorry that I couldn't wait like Momma asked me to do. I just knew that she would never get around to telling you because they covered up this thing so well that I wondered about it like you until Dorothea, who moved away with her family over to Olellean before you could talk, told me of the hate and the violence.

"You know on the news they have been talking about Miss Rosa Parks and Civil Rights. It means equal rights for all of us, Negroes and whites. We've been fighting for our rights since the slaves were freed in the 1860s like when Ol Nig got his name. Yes, from the word, 'nigger' and he never really had a real name. Miss Rosa believed in what was right and fair."

Hitting my forehead with my palm, I frowned, thinking of when I was on the bus with Momma. She made sure that I didn't sit in a seat designated for white folks.

"The guys in white sheets belonging to that 3-K club probably would have hung Miss Rosa at night if it hadn't been for the Reverend Dr. Martin Luther King, Jr. He was a peaceful and courageous Civil Rights leader who convinced black and white people to boycott the Montgomery, Alabama, public bus transit system."

I put the letter aside and started to jump rope as this was a lot to think about. The words in the letter kept roaring loud and clear to pick it up again no matter what I did to distract myself.

"Folks called them 'Freedom Riders' when they campaigned to force integration or combining the bus terminals without white folks sit and piss here and coloreds sit and piss there."

I laughed.

"That's how you started reading when you and Momma Zettie took that bus trip. I said to myself that the Lord put forth evil words for a child to say and read."

I grunted.

"Also, that stained red-paint story that Daddy Al mentions when he gets frustrated and scared was a lynching story about a Negro man named Seth, who was about to be murdered for a crime he did not commit. His murderer held a double-barreled shot gun at his chest. When Seth saw, under the flickering flames of the night torches, that the man under the white sheets had red paint on the top parts of his boots, he shook like a leaf flapping in a hurricane. These were the same boots that his boss man, Morton, always wore because Seth himself had accidentally spilled paint on them. Morton thought these to be real cute and authentic and did not reprimand Seth as they were also friends. At this point, are you still absorbing my words Tamara?"

I had to think if I was.

"Old Jambailah, a man Daddy only mentions when he's afraid, was hiding in the weeds and saw it all and he knew about Seth spilling the paint on his boss' shoes long before he saw him die. Jambailah could see Seth's eyes pop wide open as he looked down at those boots. Jambaliah on his death bed told this story to Daddy Al to serve as a warning to be cautious in his lifetime. Seth really knew it was Boss Morton and he saw his hands tremble at the gun trigger. Morton had been bullied into doing the dirty work by a fellow sheeter who knew their closeness and resented every bit of it. Jambaliah heard him say that 'it's high time Morton that you do the deed to this one. You always with us but you never strike out. You turned into some kind of nigger lover?' The other sheetmen chanted him on to pull the trigger. Seth sweated like rain and panted in fear and deep sighs and said to Morton, 'Don't do it. No, no,' as the torch bearers laughed at his words."

In the meantime, Seth literally had a massive coronary as he choked and gasped on the spot while holding his chest. A high-pitched drunken voice from one of the night men announced, 'I never seen a nigger die before he got shot or hung.'

Jambaliah heard Seth's last words as he held his trembling chest: 'What Miss Sally gonna think of you now since my mammy raised yu since yu was a suckling baby?' Jambaliah said that Boss Morton's eyes were seen flickering wet from the burning fire cross. Morton backed away, stumbled and vomited as the white sheeters laughed at him.

'Well boys, we finished for tonight's work. Let's go have turns at gulping down some White Lightning.'

The next morning, Morton never showed up outside his plantation. Miss Sally found him in his study with a fatal wound to his head. Since Butler Jimmy could read as Miss Sally had taught him, he read the note to himself. He tells it to Jambaliah that it went this way:

My Dearest Sally,

You have to know this so you can change their ways. Reform. Reform. You always wanted to do it that way. I been too weak to do so. I couldn't live any longer because I killed the man who was more of a brother to me than my own flesh and blood. His momma raised me from her own breast when I was so puny and everyone said that I would die. He is gone now. He's gone and I was told to pull the trigger. When the head man said that it was my turn now, I had to either do it or die right along beside him. They would have called it a hunting accident like when Evert Moss stood up for one of his boys. You the strong one in the family. I couldn't look at you in the eyes knowing what I been a part of. I really died last night, not this morning.
I love you forever.
Your husband and friend to the end,
Morton.

Suddenly, Momma Zettie's voice bellowed, "Where are you, Tamara!!? Find your way out here and help me, Hortense, and Miz Siddie with some of these quilt pieces."

"Yes ma'am, Momma."

Chapter 33

Where is Cousin Delmar?

The year passed with memorable events. I had been wisened about racial injustice and interrogated Momma so she could replay in her mind what really happened to our dear Cousin Delmar.

Althea had written back to just about everyone in Corn Hollow and weekly to Momma Zettie. Much of the country was in a state of unrest. Momma and Althea were still in shock about John F. Kennedy's assassination, and Althea continued to write about it.

All the black families of Corn Hollow were using new words that they were once frightened to even think about.

It was the promise of Kennedy that shone the light on the new terms. The speeches of Dr. Martin Luther King, Jr. gave even greater hope. Lots of changes were inevitable, like it or not.

After Christmastime, all the black families witnessed a time of year when crops had been picked and new ones were not yet sown. There were occasional snowfalls, but mostly plain cold weather.

After althea telling me about the K Club, it made me think. I recall when I was in grade school that on a Monday morning our one-room Corn Hollow Elementary School was missing its teacher, Raymond Delmar. Even though he was a cousin to us Banks and the Ludgess,' all the kids, even those that were not related, called him Cousin Delmar.

Raymond Delmar worked in a beautiful, surrounding flat farmland view from the hillside one-room schoolhouse that was approximately one and a half miles from the Banks residence. Unlike the company store, the cotton gin and the churches, the schoolhouse was a center for freedom. Corn Hollow kids' minds could expand.

At the foothills were dogwoods galore that were the curtains for the picturesque clay mountain like hills that were full of evergreen and cedar.

Deciduous trees, including the black walnut tree, grew prevalent in the hills. When the leaves would fall, they looked like golden snow. When spring came, vivid expressions of wildflowers popped out of the ground. The wild cherry blossoms and dogwoods lit up the hills like vernal Christmas trees blossoming as light.

Water would gush up from unexpected places like geysers from heavenly fountains. The perfect addition to having Cousin Raymond Delmar as a teacher was the assured permission to be excused from the schoolhouse room to consciously focus on such things, especially filling the water pails from the spring. Fresh spring water fed into a ground box from the veins of the hills. This liquid tasted differently as the essence of purity slid down one's throat. It seemed that no kid could ever get enough as they filled their bellies-a-plenty and dehydration was never an issue. After taking sips and sips and looking down at a swelled stomach, an end had to be declared for the moment.

At other times Cousin Delmar would give us free time to quietly read or write or look at books. We would pry open an old hand-me-down encyclopedia that illustrated the reproductive system or find something as magnificent as the Taj Mahal.

Luella and I were competing to be the school Spelling Bee champ, and found ourselves raising our heads from the study list on occasion. It was as if a passionate rush of spring fever called us from our seats. Being excused to the outhouse was doubly important. The sun sparkled on the tree leaves of the hilly forest where the closest dog-woods resided near the pottie house. It occupied at least ten minutes of gazing time even though the faint, smelly, puce-scented, organic matter olfactored as a reek with the slightest air current. As this reminded me of the reason to proceed with the called-on duty, my eyes were often over-powered by the beauty and the mystery that unfolded.

The dark pink lines trimming the petals of white were stared at until the grove moved with a family of deer grounded like thin stalks. On a moment's notice they could run away if slightly spooked. "Ding-dong," a bell clanged and the dogwood trance vanished. It was recess. The toilet was used and the playground was the next occupied space.

Yet, on this winter Monday morning, Cousin Raymond

Delmar was nowhere in sight.

Since Cousin Delmar infrequently preached sermons and married folks, perhaps he had a late evening and would show up later. When Luella and I started shivering, and then the younger ones got even colder, home was on our minds. Cousin Delmar had always arrived early, threw in big chunks of black coal in the big potbelly that warmed up the big, high ceiling room in about one hour, which led to shedding coats and sometimes sweaters by the second hour. We looked at the school door and next thing we were all fast-walking home.

Momma had a chilly-gripping thought when she heard the Ludgess kids ask, "Where is Cousin Delmar?"

"Momma! Did he tell you to substitute teach today and you forgot?"

"No!"

"He knows his preaching schedules two weeks ahead and gives me ample notice."

"Your Daddy Al and Mr. Daniel said they'll run over to Granton early in the morning if he don't show up. Just a 30-mile drive and you chiren know that he lodges with Mr. Daniel and Miz Siddie Goodson during the week and even they haven't heard about him being absent on Monday. I'm worried."

Momma told me that her mind flashed back to two weeks prior when she gave him two poems that Althea sent and wanted her to also share with her dear Cousin Delmar. They were poems written by Langston Hughes:

JUSTICE
That justice is a blind goddess
Is a thing to which we black are wise:
Her bandage hides two festering sores

That once perhaps were eyes.
STILL HERE
I been scared and battered.
My hopes the wind done scattered.
Snow has friz me,
Sun has baked me,
Looks like between 'em they done
Tried to make me
Stop laughin', stop lovin', stop livin'—
But I don't care!
I'm still here!

Momma Zettie also remembered their conversation when he finished reading the poems.

"Zettie Mae, I'm going to use these in my special speech in Memphis the week before Dr. King really excites us."

"So youse preaching them Civil Rights sermons, Raymond? You knowd you been warned to stop 'em and I'se beggen yew and it's so dangerus."

"Now Zettie Mae, you know how I feel from way back in my boy days in Mississippi when I used to run with them white boys of our homestead owner, Mr. Shabner. His two boys, Jim, Rick and I were around the same age. We rode horses, rustled cattle, and played in the mud like kids do. When Jim reached his 18th birthday, his daddy told me that I had to call him Mr. Jim or Mr. Shabner. When I answered, 'Does that mean that he goin' to call me Mr. Raymond or Mr. Delmar?' Mr. Shabner pulled me off the horse and kicked me in the belly. Jim and Rick and Mr. Shabner all laughed at me. They demoted me back to a kid as they were supposedly men."

"Yes, I know you been hurt ever since and you gotta let it go forever." Momma spoke quietly with tears in her eyes.

"So Tamara, Luella, and every Negro youngster alive have to experience such disgrace, abuse, and other pejoratives? And what about that poor boy Till that did no harm to anyone? There wasn't a mean bone in his body."

Momma started crying.

Out of respect for Zettie Mae, Raymond cleared his throat and said, "That s---   has got to be stopped now."

Momma kept telling me more about what Daddy said that happened.

Meanwhile, on the search for Raymond Delmar, after politely questioning a white farm worker, Mr. Daniel and Daddy Al discovered that he was in the white hospital. The farm worker had found him outside his car all crushed up. He and his neighbor took him in to the hospital.

"You know we wouldn't let our kind just bleed to death or die on the road," said the white farmer.

"Y'all work for him?"

"Yah sir," Mr. Daniel shockingly mumbled.

Daddy Al nervously mumbled, "Can you take us to 'em?"

"You have to let me get my pickup down the road and y'all can hop in the back and leave your cars parked here rather than drive 'em in to the hospital parking lot unless you want to follow me and park about a quarter mile away from the hospital and meet me in the parking place."

Daddy Al obligingly hollered, "We'll follow you."

Until the truck arrived for them to follow, Mr. Daniel and Daddy Alfonso were almost afraid to talk as they just walked around Cousin Delmar's light green, four-door sedan Buick. Except for the spots of blood soaked on the dead grass and weed stalks, they couldn't see any signs of a car crash: no dents, nor broken windshield. There were a lot of tromped, down dead weeds, like from a bunch of people or mules that had congregated in one place.

Trailing the pickup to Memphis was like a death ride of silence and deep, shallow breathing that expelled fear. Would Raymond Delmar be dead or alive?

"This is it, boys. It's mighty decent of you checking on your boss when he hurt bad."

Mr. Daniel described their experience: Upon entering the hospital, they removed their hats and held them over their flies and bent, sorta bowing their heads, and moved slowly, as everyone stared at them. They told the receptionist that their boss man been hurt really bad and they want to talk to him. The receptionist beckoned the black doorman to take them up the back steps to the intensive ward and announced, "Two negras comin' up the back steps to see their boss so give 'em three to five minutes and send them out."

There was Raymond Delmar with his recognizable big feet lifting up the top sheet way in the air and breathing with a tube in his neck. His face was so smashed and swollen that Mr. Daniel held his mouth when he saw it.

Alfonso whispered to Daniel, "We better get outa here and tell Miz Faye and them kids and not be bothered explaining that he really ain't white, even though his daddy musta been and his Momma surely was not."

Five days passed but the family knew better than claim their kin or he'd be released to the recently established colored wing and perhaps die since the doctor comes around once a week and two benevolent Quaker nurses who volunteer to do the rest.

Puzzled, Mr. Daniel and Daddy decided to drive over to Miz Sally's, widow of Mr. Morton, who shot himself. Although she was getting real old and feeble, they knew her ways were favorable. She would have her cousin run in to the Memphis hospital and give reference to Raymond being family kin and to be released to the cousin and driven to his home, where he could be with his wife, Miz Faye.

At the same time, back in Corn Hollow the tension was so thick it was like seeing black apparitions swelled up with anger, walking in and out of a thick fog of frustration. They wanted to cry out "Mercy" or lash out in anger as they stuffed and contained their fear that some did not understand. Corn Hollow Negroes seemed helpless.

Upon hearing of the circumstances of Raymond Delmar's hospitalization, Miss Fruke's blood pressure rose. She bellowed over this incident as if she was a close family member. The bond between Miss Fruke and Cousin Delmar was like loving something you could never have. Miss Fruke had a stroke two weeks later.

The children talked about Cousin Delmar as if he was dying or dead, thinking he was just in a car accident.

It was a month of substitute teaching for Momma Zettie, starting off the day with a prayer and stories about Cousin Delmar before teaching the lessons. There was a stack of extra assignments in a special corner in case he had to miss teaching any day. It was accompanied by a list of things for the kids to read and write for themselves and have them ready when he returned. Cousin Delmar had planned for the next crop lay-by season for Momma to come early and spend an hour with him twice a week to teach her some basics while he had us doing math problems. He didn't want to put any pressure on Momma Zettie's lack of education.

For the first two weeks it was, "I remember when Cousin Delmar paddled our bottoms for staying up on the hill skates that June Bug had made for us out of old desktops. He knew we were sliding those dirt sleds into a pile of leaves and we traveled at high speeds down the hill."

With a smile on Luella's face she recalled the rides and paused and continued to speak.

"We were ten minutes late after he rang the lunch bell. I can feel the paddle burns just by mentioning that day."

"I recall the kindness Cousin Delmar bestowed on me when I was hit in the belly last year by a baseball. I was the catcher for the recess game. When I looked away all I remembered was a fire in my belly. I keeled over and rolled as I couldn't get my breath right away. Next thing I knew, a voice said, "That's right, just let it out. My belly was being rubbed at the same time. It was the same as Momma Zettie would do. Cousin Delmar helped me to feel better."

"Oh! You remember being late and I felt my butt being cut by a nail that pulled up from the foot stop. Since we rode tandem and my partner jumped off when we hit the pile of leaves, my body slid sideways as my back met the hill skate and a loose nail was jostled up and I slid over it. It hurt me so bad I couldn't get a scream out at first."

Momma took her turn also.

"Well, I won't forget that one either, because Miz Siddie helped me to make up a special salve that helped to suck out any of the back-teria from your nailtorn-up skin. It looked like what might happen to a peach skin if you took a nail head and forced it in and tore the skin away."

"Speaking of salves, how did Cousin Delmar know what to do when the yellow jackets and the bees stung us? Did Miz Siddie have something to do with providing him with the right care supplies?"

"Do you think we wouldn't furnish what was needed?"

"No, Momma Zettie, we know better."

After a month had gone by, all students were warned that Cousin Delmar's face was torn up from the accident.

What they didn't say is that he would look like a monster-man.

His tall body, his robust muscles, his big feet, his naturally semi-straight hair, and nearly white skin with its sun tone were still the same. His voice, however, was different. It sounded like he was talking on the other end of a string inside a tin can.

It was easier for the children to stare at the hole in a tin can. It wasn't easier for us children to stare at the hole in his neck when facing him as he had only one green right eye, not two, for the other one had been poked out and his eyelid was sewn shut. About every two hours, he had to put eye medicine in it and shortly after a yellow goo would run down his face. Momma Zettie explained to us that our Cousin Delmar also had some damaged nerves which meant that he couldn't feel it when the fluids run down his cheeks. We were further warned what to do by several Corn Hollow women.

"We are just making him lots of handkerchiefs to keep near his chair and in his pockets. You kids can help him by taking one out of the box for him if he fails to wipe his face. He will understand but whatever you do at school, don't baby him. He's still in charge."

Things seemed to be normal as Cousin Delmar practiced his same routines and said the same familiar words, yet barrel-toned. The usual timetable repetition that each class member had to repeat and be orally tested on still continued. The math blocks or mind freezes continued to exist as well.

Things seemed the same yet they were obviously a bit contrasted now. The sweet smelling nectars and the beautiful plumage were there but our usual Cousin Delmar was not.

It surely made Momma wander off in her thoughts a lot with Raymond Delmar's adversity when she washed the morning dishes. Could her Althea be a psychic fore-knower having sent those Langston Hughes poems which described Raymond: "I been scared and battered ... I'm still here." And the other one called JUSTICE saying it, "is a blind goddess, her bandages hides two festering sores, that perhaps were eyes."

Then as Momma washed the dishes after sending us kids to school, Cousin Hortense tried to console her. She told us that Momma Zettie would cry almost every day for three months. Her tears would drip and blend with the suds into the dishwater.

Chapter 34

Sis Got the Job

I decided to be the first in the family to attend college. Taking advantage of all the equal opportunity grants and dressing myself with a persona of radiance and pure joy, I set on my path. Momma was so proud of me preparing to make something of myself.

Daddy Al would only mutter, "I'd give them hourly wages to help me in the fields."

This would make Momma buck her eyes at him, turn and walk away from Daddy Al's impetuous ramble. "Think I'll drive to the store and pick up any mail and get a bag of sugar."

Meanwhile, my gloating subsided when I sat down and read the fat enveloped letter from Althea:

Dear Sis,

I'm so proud of your choice to attend college. I'm proud that I got that Level 3 job at the Underwood Subsidiary Corporation. This means that I get to work in their fancy office building and receive a bigger paycheck than before.

It really wasn't hard to get because the employers were looking for African Americans so they wouldn't get sued on racial discrimination hiring charges. The preferred sex is female. They seem to pose the least threat to white males.

Considering my psoriasis-ridden anxiety and the mental ping pong that was going around in my head, it took two days to find out. Hey Sis Tamara, tis about reversals rendering separate but equal lip service. Get used to it, especially if you are the only dark-skinned one on staff. If you were right here I could imagine you saying, "What do you mean?" What I mean is every mail slot including yours is filled with an invitation to this grand private party sponsored by one of the richest staff members at one of the swankiest hotels in town requiring a tux and gown attire. Well, I got one and my mind sizzled with glee at the thought of wearing that strapless gown I managed to snag for a cheap price at a "going out of business sale" this past summer. Perhaps I could even sew one up on the weekend. You know how fast I can stitch up a garment.

As I was just thinking about my attire, the inviter came near my desk. I thanked him for the invitation and said that my RSVP would be a "yes." Well. This country gentleman turned out to be a classic, biased jerk. He said to me, "Oh, I want everyone to come but I know with where you live it will be impossible for you to drive that far, especially since you give Maye in the next building a ride every day. It will be midnight by the time you get home to change for it." As my heart was breaking, my lips wanted to utter, "Raleigh, Maye said she will catch the transit if ever I needed to stay in the city and her Cousin Fanny, who lives in the city, can offer me an occasional couch." Instead, all I could say was, "OH!!" He actually let it slip by saying, "Glad you understand."

This, Tamara, is what you might toughen up to. The hardest thing about this is that it will catch you by surprise. Well, from the invitation that I am enclosing, it really does look enticing. Read it and tear it up. As for the Art Museum exhibition, cherish it. You see, whenever I see one of those things called invitations now, I use it as a shield to actually go to public art openings and museum exhibitions. I socialize with the elite public that I would never have dared to meet. So when the office socializes, I socialize too.

I must admit that it is real scary when I enter an unknown place where the people are unknown. What I do is read information about them and their work before I attend. It helps me to feel comfortable and start a conversation. The first half hour is just dissolving the jumpy feeling in the pit of my gut. There's always someone with their nose turned up when they see me and there are also those who welcome diversity. It is like that lesson from Turkey Ridge High School that you shared with me about your English teacher vs. your psychology teacher, Miss Hendy.

You know, Tamara, at the last art opening I realized that someone was looking at me. When I looked back at him, I couldn't speak. I fell into a daydream world. His name is Darryl. He is every bit of my dream man. He is medium height, slightly dark, very well educated, very handsome, and seems kind. His eyes are so hypnotic that I get unresponsive and have to focus on my breathing so that I can snap out of it. I'll tell you more after our first date to the

Concert Gospel Convention Show in two weeks.

I make it a regular habit of mine to habitually browse the Art and Entertainment section of the *Tribune* every Monday. I arrive early to work and receive the Sunday paper, which posts all cultural events, and since it will be thrown away after a few folks read the funnies, I cut out at least two events that have extended dates to cover any week and weekend times of the great places that I want to go to.

There was one invitation that I couldn't get away from that occurred on an office afternoon, a surprise party for Susan, the office manager. We were all herded into the company vans and whizzed away to a big party room. Susan got drunk and started making fun of my way out country apartment where there are just too many birds and too isolated. I had the guts and the nerves in that instant to say something back to her, yet after breathing a few shallow breaths, I decided to not rain on her parade. Luckily, my brown skin-tone did not reveal a flush, blush or wink of the put-down. By now, the alcohol was raining metaphoric puke in the room. I became so unemotional that all I could do was keep the frozen, fake smile. I took a big deep breath and was functional again.

Sorry about all this talk. I really must quit babbling. As you can tell, my counselor is on vacation again so I will give her a carbon copy of this letter. She will understand without me digging into something that will have passed by the time we speak and I don't have to hold on to it.

Thank you, Sister, for letting me be myself. My work is really good and I over-excel in order to validate my capabilities. It's just that being accepted within the office building is one thing and to be a newcomer and an African American is hard for folks to accept and to reach out to. I learn to cope and manifest comfort within my office space. I know that I must keep a fresh change of polyesters. God forgive me for having a pair of those things folded under my desk whenever I have to be a part of the office open house. I even keep a necklace and earrings in my purse because I can't count on any of the ladies living nearby inviting me to their apartments or homes to change and freshen up. The company bathroom is where I brush my teeth and refresh myself. I have witnessed other employees offer the opportunity to those who live in other suburbs of the city.

So picture this. You are all seated together and you are to make conversation and pretend you are a part of this group for only 300-600 eyes are watching you at one given time. I smile, converse, so that I can show them that I might be fitting in. All the seats to my right are empty until the office latecomers arrive and are forced to sit next to me. I feel the heartlessness, the insensitivity, the ignorance among the so-called intelligent. I know that I deserve and need the job so I tolerate with social injustice. Be cautious in matters, Sis. When you get a fine job, just absorb or find other pathways out so you don't have to become the victim. Just be an over-achiever if you want to and then go do your own thing.

To really sum it all up, I have graduated into the psychological club ... being clobbered in ways to make me feel nervous and unsettled. If I buy into that trap, then I'm a powerless, second class caste.

Well, my focus is on that milky chocolate, deep-voiced, intelligent, hunk of a man. I love hearing him speak. So long, Sissy.

From One Dearest Sister to Another....

Love,

Althea

As I lowered the letter from my eyes, all I could say was, WHEW!! And I rubbed upward on my forehead.

I thought silently by giving Althea a thanks for warning me, as it was too deep for me now but in four years, after I've completed college, I'll re-read the letter for strength. I unlocked an old over night luggage case, dropped the letter inside, and put it away under my bed.

"Wonder if Thea and that Darryl guy will really click?"

Chapter 35

College

After transferring from Grentwood Junior College, I met a lot of new friends at Southeast Tennessee State located about 100 miles away from Corn Hollow. My roommate was named Jacquilla and liked to be called Jackie. She and I often stayed up late just talking.

"Wonder what my Momma Zettie will say to me about my big afro, Jackie?"

"She shouldn't say a thing. You're a junior in college and you don't use drugs even though you might dress like you do."

"What?"

"Just teasing."

"I know, girl. Look at you, Jackie."

"Look at you, Sunflower, those thick-heeled shoes, the wire, rimmed glasses and your tie-dyed shirt and … bell bottom pants. Oh yeah, Mary Ann saw you and that Phillip guy going into the library together. Anything you want to tell me?"

"Yes. All students go into the library and they study. I went to the library with Phillip just to do such. He tells me such funny jokes and I like hanging around him. He asked me to work on a project with him for chemistry class. I said okay so we have a report to give next week."

"Well, Tamara, he does have cute dimples."

We both chuckled and caught a glimpse of the clock.

"Oh, Jackie I didn't tell you what Phillip taught me how to do last last week."

"You don't mean?"

"Quit thinking dirty thoughts. He taught me how to hit balls with irons and clubs. Phillip is a part-time caddy at the country club the college uses and he teaches me on the days they shut down to water and mow, as long as we play on the side where the maintenance men are not working. He's going to teach me some more when he gets a chance. I have to write Thea and I can imagine what she might say. 'Well that's okay, Tamara. That's really cool. I never ever thought I would see that day come. So many things we can do now' and I bet I'm pretty close to her words. Now let's stop this, girl, and get some sleep or we'll be late tomorrow for the African American Club meeting."

"You are right, Tamara."

Standing in the back room of the old Baptist Church for minority services, without a bit of heat, the MC began to speak.

"Sorry we must meet in the cold and at 9:30 this evening. It has to be this way or the Dean of Students will find a reason to shut us down. So, I must be brief. Since our world leader, the Reverend Dr. Martin Luther King Jr, was assassinated eight blocks from here this past April, God rest his soul, we've got to rise up and march."

This frightened me, so I eased back to the door and left the room. I explained my feelings to Jackie before I went to bed. I said that I did not want to be threatened or even killed and expressed my fears of what Momma felt and those stories that Althea told about the KKK that made me shiver.

"On this campus is one thing to look like Sister Angela Davis, but it's quite another to march in the streets and be shot dead as a revolutionary by some KKK member."

"I suppose it will be forgotten that good things such as sickle cell fundraisers and breakfast programs in the ghettoes were part of the Panther Movement."

"Probably so, Jackie."

After hearing of Robert F. Kennedy's murder by Sirhan, everywhere I turned, I felt sick. I couldn't keep from contemplating Momma's stories about wrongful killings.

I then put every thought of Momma's into my studies and received A's and B's in most courses. However, being the product of both high school and college integration, I still faced the D's on my transcript by professors who resented Civil Rights and hated Negroes. Even so, I was not discouraged. Set up for misjudging my capabilities was just an untrue legacy that would follow me and I would have to live with.

"Inside, I know, Jackie, that someone will recognize this deception."

Taking interesting courses such as Music Appreciation increased my tolerance for hanging out with various races and hearing their songs. Being the curious sort, I took my saved up work-study dollars and received a private astrology reading from my professor, knowing that I still had federal grant money for my full ride.

Realizing that other than having my Sun sign truly in Pisces, it also explained some creative urges and mystique. The professor interpreted the manifestation of my showy side as a rising sign that was in Leo, like the Lion, while my Moon sign of Aries gave way to my persistent and "get it done" nature. The big message was that the planet of Uranus was in the midheaven and that great creative energies would pour out, especially for three years.

After dreaming on this reading, I felt more confident that I would not fail in life. I truly became more interested in the arts and cultural studies. It was such a good feeling to have finished my junior and senior college years majoring in Visual Arts with an emphasis on Textiles.

By graduation time I had thrown my self-designed bell bottom jeans and my thick, heeled boots aside. I desired being near art galleries on campus, in the city halls and in fancy neighborhoods.

At college graduation, Momma was all dressed in finery and proud of my achievements. Althea, James and Trish, Cousin Hortense and family were also in attendance. Most everyone, except Thea and Momma, looked and stared at everyone and everything else with twisted lips and jaws and were real quiet.

Daddy Al sat in the car by a shade tree. He indicated that he could see all the action from the car where he was later found asleep with a bottle slipped inside a paper bag. James had cleared it away before Momma saw what he had been up to since it was his usual Sunday way. Trish tried to whisper to him but was unsuccessful. "Daddy-in-law Al, that stuff makes yow face look real yellow. Gotta stop drinking that poison."

I had to change the impending gloom.

"Thank God!! Thank you, God!!"

With this, Momma's face lit up.

Throwing my cap and gown across the back car window since the ceremony was over, I started jumping up and down like a little girl. James "June Bug" threw a dirt clod under my feet on a jump. Althea hit James. Luella and Trish were blasted.

Momma's hypnotic words stopped the play.

"Hey, let's wipe it off and go to that dorm fridge where the dorm supe said it was okay. We gonna spread a cloth out on some of that lawn and chow down on fried chicken, turnip greens, and corn bread!! Find us a good place, Tam."

"Yes, Mammm!!"

Chapter 36

In the Car with Momma

It was the early seventies in Corn Hollow. Momma was getting older and Daddy Al had passed away after one week of being twisted up with a stroke. Althea and I wanted to help Momma Zettie by doing something special for her. Momma Zettie's wish was to visit her mother's Creole relatives. Althea and I drove Momma back to Louisiana.

Everyone made it easy for Momma, especially those involved in the strong ecclesiastical mode of the A.M.E. Church. The young steward, Jack Motley, convinced Momma that he would protect her house while she was on her short sojourn and even mow the lawn before she returned.

Jack called up the old Louisiana General Mercantile to leave word with Mr. Floyd and Mrs. "Nessa" Vanessa Hollister to expect a visit from Mrs. Zettie Mae Banks in a couple of days.

"You did that for me?"

"Why not? You are the mother of the community and an elder."

"Well, thanks, son."

"Tamara and Thea! Can't be gone over four days, makes me nervous and irregular with my bowels. I don't want yo'all getting pigheaded and taking me all over the country. By the way, thank you girls for doing this for your poor old Momma."

"You are our Momma and we are glad to do it for you."

Momma's car conversations seemed to repeat themselves over and over. It was interesting yet getting a little boring.

I decided to roll down the driver's window in my new 1971 Vega that my brother James, and even Althea, called "a lemon." James attributed that my inexperience with purchasing a car from my first year's salary (as a managing editor for a cultural arts magazine in St. Louis, Missouri) to why I was sold a Vega.

Althea teased me.

"Could it be because of its honey-banana hue that makes your car a yellow fruit?"

"It's brand-new and it will get Momma where she wants to go, even to Louisiana and back."

Momma had tried to not let the wind in her hair interrupt with my driving until she lost patience with patting down her hot-comb straightened and rolled hairdo. It was like some unorthodox breeze had blown in a spirit that lifted off the control valves to Momma Zettie's heart.

She started talking about her bitterness and disappointments with people and events in her lifetime.

The old A.M.E. stewards had put a halt to her fundraising plans which would raise enough money to rebuild the church.

"They did it because a woman came up with the idea. Those jealous bastards!"

Althea and I seemed shocked as our extremely Christian Momma had not forgiven those old Corn Hollow church leaders who were all dead.

"You know you girls have a brother. Course Momma, we know June Bug."

"I mean Till."

"You are not making sense, Momma. That's Miss Attie's son."

"Me and Attie half sisters and we both gots knocked up by our brutish uncle. My Mammie Inez hid this and made us two big, wide flower sack dresses. She didn't let us go to church the last three months 'fore birth saying we got hoof rot on our feet from the hog lot. Folk back then not so cotton picking nosey like now. Back then most folks just getting used ta not being in them bonds and lotsa folk don have no kin cause a slaverie putem alls over the place, even down the rivers. So anyhows, I done wents into labor first and Mammie Inez had to save either me or the baby seeing lots of blood 'fore the deliverie. Said she saw it twice in her life. She tied my feet down and my hands and asked me to push. Mammie Inez felt the head and said we gots to do it or else. She made me breathe in a cloth sack where she had put some herbs and 'bout 6 drops of some kinda stinky tonic. She held it to my nose till I breathed the fumes. Next thing I was dizzy and my head went round

279

and round and I don know nothing else cept whens it over.

I woken up all tied down like a foot laced in a tight shoe. Mammie Inez sez she had to use sewing stitches to hold me together where she don cut that child outsa me. It taken two weeks of salving down to not be 'fected. I loved that ol boy buts he hada milk Attie since I kuldn move for two weeks. Thens Attie done pained out and had a boy too. Two days later her boy died in his sleep. I loved my sister so much that I gave her my Till. Four months later Mammie Inez died of pneumonia." Momma stopped talking and got quiet.

"Then what, Momma?"

"After her funeral, Attie asked me to leave and not ever know her in publick and don't claim Till as she named him. Attie had her own ideas how to make it and two men to show her how. I never ferget them words of hers. 'Don ever come to see me less you need help livering a new one to the world or letting one out early.' Attie had the touch liken Mammie Inez. So alls of yew chiren gots Attie to help you come out. I fake that I went into the hurts too fast to have Miz Camille from Olellean to hitch a mule and get to Corn Hollow. My eyes would meet Attie and I knew our sisterly bond would never fade from our hearts. Now Till is dead and you never knew him. He was smart and he knowd things others kudn know nor see."

Althea and I were so shocked and full of tears at what Momma told us. We sniffled, blew our noses and didn't want to interrupt any more of Momma's withheld family secrets.

"Keep talking, Momma."

"We hear you and we are listening."

"And many a time I had to act so corpselike just to please your Daddy."

"When the youngish folks were out visiting June Bug and Tricia, I dialed some finger-popping music on WBIA. Nobody was home but me and your Daddy resting on the cot. I wanted things to happen. I get myself in a rhythm spirit for being close with my Alfonso. He then turns sour and insults me that his knee is killin' him so he can't dance. He just turns around and farts."

Althea noticed that I was jolted by Momma's talk, so she took a turn at the wheel and could barely open her mouth to speak.

"Keep your eyes on the road, Sis, and turn the radio off so we can hear Momma better."

Momma continued.

"I knowed that he been with Attie, my own sister, or that old whore down in that mosquito squalor of the new ground ... Just too tired and sickening to muster up time with me. If it was Attie, she goes outs her head when she turns up the bottle and donts know who anybody is and donts care. I would just drop into the old Momma's chair and stare, and not blink, nor cry, nor feel. I was as close to dead as I could be because it didn't do me any good to feel life flowing through me."

"And those many times when he was getting forgetful and growing with more meaness, I had to listen to or patch over his crap. Once he left his wallet in the truck and some punk came and lifted it causn he forgot he left the windows down, left his Christmas watch in a restroom in Olellean. Luckily he got it back and he once told me that a Corn Hollow feast was on a Sunday, when asking other folk, it was really Saturday and on and on. He got really mean when I would ask him questions about any of it."

Through my trembling voice I asked Momma a question.

"Momma! Is that why you didn't cry at Daddy Al's wake, his funeral, or his burial services? And I didn't even see you cry at home. You seemed relieved and this frustrated me so much. I've often wondered if those peach tree switches on our bottoms had any bearings with letting out some of your disappointments with Daddy Al."

"Maybe honey. It's been so long ago."

"Did Daddy Al have some Indian in him? I know these high cheekbones of mine didn't come from Daddy Al nor your yellow-skin that matches three generations of plantation owners. Does that mean that I am part Indian? And Althea and others are really Cherokee? White? And seventy-five percent African American?"

"Yeah, you know the truth. Some of your daddy's kin been driven off to a squat corner of some so, called reservation."

"You'alls Daddy did horrible things to them mules."

Hearing Momma's disclosures, I thought she might be having a nervous breakdown.

"Do we just let her talk or look for a hospital?" Althea whispered as if she read my mind.

"Keep talking, Momma."

"Yow Daddy could break wild mules in a special way 'til one stubborn one rode on his mind all the way to his grave. Mr. Jeffers told Alfonso, gotta make it move or the mule loses."

"Now you'alls Daddy was gentle with the crop until he commenced to beat the poor animal to deff. That one more mulish than ten mules. He wount not move a plow. He could walk anywhere you led him but out right spurned work. Daddy Alfonso beat the mule so hard that he brought the critter to his knees, bellowing for mercy. He was fitting into his grandpappy's shoes of a slave whipper. His eyes come filled with water as he done tole me sorrow."

'Was hearin' Grandpappy's spirit in the ears. I din't tend da do it. The blood kept on popping and I hadsta keep on knock the whip cross hisen back till the buck give in or twas hauled off. Twasn nuthin elsen da do cept they rope my neck.' Momma paused for a deep breath of air and was still full of words.

"Anytime anyone mention that day, he would rub his brow, get all low in spirits and walk away. Then he started drinking more than on Sunday morning and took his sore heart to the whores and more bottle turning."

A deep silence prevailed in the car for at least twenty minutes as eyes were on the road or gazed out the window.

"Two years later had another stubborn mule."

"But Momma!" Althea whined.

"I do remember him saying …"

"Saying what, Thea?"

"He said this time, he had to run his hand along his backbone and under his belly before he did anything. He got really happy because he started using the heavenly name."

"You right, Thea. Lord knows if that other mule had some kinda backbone nerve pain or some pulled down entrail that given him heap-of-pain when he hafta pull anything. I heard 'em tell Mr. Jeffers, as his jaw was dripping sweat, that the critter was sick. That was when Jeffers gave the mule to Daddy Al and he let us play on him and told us to rub its back when we feel like it."

With a big smile to share other sides of Daddy Al, I declared, "Daddy was also known for marking the finest hardwoods that most men would not tackle, much less identify. I remember the persimmons that he found and we ate 'em and put the seeds on a shelf to dry out. When his wood season was over, he would do a lot of good things with us children. I can't forget every night for a week, Daddy would sliver a persimmon seed with a thin, sharp, small knife and display the silverware that was revealed in the seeds. And he would tell stories about the woods and what the trees would eat to make them so hard and with different shapes and ripples inside."

"Oh yeah, Sis! He also told how the tree spirits held onto the fork and spoon and remember the fire. One night, a log pushed the stove door open. The fire coals and burning wood popped out. Daddy Al used his bare hands and threw the glowing ember chunks back into the stove's ravenous, redhot inferno. He said that it didn't hurt not unless you think about it being hot."

"Evens though the Ol Buzzard had some faults, us had a bettern house than most in my early days," Momma commented.

"Oh yeah, Momma! Unlike most houses, our house was well-made with three bedrooms. Its rusty corrugated tin roof and big front and back porches respectively housed our huge swing and the back porch with its wringer washing machine. The big barn, hog lot, chicken yard and henhouse, not to mention our truck patch vegetable garden and grand front yard, made us seem as you once said 'rich for colored folk in Corn Hollow.' You always took advantage of your status and called it your 'sponsible duty' for meetings held at our house. I deeply felt you loved doing so. As I always remember, the topic was always the Grentwood County Fair." I then continued with other talk.

"From my eavesdropping and waitress service moments, I think the Community Circle was basically a place to confront others with pent-up feelings, accusations, and outright arguments. It was you, Momma, that cooled down the talkers. And you always concluded with a blessing by a Reverend before the end of the evening."

Thea spoke out. "You got that right, Tamara. Corn Hollow either fit in these categories owners, workers, or outcasts. You knew where we fit and Momma made sure of that. Our little Tennessee town is in a small cotton belt region of the mid-South where the coloreds used to be called blackies. I now understand that Mr. Clifford and his brother, Mr. Jeffers, owned so much land and controlled everything that colored people did and didn't have. These brothers managed to stay wealthy due to illiteracy and putting fear of what could happen if anyone contested. I am so proud of you, Momma, that we own land in Corn Hollow."

"Yes daughters. It's me granpappie who was sired by one of Clifford's uncles. Nows we ends up being the only coloreds who had some say, so over the piece of land given us. We had to shut up about … 'bout."

With tears in Momma eyes, she turned her head.

"I'm getting hungry, girls, and I am sick of fried chicken."

"Okay, Momma."

"We'll stop as soon as I see a place."

"Momma! What ever happened during those three days that Esther was somewhere?" I queried.

"What happened was that Miz Quintilla lost part of her mind and Mr. Leo never shouted back at no white man again."

I slithered my yellow Vega into a diagonal parking space. Looking up at the sign, Momma quietly raised herself from the car.

"Woolworth's- Five and Dime, huhn."

Althea had made her way through the door and was headed towards the food area booths. There was a long counter with round silver stools upholstered with thick red vinyl. Under the rim of the counter were red diamond tiles inlayed around black tile and trimmed at the tops and bottoms with white tile. Food menus were stuck into metal frames between every three stools. One waitress was pouring coffee to an African American man at the counter and another was taking an order from the cushioned seats.

"It's okay, Momma." I assuredly expressed to her as she stepped back at seeing the lunch counter and booth seats.

"Oh, NO."

"Oh, YEAH!! Look over there and see one of us."

Momma looked over and saw an African American man eating lunch. He nodded at us and smiled.

Sitting on the vinyl twist-and-turn counter chairs, Momma swiveled with joy. She refused a booth seat as she wanted to try out something she had seen on television.

"There was a time when we would have to ..."

"We know, Momma. Those times are over now."

"Pinch me. Is it real?"

"Then if I do, you will be mad and won't eat your lunch."

"Hush."

Momma's eyes sparkled when we left Woolworth's. She looked like she was filled with the Holy Spirit for five Sundays in a row.

"You ate at your first restaurant, Momma."

"Yep," Momma proudly snapped.

We hopped into the Vega.

"You don't mind if I listen to a cassette, Momma, because I have to find at least three sentences that I can quote for my next month's club meeting?"

Momma shook her head with approval. The cassette

player started with:

Ain't I A Woman by Sojourner Truth that was delivered in 1851 at the Women's Convention in Akron, Ohio.

"Hallelujah!!"

Momma sounded happy and then suddenly dozed off to nap. Althea then played some smooth jazz as Momma Zettie snoozed.

Upon seeing a road sign, Althea and I let out a synchronic chuckle which actually awakened Momma.

"I like to hear you kids sound happy."

The sign read: "A Good Place to Take a Leak-Livingston Radiator Shop."

Momma lifted her head.

"You mean we are almost there? And by the way, children, while here on this earth, always have a piece of land you can call your own with your name on the deed. You can put up a tent and make a house of sticks and someday it can be brick. It's the land that matters."

During the time that the car got closer to Louisiana, Althea and I kept listening to Momma talk about kin folks have to always stick together.

Upon arrival, everyone's hearts melted into one family mass. Mr. Floyd was all white-haired, humpbacked, and toothless and Mrs. "Nessa" with her nappy braids and poor eyesight, was like looking at two stars in heaven.

"I hear you Zettie Mae."

"Come closer so I can see you"

Listening to stories about favorite times while visiting old and dying relatives as well as trimming their toenails and bringing glasses of ice water from the Frigidaire was the expected task for us like the Community Circle days.

In conversation after conversation, Momma chattered until the sun went down and did the same the following days.

"Thea, do you think Momma is really keeping track of the days? If she is not, I would like to have another day to feast on more Bayou shrimp and rice."

"Don't count on it, Sis. She knows."

Being awakened by Momma at 5:00 this morning and seeing her all washed up and fully dressed evidenced that it was time to return to Corn Hollow.

I yawned. "What time is it?"

"It's time to go home. Yes, girls, home."

Shortly after a grand breakfast that was already being cooked and the goodbyes and, "Don't worry we'll bring her back for another visit," we were off and traveling.

The Vega pulled over to a rest stop where we emptied ourselves of the juices and coffee from breakfast.

As we waited for Momma to exit the bathroom, we nodded and agreed that it was time to deal with the issues, once and for all.

Momma heard me call out before she had walked all the way to the car.

"Momma! You want to lead the Corn Hollow town hall fundraiser that's coming up in six months?"

"Why, Sarah Hawkins is doing that."

"You mean she was doing that," remarked Althea.

"You girls are talking crazy."

"We called up Sarah Hawkins when you and Mrs. Vanessa were talking up a storm about old times. She said she wanted someone with community experience and wisdom to be chairperson of the fundraiser; someone who could recognize who could run which committee."

"You know there are six key people in Corn Hollow who have the wits to do that."

"You mean that you will do it?"

"Well, you know in six months, we could raise enough money to build two town halls and community centers, dear children."

"We'll help you in any way, so you now have eight key people you can count on. It's your project Momma. Can you do one thing for us?"

"What's that, honey?"

"Forgive those dead A.M.E. stewards, our Daddy Al, and me." Althea pointed to her own heart.

Momma let out a big sigh that sounded like a semi-deep bellow from her gut. I lead her to a bench that was shaded by the leaves of a lightly winded maple tree. Putting my hands on Momma's back, I let her weep and weep.

Althea repeated the Lord's Prayer.

"Momma, name those stewards!" Althea softly commanded.

"Mr. Daniel Goodson, Mr. Jake Barnes, Mr. Leo Hickle," and so on.

Momma whimpered in a grieving tone.

"Have mercy on me and accept my forgiveness as the Holy Spirit digs through the dirt, the dust, and them ashes of your souls, gentlemen."

"And now Daddy Al, Momma."

"That old fool? I loved him so much and he still swaggered with whores."

"Momma, he's dead. Forgive him."

There was about a minute of silence which seemed like an hour. Momma let out a big huff.

"Lord, Release the words of forgiveness from my lips and my heart. I bury my hatchet now with you, Alfonso, and forgive you. You were a great father to our babies and always found a way to provide for the famlee."

"Mercy, mercy. And now me, Momma."

Momma looked up.

"Why you say that, child?"

Althea didn't answer back. She just looked into Momma Zettie's eyes with tear-filled depth as then she got on her knees in front of the bench and laid her head on Momma's lap.

"I know me and Al weren't all good to yew on some of your visits home. We got all jealous that you had it made. Then when I sensed when somebody tampered with you, because you flinched around some of the men folks. I had something to hold 'gainst you for being overtaken, even though I know how I raised you. It couln'd been your fault. Didn't want to see you suffer but I let you do so rather than hold you in my arms. You still somebody and don't let evil folk spoil your thoughts and ruin your life."

"Well, Momma, I had a lot of burdens and pain to bear just being who I am and being the only dot in an office and tolerating with injustice on the front lines as I forged through to make something of myself. I could have used every bit of your love and compassion. But just know that the times I had to pull myself through, I did so because you taught me to be strong."

Momma's eyes filled with tears.

"I forgive you for succeeding, like I always wanted to. I helt it in me 'cause my early days of getting into family way stopped me and the times in historie stopped me. Stand up, honey! You are somebody and you made somthin' of yourself. I love you sweetie, and I love you, Tamara."

"I know, Momma, and we love you. Since we are forgiving everyone, let me tell you that I lived in a wild and sheltered world, never knowing the contradictions with the KKK and moonshine whiskey right under my nose. I grew up really understanding the true bitterness that some community and family members, particularly those older than me, carried a lot of hate for anyone white. I confess. I don't hate them."

"It was so many evil rotten things the sheet killers bent doin' honey. I probably would have let go and said the wrong thing and been kilt myself so I kept quiet to spare us pain. Didn't mean no harm by holding back from you, Tamara."

All eyes were in tears and met tears of forgiveness for the other.

I requested that everyone repeat after me.

"I forgive those white folks for using us, scaring us, and trying to keep us from advancing in America ... And forgive us for the thoughts and things we held and done against them ... Forgive us all for everything."

A little white boy was walking across the rest stop lawn to retrieve a ball and momentarily stopped when he heard the words "white folks" and then proceeded to play.

"Whew!! I think, girls, that we done 'nough repentin' and forgiving for three life times."

"It's what you taught us, Momma."

"I musta done well!"

There were more tears, snotty nose-blowing, and laughter. The three of us were so light and relaxed that mostly everything was just plain funny. Each of us started walking towards the car and almost simultaneously pointed at the yellow car and broke out into an ecstatic laughter and even some corny hollering and murmurs.

The car doors slammed.

"We are the Corn Hollow ladies."

Some rest stop folks heard chuckles, giggles, and quickly glimpsed our rhythmic body motions in the yellow car as a cassette blasted. "Oh Glory, Hallelujah!!!"

Momma was clapping her hands and shaking her head to the tunes as well. She then announced, "I think Corn Hollow is calling us."

Bibliography

Brunner, Borgna and Haney, Elissa. "Civil Rights Timeline 1954-1971." *Infoplease.* <http://www.infoplease.com>.

Hughes, Langston and Rampersad, Arnold (Ed.). *The Collected Poems of Langston Hughes, "Still Here"* and *"Justice."* New York: Alfred A. Knopf, Inc,,1994.

McLeod, LaVerne. *Corn Hollow,* "Crying Souls." Big Sur: Purple Feather Press, 2006.

McLeod, LaVerne. *Corn Hollow,* "Cycles." Big Sur: Purple Feather Press, 1992.

McLeod, LaVerne. *Corn Hollow,* "Truck Patches and Canning." Big Sur: Purple Feather Press, 2004.

Simmonite, William Joseph and Culpeper, Nichol. *Herbal Remedies.*
London: W. Foulsham & Co., Limited, 1957.

The Holy Bible, New Testament, "Matthew 14:15-21." London and New York: Collins' Clear-Type Press, 1958.

Image Credits

Author photograph on back cover © 2014 Patrice Ward

Chapter 1- "Vintage Fashioned Radio." Stock image. ©Jannoon028, August 18, 2011. iStock.com.

Chapter 2- "4-Queens Quilt Pattern." Color design and photo image. ©LaVerne McLeod, March 2016.

Chapter 3- "Vintage School Books, Bell, and Desks." Stock image. ©Richard Goerg, June 29, 2007. iStock.com.

Chapter 4- "Lemonade."stock image. ©Mitchellpictures, April 12, 2013. iStock.com.

Chapter 5- "The Still." Stock photo. ©Kaye Grogan. Shutterstock.com.

Chapter 6- "Old House on Fire." Stock image. ©JoeDphoto, March 24, 2010. iStock.com

Chapter 7- "Violent crime concept with a close-up of an eye ball crying with a tear of blood due to criminal violence as child abuse and violence on women or other victims of physical injury." Stock photo. ©Lightspring. Shutterstock.com.

Chapter 8- "Old Shack." Stock image. ©simonmcconico, August 24, 2006. iStock.com.

Chapter 9- "Retro Bus. Vintage Bus." Illustration. ©etraveler, February 11, 2015. iStock.com.

Chapter 10- "Apartment Building in a City." Illustration. ©4x6, November 10, 2009. iStock.com.

Chapter 11- "Old Southern Baptist Chapel in an Historic Village." Stock photo. ©Sean Pavone. Shutterstock.com.

Chapter 12- "Freehand Drawing Vegetables." Vector illustration. Seamless pattern. Isolated on white background. ©Lyudmyla Kharlamova. Shutterstock.com.

Chapter 13- "Little Girl Running Away." Stock image. ©Andrew Lytwyn, June 21, 2010. iStock.com.

Chapter 14- "African Americans Picking Cotton in the U.S. South in 1887." Wood engraving from a drawing by Horace Bradley. Stock photo. ©Everett Historical. Shutterstock.com.

Chapter 15- "Ferris Wheel at Dusk." Stock photo. ©Joseph Sohm. Shutterstock.com.

Chapter 16- "Set of Pig-Slaughtering isolated on background." Stock vector illustration. ©BORTEL Pavel-Pavelmidi. Shutterstock.com.

Chapter 17- "An Image of Desperate Women in Autumn Park." Stock photo. ©Photographee.eu. Shutterstock.com.

Chapter 18- "Scared Young Girl with an adult man's hand covering her mouth." Stock photo. ©Luis Louro. Shutterstock.com.

Chapter 19- "Cotton Sharecroppers Weeding their Small Cotton Crop in Greene County Georgia." July 1937 photo by Dorothea Lange. Stock photo. ©Everett Historical. Shutterstock.com.

Chapter 20- "An Ear of Corn isolated on a white background." Stock photo. ©Maks Narodenko. Shutterstock.com.

Chapter 21- "Group of People." Vector illustration. ©syntika, January 12, 2015. iStock.com.

Chapter 22- "Golf Player Hitting the Ball." Stock Vector illustration. ©Visual Generation. Shutterstock.com.

Chapter 23- "Seamless Pattern with Ink Hand Drawn Lavender Sketch." Vector Illustration. ©Levgenila Lytvynovych, June 9, 2015. iStock.com.

Chapter 24- "Woman with Curly Hair." Stock image. © Andresr, Dec 4, 2014. iStock.com.

Chapter 25- "Cowboy Boots." Stock image. ©ppart, January 10, 2012. iStock.com.

Chapter 26- "Bus-rear view." Stock image. ©jondpatton. iStock.com.

Chapter 27- "Exterior of English secondary school building, Scarborough." ©Atlaspix. Shutterstock.com.

Chapter 28- "Cocker Spaniel Puppy Sitting in Profile and Looking Up," isolated on white background. Stock photo. ©Ermolaev Alexander. Shutterstock.com.

Chapter 29- "Gravestone with Christian Cross under Cloudy Blue Sky" – 3d illustration. Stock photo. ©Jorg Rose-Oberreich. Shutterstock.com.

Chapter 30- "A Hand Behind Matted Glass" B/W. Stock photo. © Nomad_Soul. Shutterstock.com.

Chapter 31- "Young Mixed Race Woman Girl with Finger on Lips showing hand quiet silence gesture isolated on white." Profile side view. Stock photo. ©Voyagerix. Shutterstock.com.

Chapter 32- "Cartridges Hunting Ammunition. Old style, sepia."
Stock photo. ©Alexander Leonov. Shutterstock.com.

Chapter 33- "Grass." Stock image. ©LenaKozlova, May 30, 2011.
iStock.com.

Chapter 34- "Envelope Mail icon." Vector illustration. Flat design
style. ©Flat Design. Shutterstock.com.

Chapter 35- "Graduation Cap and Diploma black web icon."
Vector Illustration. ©edel. Shutterstock.com.

Chapter 36- "Counter and Barstools of Vintage Roadside Diner."
Stock photo. ©Christina Richards. Shutterstock.com.